Your
Destination
is on the
Left

Your Destination Is on the Left

LAUREN SPIELLER

SIMON & SCHUSTER BFYR

NEW YORK · LONDON · TORONTO · SYDNEY · NEW DELHI

An imprint of Simon & Schuster Children's Publishing Division
1230 Avenue of the Americas, New York, New York 10020

For information about special discounts for bulk purchases, please contact
Simon & Schuster Special Sales at 1-866-506-1949 or business@simonandschuster.com.
The Simon & Schuster Speakers Bureau can bring authors to your live event.
For more information or to book an event, contact the Simon & Schuster Speakers Bureau at 1-866-248-3049 or visit our website at www.simonspeakers.com.
Jacket design by Krista Vossen
Interior design by Hilary Zarycky
The text for this book was set in Minion Pro.
Manufactured in the United States of America
First Edition
2 4 6 8 10 9 7 5 3 1
Library of Congress Cataloging-in-Publication Data
Names: Spieller, Lauren, author.
Title: Your destination is on the left / Lauren Spieller.
Description: First edition. | New York, N.Y. : Simon & Schuster Children Books for Young Readers, [2018] | Summary: Offered her longed-for opportunity to leave the RV caravan and study art, seventeen-year-old Dessa Rhodes questions whether she is ready to leave her family, the open road, and the boy she loves.
Identifiers: LCCN 2017025533| ISBN 9781481492126 (hardcover : alk. paper) | ISBN 9781481492140 (eBook)
Subjects: | CYAC: Coming of age—Fiction. | Artists—Fiction. | Self-confidence—Fiction. | Family life—Fiction. | Nomads—Fiction. | Recreational vehicles—Fiction.
Classification: LCC PZ7.1.S71453 You 2018 | DDC [Fic]—dc23
LC record available at https://lccn.loc.gov/2017025533

For my dad, who taught me to never give up

We've been on the road for five hours already, our skin sticking together in Cyrus' overheated RV. I scoot closer to him on the threadbare pullout couch, where we're squished between a basket of wrinkled laundry in desperate need of folding, and a precarious stack of books and auto magazines. The exit for Asheville is only a few miles away, and as soon as we step outside, I'll have to go back to pretending that the way he plays air guitar when he doesn't think I'm watching, the way he always smells a little bit like motorcycle oil and Woolite, the way he smiles with only half of his mouth . . . I'll have to pretend that none of that makes me want to roll over and die of happiness.

His brown eyes lock with mine, flooding my body with the sensation of a cold shower on a hot day.

"You're staring at me, Dessa," he says. "You know that, right?"

I jerk back in my seat, and my head slams into the low-hanging cabinet behind the couch. The sports equipment inside rattles. "Ouch."

Cyrus nudges me, his black skin smooth and warm against my winter-paled shoulder. His lips curl into a playful grin. "I didn't say you had to stop."

I look out the window before my blush can give me away. As much as I'd like to let our eye contact linger, I have to stick to my number one rule for surviving nomadic life: don't kiss the gorgeous guy you travel with. It comes right after "don't get too comfortable in any one place," and before "always have a stash of extra toilet paper."

"I was just thinking about the last time we were in Asheville," I lie. "It's been a few years. Remember that hot chocolate place, the one with the line that wrapped around the block?"

"Yeah . . ." Cy's smile fades, and he tugs at the thick leather cuff he wears around his wrist. At first I'm not sure what I said, but then I remember that the day we had hot chocolate in Asheville was the same day I announced to the families—mine, Cy's, and the McAlisters— that I didn't want to travel anymore after I got my GED. That I wanted to apply to art school instead. That I wanted to settle down and get to know a place for more than a few weeks.

In other words, High Nomad Treason.

Cy's quiet for a moment, his eyebrows pulling together. I run my fingers along the hem of my tattered jean shorts, even though what I really want is to cup his face in my hands and tell him not to worry. But saying everything is going to be okay won't change the way he feels about me leaving, and even his pack rat RV isn't crowded enough to excuse touching his face. Especially not with his dad sitting only a few feet away in the driver's seat.

Cy bumps my knee with his. "Aren't you supposed to hear back from UCLA soon? They said they'll announce who got off the wait list in the beginning of May, right?"

I squirm in my seat, which is awkward since we're sitting so close together. "I guess."

"Come on, Dess," he says quietly. "I know you're bummed, but a *few* rejections don't mean anything. You're a fantastic artist—you'll get in somewhere."

I nod, but what Cy doesn't understand is that it's not just a few rejections. It's everywhere else I applied. The only school left is UCLA, which just happens to be my reach school. If they don't let me in, then that's it. I'll finally have proof of the one thing I've always feared: that I'm not a real artist. I'm just some nobody with a paintbrush.

But I'm going to get in. I have to.

"We're here," Cy's dad, Jeff, calls from the driver's seat. He pulls the RV off the freeway at the last possible second, narrowly missing the guardrail. Cyrus leans into the curve, squishing me against the towering pile of books. "Mashed potato!" he yells.

I make a show of pushing him off, and he laughs. Five years of traveling together and he's still playing the same games we loved when we were twelve.

Jeff pulls into a gas station and parks near the convenience store. I climb out of the RV, my knees stiff and achy from sitting for so long. "I'll see you later?" I call back to Cy, who's now standing in the doorway.

He gives me a frustrated look. "But we just got here."

"Math homework."

"You're still not finished? That pre-calc is easy."

"We can't all be Albert Einstein."

"You know Einstein was a physicist, right? Not a mathematician?"

"Shut up!"

"You should have taken the GED with me last year," he calls after me, but I'm already jogging across the parking lot to join my parents, arms wrapped around myself for warmth. The heater in Cy's RV only runs on high, so it's easy to forget about the cool mountain air outside. I probably look like an idiot running around out here in my tried-and-true travel ensemble of a T-shirt and shorts, while everyone else is wearing a sweater and jeans.

My dad is standing at the pump when I reach him, his thick eyebrows pulled together in a frown. "Gas has gotten too expensive," he grumbles.

The numbers on the pump tick up, up, up, with no signs of stopping. "Yikes." I look at Dad. "I need help with math."

He sighs, his eyes still glued to the numbers. "Don't we all."

The door to our RV opens behind us, and Mom steps out. She blinks and throws up a hand to shield her eyes from the sun. Her silver rings shine in the light. "Dessa? What are you doing here?"

"I live here, remember?" I knock my knuckles against the side of the RV. "Plus I have homework."

Mom waves this off, her stack of bracelets jangling. "The school year's basically over and you've already applied to colleges. Go have fun."

I know a lot of parents are strict about homework, but my parents haven't been in years. They didn't have to be. If anything, they had the opposite problem. I can't count how many times I've had to refuse to join them on yet another hike through the woods, or into some random neighborhood to try what Mom promised would be *the best vegan mofongo you've ever had*. It was hard to turn stuff down—well, the hikes anyway—but I had to stay on top of my homeschool work. No way was I letting something like biology homework get in the way of finally going to college.

Across the parking lot, Cy stretches and waves.

"I guess I could take a *little* time off," I say. "Dad, help me with my math later?"

He's moved from frowning at the pump to frowning at his receipt. "Mmm."

"I'm changing, then I'll go," I say.

Mom tightens the shawl around her shoulders, as if she only just noticed it was cold, and steps to the side so I can squeeze past her. I jump the two steps up into the RV, nod to my ten-year-old brother, Rodney, who's sitting in the middle of the floor playing with his Game Boy, and grab a hoodie and a pair of old jeans I find in the clean laundry bag hanging on the back of the bathroom door. I don't have to look to know exactly which pair I've grabbed. When you travel like we do, you wear the same thing over and over, because there's not enough space for anyone to have more than two or three pairs of pants. I'm used to it now, but I missed my double closet when we first started traveling.

"Will you guys be here for a while?" I ask once I'm back outside, having quickly changed clothes in my parents' bedroom. Aka the *only* bedroom.

"A few hours," Dad says. "I'm going to park the RV against the fence over there and take a nap, and the McAlisters are bringing their girls over to that jungle gym." He jerks his chin toward a playground across the street. It looks dingy and depressing, even from far away. There are swings missing from the set, and the monkey bars look distinctly crooked.

"Should I take the twins on a walk instead?" I ask, glancing over at the third RV in our caravan, then back at the death trap we're all pretending is a playground.

"You worry too much," Mom says, handing me a large canvas tote bag. "Do me a favor and pick up the ingredients for spanakopita."

"Okay."

"But only if you find a farmer's market."

"Okay, Mom."

"And Dessa, make sure the spinach hasn't been frozen. Ask them—"

"Before I buy it. I know."

I kiss my mom on the cheek and walk to Cy's RV. I just hope the McAlisters remembered to get the girls a tetanus shot.

When I reach Cy, he's leaning against the door, arms crossed over his chest, his face tilted up to the sun. "I'm thinking hot chocolate," he says, not opening his eyes. "What about you?"

The Chocolate Lounge is one of the most popular spots in downtown Asheville. It's full of squishy leather armchairs, worn wood tables, and tons of people devouring every kind of chocolate under the sun. It's the kind of place where I can imagine hanging out with friends after school. We'd do homework, talk about guys . . . the kind of normal stuff people do in high school. Or at least, what I assume they do. I stopped going to normal school the summer after seventh grade, so the only experience I have with high school life comes from movies.

The line starts halfway down the block, but it only takes about ten minutes before we're standing inside. I squint at the chalkboard menu, scanning the options. There are five kinds of cake, a dozen different truffles, three kinds of brownie, a bunch of cookies and tarts, chocolate mousse, something called *pot de crème* . . . and that's all in addition to a never-ending list of hot chocolates. Cyrus and I turn to each other and grin. There's no way we're not each trying at least two things.

The line moves forward.

"Did you ever hear back about that internship you were talking about a few months ago?" Cy asks.

"With Fiona Velarde, the artist in Santa Fe? I wrote the essay but I never sent it in."

"Why not? You could've gotten it."

I shrug. "She probably got a ton of applications from people with way more experience than me. There's no way she'd pick someone whose formal art education stopped in seventh grade."

"Oh, come on," Cy says. "You take all those online classes. They totally count."

"They're only okay."

The line moves again. I stand on my tiptoes and peer up at the board. Maybe I'll try a fancy hot chocolate. Or a little cake. I tap my foot with impatience.

"You should have applied," Cy says. "You never know."

"With any luck I'll be leaving for college soon anyway."

The family in front of us finishes, and Cy steps up to the counter. He orders an almond butter cookie, a French raspberry truffle, and cayenne cinnamon hot chocolate. I roll my eyes at his over-the-top choices, but he just shakes his head and moves to the side so I can order next.

The girl taking my order is short, with a green stud in her nose. "What can I get you?"

I look back up at the board. I've been staring at the menu for what feels like forever, but there are so many choices, it's overwhelming. "Uh . . . can I have a chocolate chip cookie and . . . a regular hot chocolate?"

"You can get that anywhere," Cy whispers. "You sure you don't want to try something different, like the one with maple and sea salt?"

"But what if I don't like it? It's not like I can return it."

The man behind us inches closer to me and clears his throat. Cy gives him a look, and the guy backs off.

"The original hot chocolate is really good," the girl at the register says with a patient smile. "It's made with ganache and organic milk. It's way better than the plain hot chocolate you get at other places."

"That sounds great," I say, handing her my money. "Thanks."

"Wait," Cyrus says, "can you add two milk chocolate truffles?" He turns to me. "I wanna give them to the McAlister girls."

He pulls his wallet out again and grimaces. "Actually—"

"Make it three," I say, handing over my last ten to the girl. "I'll get one for my brother, too. Rodney loves anything sweet."

Cy bumps me with his shoulder. "I'll pay you back, Dess."

"That's okay," I say, accepting my change. "I probably owe you some money anyway. Plus, this way, you have to share the credit with me."

We take our food and step to the side, where the other employees are calling out the names of people who ordered drinks. I wander over to a corkboard that's covered in flyers for guitar lessons, babysitters, and other local stuff. I act really interested in a missing cat poster, but really I'm avoiding talking to Cyrus about him paying me back. We both know I don't owe him any money, just like we both know he would have said the truffles were from both of us anyway. But he spent the money he made helping his dad fix motorcycles on taking Rodney to a movie last week, and he doesn't have a grandma who sends him a twenty-dollar bill every holiday like I do.

When Cy's cayenne hot chocolate's ready, he holds it out to me. "You try it first."

"It's going to be too spicy."

"It might not be."

The guy behind the counter calls my name, and holds up my regular hot chocolate. I take a sip, even though it's way too hot. "Mmmm," I say. "Whatever ganache is, it's freaking delicious."

Cy shakes his head.

We sip our drinks as we walk to the Asheville farmer's market, where we pick up groceries for my mom. On our way back to the RVs, I take my time, enjoying the way the cool air makes my skin tingle. Half a block ahead, Cyrus swings his plastic grocery bag around and around, letting the loops twist against his wrist. "It's going to rain," he says, staring up at the darkening sky. "We should walk faster."

My cell phone buzzes in my pocket. "Just a second." I click the email icon on Dad's hand-me-down smart phone. My breath catches in my chest at the sight of the subject line.

Application to UCLA.

I open the email, my fingers shaking so hard I almost drop the phone.

Your UCLA application has been updated. Please click here *to check the status of your application.*

I tap the link, and wait as the UCLA website loads. It happens painfully slow, my phone struggling to find a signal this close to the mountains. The loading symbol spins and spins, my stomach churning with it. This is it, I can feel it. It's not going to be like all the other places. I'm finally going to get into college. I'll be able to show my parents that art deserves to be studied, not just created. There will be no more sitting alone in the RV, searching the internet for tips on using negative space in paintings while my family explores yet another small town on the East Coast. No more squeezing my legs together while I wait for my brother to finish using the damn bathroom in the morning. Instead, I'll be surrounded by other students, holding my breath as a real live art professor leans over my work, critiquing the composition, commenting on my use of light and shadow. And at the end of the day, I'll go home to my dorm, to my one and only roommate, and we'll talk about how incredible our new lives are. I'm finally going to start living the life I'm supposed to have.

The life I want.

The website finishes loading. I scan the page, searching for the words "Application Status." At the bottom of the screen, I finally find what I'm looking for.

Application Status: Enrollment Denied.

No.

Panic surges inside me, hot and wild. This status isn't for me—it can't be. I scroll up, then down again, searching for someone else's name, an error message, anything that'll reveal this is all a terrible mistake. I reload the page.

Application Status: Enrollment Denied.

"No. No, no, no!"

Cy looks back at me. "What happened?"

I try to speak, but my throat feels raw. My chest heaves. I can't . . . I can't breathe.

Cy's eyes go wide. "Dessa. Are you all right?"

My brain is fuzzy, like I've just woken up. But even through the fog of my misery I can see that he's staring at me, waiting for me to tell him what's wrong. I take a step back, my legs shaky beneath me. "I have to go—"

"Wait." Cy walks toward me, slowly, like he doesn't want to scare me away. "What happened?"

I look down at my phone, still clutched in my hand. I can't say it out loud. Won't.

"Is someone hurt? Is it your parents?"

At the mention of my family, I let out a moan. I'm going to have to tell them, and then everyone will know I failed. Ten schools and I didn't get into a single one. I should have studied harder. I should have retaken the SAT. I should have—

No. This isn't about my math scores, or my stupid grades. This is about my portfolio. My art.

Me.

"Oh god," I whisper as Cy closes the gap between us. "It's over."

Cyrus wraps his arms around me. My muscles immediately tense at his touch—it's too much, I should pull away—but he rocks me back and forth slowly, and for once I let myself need him. I let him hold me together so I don't crumble to the ground and scatter in the wind.

"It's okay," he says. "Whatever it is, it's going to be okay."

A strangled laugh escapes me. It's an awful sound, guttural and full of pain. "It's not going to be okay," I say, and pull away from him. "I didn't get into UCLA."

"Oh, man." Cyrus runs his hand over his close-cropped hair, his fingers brushing through the short black curls. "Dessa, I know you're upset. I do. But you can't let this beat you. It's unfair and stupid and they're idiots for not accepting you. You're . . . you're amazing."

We stare at each other for a moment, the distance between us somehow way too far and yet much too close. If this were a movie, we'd throw our bags down and reach for each other again.

"You'll get in somewhere else," he says. "Right?"

His eyes are worried, but also full of hope. Even though he

doesn't want me to leave him and the families, he still wants me to succeed.

How am I supposed to tell him I'm an even bigger failure than he realizes? How am I supposed to tell any of them?

There's a rumble of thunder overhead. I hitch my mom's biodegradable tote up my shoulder. "Come on," I say, my voice barely more than a whisper. "We should get back."

We walk in silence for a while, and I can feel all the unspoken words bouncing between us like a current.

Cyrus finally clears his throat. "Do you think that maybe . . ."

"What?"

He licks his lips. "Don't take this the wrong way, okay? I love your work, but . . . do you think maybe the problem was your portfolio?"

I tighten my hands into fists. It's one thing for me to think it, but I can't *believe* he'd say that to me, especially after it's too late to apply anywhere else. "You don't know what you're talking about," I say through gritted teeth. Cy opens his mouth to defend himself, but I cut him off. "I chose the pieces based off the student work they're showcasing on the college website. Clearly that's the sort of thing they're looking for."

"Okay, okay," he says, holding up his hands in surrender. "I just wonder what would have happened if you submitted that other painting you were working on."

I frown. "Which one?"

"The sunburst, remember? Those colors were amazing. It

was like the reds and yellows were busting off the canvas." He mimes an explosion with his hands, throwing his arms wide. "It was awesome."

My chest constricts at the mention of the sunburst. It was one of the fastest paintings I ever did—under an hour, while Dad was having the oil changed. You could tell, too. It was messy and bright, nothing like the careful studies in shape and color I'd been doing for months. It felt reckless and alive. I don't know if it was because I was sick of being cooped up in the RV, or because of the argument about extracurricular credits I'd had with my mom earlier that day, but from the moment my brush touched the canvas, it was like being caught in a tornado. I couldn't see where I was going. I just had to ride it out.

In the end, I loved it so much that I had planned to hang it over my bed when I got to college. But then the rejections started coming in, and I couldn't bear to look at the blazing sunburst. It's lived in the storage compartment by my bed ever since.

"UCLA wouldn't look twice at that painting," I say. "It's juvenile."

"You're the expert," Cy says with a shrug. "I'm just trying to figure out why you didn't get in, that's all."

I've been asking myself the same question over and over again for weeks, ever since I got my first rejection. I told myself it was about something other than my work. They had a lot of really talented applicants. They were looking for sculptures, not painters, like me. Budget cuts forced them to take fewer people. But now that I've been rejected from every single school, those excuses don't work anymore.

I didn't get into art school because I don't belong there.

We continue down the street, past the single-story houses with perfectly manicured lawns and freshly painted doors. Above us, the clouds sag under the weight of their collected water, their bottoms gray. We turn the corner, and the neat homes become a row of apartment buildings.

Cyrus swings his plastic bag through the air, letting it fall back against his leg with a thud. "I love when the sky looks like this," he says, staring up into the moody sky overhead. I don't look up; it's going to take more than the weather to distract me.

We round another corner, and the three RVs come into view up ahead. I stop walking and face him. "You can't tell them about UCLA. About any of it."

"I won't. But you're going to, right?"

I picture the sad sympathy on my parents' faces, and it about turns my stomach. "I don't know."

There's another rumble of thunder above us. I glance up at the clouds, but Cyrus doesn't look away. "Dessa, you have to."

"I will, eventually. But not right away. I need time to think." A trickle of rain begins to fall. I start toward the RVs. "We have to get inside."

"Dessa, wait." He catches my hand in his. "You did your best. That'll be enough for them."

I look down at our hands, his fingers laced in mine. "But what if it's not enough for me? What if I want more?"

"You've done everything you're supposed to," Cyrus says, pulling me toward him. The rain falls harder, clinging to his black hair. "Maybe try doing something you're not."

I swallow. "Like what?"

His lips curl into a slow smile, and he spreads his arms wide. "Stay out here with me until the rain stops."

"What?" I say, pulling my canvas bag to my chest. "We can't do that."

"Why not? It's just rain."

There's another roll of thunder, and the sky opens up. Rain pours down on us, soaking through my clothes. "Don't go," Cyrus says, his brown eyes serious. "Give it a chance."

Water streams down his face, turning his dark skin shiny. He's so handsome it hurts to look at him. I imagine myself closing the distance between us, wrapping my arms around his neck as he presses his lips to mine. I imagine his warm hands on my back, how I'd hold him so tight and never, ever let go—

A crack of lightning splits open the sky, and I jump back. "I'm sorry," I say, and take off running across the dirt lot toward the RV.

Cy calls my name, but I don't look back. If I do, I might turn around and go back. I might kiss him and kiss him and kiss him, just like I do in my daydreams.

CHAPTER 2

I launch myself into the RV, slamming the door shut behind me. The inside is warm and cheerful, the compact kitchen table illuminated by the electric lights. As much as I want out, right now I'm grateful for this tiny piece of home.

"Oh," Mom says, gazing at me from the passenger seat. "You're soaked."

"No kidding." I slide onto the bench seat and look out the window, hoping for a glimpse of Cyrus, but I can't see him. Only mud, wet concrete, gas pumps, and Jeff, ripping jeans and T-shirts off the clothesline attached to their RV.

I pull my dripping brown hair into a ponytail, then prop up my elbows on the table and let out a long sigh. The kind my mom says is a sign of "bad energy."

"What's wrong?" she asks.

Outside, Cyrus finally appears. He jogs over to help his dad save the laundry. It's too late—everything is already soaked—but Cyrus keeps tugging at the fabric anyway, his wet white T-shirt clinging to his broad chest.

"This rain sucks," I say, my gaze lingering on Cyrus. I force myself to look back at my mom. "Let's go somewhere else. Anywhere else."

"You've been complaining for months that we move too often."

"But—"

"You loved Asheville the last time we were here. You tried to convince us to stay, remember?"

"I know, I know." When we stopped in Asheville a few years ago, I spent all my time wandering the artsy downtown streets, a cup of hot chocolate clutched between my fingers. I loved the way the mountains towered above us, sending messages on the wind that whistled between the trees and down the streets. I'd begged my parents to enroll me in school here, like a regular teenager. We could still live out of the RV, still take short trips on the weekends, but the rest of the time we'd just be a normal family.

We'd packed up and left the next day.

"I'll tell you what," Mom says, swiveling around in her seat. "Let's give it a few days, and if the rain hasn't stopped, we'll go somewhere else. Never stop moving, right?"

I smile at her words. I can't help it. Whenever I'm tired of traveling, whenever Rodney complains about sleeping in the pullout bed, whenever we run out of gas, Mom says the same thing: *Never stop moving.* It's the traveler battle cry, and every family in our caravan lives by those words, for better or for worse. It's only a matter of time before someone asks me to paint it on our RV alongside the bright orange California poppies I did last spring. But as often as I make fun of it, I'm proud that it's our slogan. Because even in my bleakest moments, it reminds me that there's still something to love about this life: Travelers never give up.

"Did you get the spinach?" Mom asks.

I upend the damp canvas bag onto the table. Two bunches of spinach, a package of feta, a box of phyllo, and an onion come tumbling out. Everything we need for my Greek grandmother's family recipe.

"Good girl. But you'll get sick if you stay in those wet clothes. Change, then we'll get started."

I glance down the length of the RV, and when I'm sure my dad and brother are gone, I strip out of my wet clothes and into a pair of pajama pants and an old T-shirt.

"Where's Rodney?" I ask when I'm done.

"Oh, he's up in your bed," Mom says. I roll my eyes. So much for Dad and Rodney being gone while I changed.

"Sweetie?" Mom calls up to my brother. "Come down here and help your sister squeeze the spinach."

Silence.

"Rodney?" Mom calls out again.

I lean out of my seat and peer up at my bed. It's tucked into a nook over the driver's seat, but I can just make out my brother's bare foot. "Rodney, I can see you."

My brother pulls in his foot but doesn't respond.

"Rodney," I say, louder this time, "if you help us with the spinach, I'll let you stay up there for an hour the next time we move, even though you're not allowed on my bed."

My brother's upside down head drops into view, his brown hair hanging like a curtain. "Two hours."

"One and a half."

"Be down in a second," he says, then disappears again. I try not to think about what kind of havoc he's wreaking up there.

Mom carries the spinach to the sink. While she washes it, I reach under the table for the small box of broken glass I have stashed there. For months after I first saw Fiona Velarde's art, the families helped me collect glass bottles and broken shards of windowpane for a two-by-two-foot mosaic of the Santa Monica coastline. I only kept the most vibrant pieces, the ones that reminded me of the rolling waves and the clear sky. I've only been there once, back when we visited UCLA, but it's burned into my mind. I pick an aquamarine piece and hold it up to the window. The light glints against its watery surface, shining blue-white-blue. It hurts my heart just looking at it.

"Are you going to start the mosaic?" Mom asks, shaking the wet spinach over the sink.

I shrug and drop the piece of glass back into the box. Mom hands me a roll of paper towels. I tear off a long sheet, then another, layering them until the foldout table is covered. When I'm done, Mom spreads out the clean spinach, making sure none of it overlaps, then slides into the bench seat at the table.

"Remember, we have to get all the water out, or the whole thing will come out soggy."

"I know, Mom."

Outside, a cloud moves, releasing a beam of sunlight that cuts through the rain and into the RV window, splintering into a rainbow of colors when it hits my mom's chunky silver rings. She twists the one on her middle finger around and around, a sure giveaway that she's about to say something that makes her nervous. I brace myself.

"Sweetheart, I know you don't want to hear this," she says, "but I'm worried about you." She picks up a handful of spinach and squeezes, the green juice running between her fingers and soaking into the paper towels. "You've been so preoccupied lately. Sometimes it's like you're not even *here*."

I poke at the spinach in front of me. "Yeah, well, I've had a lot on my mind."

"But now that school is mostly over and you're done with your applications, maybe you should focus more on the families. On all of this."

She gestures around us, as if we're sitting in the middle of a magnificent oasis, instead of an old RV with a pile of already-withering spinach spread out between us like an uncrossable green ocean.

Mom reaches under the blue circle scarf around her neck, not caring that her spinach-stained hands are dripping green water everywhere, and pulls her silver leaf pendant free of the fabric. "Remember when we got these in Flagstaff?"

I rub my fingers along the matching pendant that hangs around my own neck. We had started traveling a few months earlier, and everything was still brand-new and exciting. Sleeping in my cabover bed was like living in my own personal tree house, and sharing an airplane-size bathroom with four people was fun. When we were ready for our first cross-country drive, Mom decided we should all find something special along the way to commemorate the journey. Rodney chose a stuffed dog from a toy store in Chicago on the second day of our trip, and Dad bought a fancy Swiss Army knife in St. Louis a day later, but Mom and I took our time. We wanted something unique, something we'd keep forever. I was the one who found the necklaces, tucked into boxes in the back of a store in Flagstaff. For years, the pendant was my lifeline. Sometimes things got hard, and I'd miss my room, or my friends back in Chattanooga. But then I'd look at the leaf pendant, and remind myself that I was on an adventure. I was lucky.

Now all I see is the life my parents chose for me, one I'm going to be stuck with forever.

"I remember," I say, tucking my necklace back under my shirt. "But I'm not twelve anymore. People change."

"They don't have to," Mom says quietly.

I pick up a huge fistful of spinach and squeeze as hard as I can. Green juice runs down my hands and arms, pooling on the paper towel. I drop the spinach and pick up a second handful.

I squeeze so hard it hurts my fingers. Mom gives me a worried look, but I ignore her and keep squeezing.

An hour later, my hands are stiff and stained green, Mom and I still aren't speaking, and Rodney is back in my cabover bed having helped for approximately fifteen seconds before he complained his hands hurt and gave up. Just as I squeeze the last bits of moisture from a handful of spinach, the side door opens and Dad climbs into the RV. "Damn this rain." He shakes his head, spraying water all over the floor. He reaches into his pockets and pulls out four Reese's Peanut Butter Cups—one for each of us. Mom wrinkles her nose.

"Stage one complete?" Dad asks as he appraises the wilted, dried-out spinach.

"Finally," I grumble. But the truth is I'm glad I had something to occupy me for the last hour. It's better than sitting up in my bed, wishing for a college application do-over.

Dad hands me the candy, then leans over and kisses Mom on the cheek. "Have you seen my wrench?" he asks her. "The McAlisters' awning is stuck again. I told them not to buy their RV from that guy in Reno, but did they listen?"

"It's in the toolbox in the storage compartment," Mom says. "Under the RV."

"I looked there, but—"

"I'll show you."

She gets up, waving off the umbrella he offers her. Outside, the rain hasn't slowed, but the sun is still peeking out from behind the clouds.

When they're gone, Rodney hangs his head down from my bed. The skin around his eyes is black and he's holding my liquid eyeliner in his hand. He looks like a raccoon. I jump up and grab the tube from him. I splurge on makeup for the first time in months and it ends up all over my brother's face. Figures.

He wipes his eyes, smearing the makeup over his nose. "I heard something while you were gone."

I drop the tube into my purse. "Oh yeah?"

Rodney grins. "Dad said Mark's an 'unforgiveable ass.'"

I clap my hand over Rodney's mouth. "Shhh. Not so loud. Who did he say that to? Mom?"

He pulls my hand away. "No, someone on the phone." Rodney points at the candy in my hand. "Can I have one?"

I open the package and give him a Peanut Butter Cup. He immediately shoves the whole thing into his mouth, then disappears back into my bed. I lean against the kitchen counter and stare out at the rain. Dad would never talk badly about a client, especially not Mark. He's one of Dad's biggest accounts, and Mark helped him find lots of other marketing work too. I've lost count of how many times I've heard Dad say that if it weren't for Mark, he'd still be stuck behind a desk in Chattanooga, working for a soulless design firm. But if Rodney's right, then something is *very* wrong. Without Mark, there's no paycheck, and without a paycheck, we might not be able to afford to travel.

I shove a Peanut Butter Cup into my mouth. As much as I want a break from this life, I've never wanted it to disappear entirely.

The next morning, I wake to a fine layer of frost clinging to the windows, and the gut-busting realization that this is the first day of my new life as a non-college-bound graduate. I close my eyes, willing myself to go back to sleep. But the cold air creeps under my blanket, and I'm forced to accept that this is real life. I'm not going to college. The end.

I peer over the edge of my bed down at the kitchen table. Dad is reading a local newspaper, a steaming cup of coffee in his hand. He's wearing his winter coat.

"Why is the heat off?" I ask, clutching my blanket closer.

He takes a sip of coffee. "Saves money."

"But it's freezing."

He shrugs. "Put on a sweater."

First Rodney hears him call his boss an ass, and now he's not turning on the heat? Not good. I pull a pair of clean pants out of the cabinet next to my bed and shimmy into them under the sheets. Then I climb down the ladder, my right hand clutching the blanket around my shoulders. When I reach the bottom, Dad hands me his cup without looking up from the paper. I take a sip and grimace. "This is weak."

"We're running low on coffee."

I wait for a second, hoping maybe he'll say something

more—*good morning, we're having financial problems but everything is under control*—but he doesn't. After seventeen years of
waking up to my dad blasting show tunes with a ten a.m. smile
on his face when it's barely even seven, this version of him feels
as watered-down as his gross coffee.

"Where's Mom?" I ask.

"Outside with Rodney."

I throw the blanket back onto my bed and pull on a sweater,
the whole time watching my dad out of the corner of my eye.
I've been so wrapped up in my own life over the last few months
that I haven't noticed what's been staring me in the face: Dad's
pinching pennies in any way he can to save money. How could
I have missed that?

Except . . . I know exactly how I've missed it. For the last
two years, every moment that I haven't spent studying, taking crappy online art classes, or exploring with Cy, has been
filled with volunteering at whatever animal shelter was closest
to where we parked the RV. All in the name of rounding out
my resume. I haven't been paying attention to money, mostly
because I rarely buy anything for myself. And when I do, it's
always cheap—a snack for the road, discounted eyeliner from
a drugstore, dollar-night movie-theater tickets. The biggest
splurges have always been on art supplies, and I save up Christ-
mas and birthday money from YiaYia for that stuff. I never even
worried about saving up for college, since I figured a combination of scholarships, financial aid, and a part-time job would

take care of tuition and whatever extra expenses I had as long as I lived cheaply. It seemed like a perfect plan. Until now.

Maybe Mom was right. Maybe I *have* been ignoring the families.

When I'm dressed, I take another sip of Dad's coffee, this time prepared for the lack of taste, and hand it back to him. "I'll be outside."

He grunts, but doesn't look up from the paper.

I find my mom and brother behind the McAlisters' RV, both standing silently, facing each other. I wait for a second, then realize they're having one of their epic staring contests. Never let it be said that nomad life isn't thrilling.

"Mom, I need to talk to you," I say when I can't stand it any longer. "Can you . . . maybe . . . pause the game?"

Rodney shakes his head, but doesn't break eye contact. "No pausing."

"Is it important?" Mom asks without looking away from my brother.

I think of my dad, sitting alone in our cold RV, a frown the size of Mississippi pulling his face into an unrecognizable shape. If I'm right, and he's in trouble, then we're all in trouble. "Yes, it's important."

Mom exhales. Then she closes her eyes.

"I win!" Rodney says, throwing his hands into the air. "You blinked."

Mom laughs. "Take a walk?" she asks me.

We link arms and walk around the perimeter of the giant gas station, leaving my brother to celebrate his victory. It's early, so there aren't many people around. Just a lot of gasoline puddles and a few stray beer cans rolling back and forth across the concrete. Not exactly scenic, but there are birds chirping and the breeze smells like the freshly roasted coffee they're serving inside the convenience store. It reminds me of the parking lot a block away from our old house in Chattanooga, where I learned to ride a bike. Mom would stand in the middle of the asphalt, a chipped mug of coffee clutched between her cold hands, and watch me ride around and around in a wobbly circle. We did it every Saturday for a month, until I was good enough to ride over to the parking lot on my own. I felt like a real badass, flying down the street, past the parking lot, and into downtown Chatt. It wasn't until years later that Mom revealed she'd followed me in the car for months before she finally let me go out on my own.

"What's up?" Mom asks.

I glance at her. If I ask about money straight out, she'll just wave me off and say not to worry. But maybe there's another way. "Remember how I asked you last month about getting a job?"

"Yes. I also remember telling you to enjoy yourself for a few months after school ended. Take a *break* for once. You're wound too tight."

I resist the urge to roll my eyes. "I appreciate your concern, Mom, but I'm serious."

She sighs. "Dessa, what would you even do? You know how hard it is to find work when we're always moving."

"I'll think of something," I say as we take a right at the gas pump.

"Why the sudden interest in getting a job?"

I shrug. "I want to help out around here. With the bills, the gas . . . traveling isn't cheap."

"You don't need to worry about any of that. We're doing just fine."

I want to protest, but she sounds so confident that I don't. Maybe Rodney heard wrong. Maybe Dad's just trying to toughen us up by not turning on the heat. It is May, after all.

"Dessa!" Rodney shouts across the parking lot. "It's your turn to take out the trash."

"She'll be there in a second," Mom yells, then turns back to me. "Was there anything else you wanted to talk about?"

College. Rejections. Shame.

I shake my head. "Nope."

CHAPTER 3

Sunny Point Café is packed when we arrive at nine. They push three tables together so all ten of us can fit. As usual, Cyrus and I sit at the middle of the table, with the McAlisters' twin girls across from us and Rodney on my left. Mr. and Mrs. McAlister take the head of one half of the table, while my parents and Cy's dad take the other. It's practically assigned seating at this point. Sometimes it bugs me—what if I want to sit next to someone else for a change?—but today it feels comforting. Like something that needs to be protected.

A pretty Chinese waitress comes to the table. "Good morning," she says in a cheerful voice, a stack of laminated menus cradled in her arms. Her eyes trail over Cy's face and down his chest.

Here we go again.

"Hey," Cyrus says. The waitress tries to hand him a menu, but he shakes his head. "That's okay. We'll have pancakes all around plus four sides of bacon." Cy glances down the table at my mom, who grimaces at the mention of meat, but he doesn't change our order. The only time I get to eat meat is when someone else cooks or orders it, so we have a longstanding deal that when it's Cy's turn to order breakfast, we have bacon, and when it's my turn to order, I make sure he isn't forced to eat scrambled eggs.

"Everyone will have coffee except the twins and Rodney," Cy says, gesturing to my brother. "They'll have orange juice."

Rodney crosses his arms over his chest. "I want coffee."

"You can have a sip of mine," I whisper.

The waitress scribbles down our order, glancing up every few seconds to look at Cyrus.

"Can I get you anything else?" she asks Cy, taking a step closer so her apron grazes his arm.

Cy and I look down the table to see if anyone has something to add, and I notice Dad looks uneasy. At first I'm not sure what's wrong, but then something awful occurs to me: Can we afford to help pay for all that food? I want to interject, but I can't embarrass Dad in front of everyone, especially when all I have to go on is Rodney's word, one cold morning, and a cup of shitty coffee.

"I think that's it." Cyrus looks at the name tag pinned to the front of her uniform. "Thanks, Alice."

She blushes, and I feel a tug of annoyance so strong it manages to trump my money worries. Every diner, every city—it's always the same. We end up with a waitress who has an instant crush on Cy. It's hard to blame her. He's stupidly cute, with his warm brown eyes and quick smile. But do they all have to be so obvious about it?

Alice returns with a tray of plastic water cups. I take a sip from mine, hoping to wash away my irritation before Cy notices. It never used to bother me when girls flirted with him. Sure, he'd go on the occasional date, but nothing ever went anywhere since we were always going *somewhere*. But it's been harder to ignore lately. Every time he smiles it's like there's something drawing me toward him, like a satellite stuck in a planet's orbit.

I really need to get my shit together.

At the end of the table, my dad taps his fork against his plastic cup. "There's something I'd like to say."

My mind immediately goes to what Rodney told me about Dad's business. I glance over at Mom for confirmation, but she doesn't look upset, worried, or even embarrassed.

"As you all know," Dad says, "things have been difficult recently. A few months ago, we lost one of our own."

I can practically feel Cyrus roll his eyes. He's sick of hearing the adults talk about his twenty-year-old sister like she's dead, instead of just settled down in Colorado. But I kind of get it. Ever since Cy's mom *actually* died when we were thirteen, Jeff's wanted to keep his kids close. It's hard to blame him.

"We knew Meagan wouldn't stay forever," Dad continues, "but none of us expected her to leave the traveling life so soon."

Jeff sighs, and closes his eyes. Mom pats his shoulder.

"And now," Dad continues, turning to look at my side of the table, "we're preparing to lose another."

I slide down an inch in my seat. This isn't about money. This isn't even about Meagan. This is about *me*.

"I know it's been hard waiting to hear from schools," Dad says, "but you're giving it everything you have, Dessa. We're all very proud of you."

I squeeze my hands together in my lap and force a smile. I wonder how *proud* they'll be when they find out I failed.

"You'll get in somewhere wonderful," Mrs. McAlister adds. "My niece got into college last year, and she wasn't half the student you are."

Her words are like a gut punch, but before I can recover, Mom speaks up.

"Personally," she says, twisting her rings around on her fingers, "I don't think Dessa needs art school to be successful. She's *already* an artist. I shouldn't have to lose my baby just so a few professors can tell us something we already know."

"Hear, hear," Jeff says, leaning back in his chair.

I dig my nails into my palms and take a slow, deep breath. "Mom, I've told you a million times that's not all art school is for. It's also about getting a degree, and establishing myself in the art community so I can go on to have a career—"

"Your dad is a web designer, and he doesn't have a degree."

"Mom, please—"

Cy stands up. "I have an announcement."

Everyone freezes.

He rubs the top of his head, like he always does when he's nervous, which makes *me* nervous. "Dessa, will you stand up for a second?" he asks.

"Cy . . ."

"Trust me," he says, pulling me to my feet. I stand next to him, my hands shoved into my pockets.

"Well?" Jeff calls down the table, a big grin on his face. "What happened? Did you two get hitched or something?"

My mom's eyes go wide.

"No!" I say, before she gets the wrong idea. It's an unspoken rule that we can never date. It would be way too complicated. At least, I assume that's how everybody feels. It's not like we've ever had a reason to talk about it.

Cy clears his throat, and I blush. Thank god he can't read minds.

"A month ago," he says, his voice oddly formal, "Dessa told me about an internship in Santa Fe with an artist named Fiona Velarde who needs help preparing for her upcoming gallery exhibit. The internship was the chance of a lifetime, but Dessa didn't apply because she figured there was no chance she'd ever get it. So instead, I applied for her."

I stare at him. "You did *what*?"

"It was hard to choose which piece of art to send since she only wanted one sample," Cyrus continues, ignoring me. "Competition was fierce. Apparently, almost a hundred people applied."

My mind is flooded with questions. I want to know which piece he sent in, whether he used the crappy digital files I sent to him in an email a few months ago. But more than anything I want to know what the *hell* he was thinking sending in my work without asking me first.

"When do you find out if she got it?" Mr. McAlister asks.

"Actually, I already know," Cy answers. "She announced it on her website this morning."

Everyone at the table is staring at us, and I can feel my heart pounding in my chest. Please don't let this be another rejection. Please don't let this be another failure.

Cy grins, his eyes crinkling at the edges. "It's you, Dess. You got it."

My mouth drops open, and for a moment, the whole world disappears. My favorite living artist wants *me*. *Fiona Velarde* chose *me*. It's as if I've been filled to the brink with warm air, and I'm floating toward the ceiling.

Cyrus folds me in a tight hug. His scruffy cheek tickles mine, and I can smell his shampoo. I lean into his chest, and his hand curls around the back of my neck. His touch makes my skin feel like it's on fire. I've kissed a few guys before, including a scruffy hipster in Portland last summer, but none of them have ever made me feel the way Cy can just by touching me.

Someone at another table laughs, and I remember everyone is watching us. My joy at Cy's embrace turns into panic. I pull away, ready to make excuses, but Mom and Mrs. M are hugging, and Dad is smiling extra big. Cyrus winks at me.

"Good work, kid." Jeff leans across Rodney and holds up his hand for a high five. I slap my palm against his, relieved that no one but Cyrus seems to have noticed how happy that hug made me. "Thank you so much," I whisper to Cy. "I owe you."

"Nah," he says. "Just dedicate your first masterpiece to me, and we'll call it even."

Cy and I sit back down just as Alice returns with the coffee and orange juice. When she places Cyrus' mug in front of him, I notice she takes an extra second to turn it so that the handle is facing him. When she puts mine down, the coffee sloshes onto the table. Maybe someone noticed our hug after all.

"So, Dessa," Mr. McAlister says as I wipe up the coffee with my napkin, "does this internship pay?"

"She should save the money if it does," Mrs. M says, staring hard at me over the rim of her coffee cup. "You never know when you'll need a little extra."

"Or give it to me," Rodney says.

"It doesn't pay," I say, but no one hears me. They're too busy arguing over what I should do with my imaginary paycheck.

"I think Dessa should buy herself something fun," Mom says. "Maybe a yoga mat."

Jeff shakes his head. "She should be helping out, like Cyrus does. Contribute to her family."

"She doesn't need to do that," Dad says immediately.

"Why not?" Jeff asks. "It can't hurt. And it'll teach her a sense of responsibility."

"Dessa is already responsible." Dad wipes his mouth and drops his napkin on the table. "And we don't need her help."

Next to him, Mom nods. "That's right—we're just fine. But that's very sweet of you for offering, Dessa."

"But I didn't—"

"I said we're *fine*," Dad snaps at me.

The group goes quiet. My dad never raises his voice, never gets mad. I glance over at Cyrus, but his eyes are glued to the table.

"Sorry," I say quietly, even though I have no idea what I'm apologizing for.

"Well," Mrs. M says, reaching over to pat my hand, "the point is that Dessa has a fantastic opportunity, and that's just great."

Alice appears behind Cyrus, a tray of plates balanced on her shoulder. "Who's ready for pancakes?" she says, and the McAlister girls' hands shoot into the air.

Alice gets to work distributing the pancakes, and everyone launches into conversation, talking all at once. It's like the tension at the table has cracked right down the middle, along with any resentment I had toward Alice. When she places my plate in front of me, I smile up at her, and say, "Thank you."

When breakfast is over, we slowly walk to the church parking lot where we left the RVs. I feel buoyed by the news. But when we arrive at the lot, Dad looks anything but happy. I kept an eye on him when the check came, but he split it with Mrs. McAlister and Jeff, so it didn't end up costing too much. But maybe I missed something. "What's wrong?" I ask.

"Nothing, nothing," he says, running his hands through his hair. He gestures for me to follow him, and we walk away from the group and stand in the shadow of our RV. When we're out of earshot, he says, "I'm just wondering when this internship starts?"

"Oh," I say, relieved. "I don't actually remember."

I motion for Cyrus to join us, and he ambles over. "What's up?"

"When does my internship start?" I ask him, feeling foolish that I don't already know.

"Well, that's the complicated part. It actually starts in four days."

"*What?*" Dad and I say at the same time.

"Yeah . . . when I applied, I didn't realize how quickly this Fiona woman was going to want Dessa to start. But . . . you know. *Artists.*"

The rest of the group joins us, leaning against the RV or sitting on the steps. Mom puts her arms around Dad's neck. "Everything okay?"

Dad clears his throat. "We're going to have to leave for Santa Fe a little sooner than I realized."

"How soon?" Mrs. McAlister asks, hoisting up one of the twins to sit on her hip.

"Right now."

The whole group immediately starts talking, and I feel the

first pinprick of worry. We're used to picking up and moving, but it's always because we want to. Never because we *have* to.

"Now hold on a second," Jeff says, raising his voice to be heard over everyone else. "We just got here, and I was going to put in a bid on a new bike this afternoon. I'm not ready to leave yet."

I look back and forth between my parents, willing one of them to argue on my behalf. But it's Cy who speaks.

"Dad, come on," he says. "We can find a bike in Santa Fe to fix up."

"That's right," Mrs. McAlister says, shifting her daughter onto her other hip. "Never stop moving, right?"

"We should take a vote," Jeff says. "That's what we always do before we move."

I shake my head. "This is totally different. It's not some random trip to the Ozarks."

Jeff crosses his arms. "Travelers decide together, or not at all."

Mom steps between us. "Let's not get worked up," she says. "Dessa, I understand how important this is to you, but fair is fair. We should vote."

"Mom!"

"I'm sorry, but Jeff's right. Travelers decide together. I'll get the hat."

She unlocks the door to our RV and disappears inside, leaving me to glare at Jeff. We have the rules for a reason; without them our caravan would fall apart. But this is exactly why I want out of this life. If I had normal parents with normal priorities, I'd be on a plane to Santa Fe right now. Instead, my future is about to be decided by a vote, and my mom, the one person who should always be on my side, is going to be counting the ballots.

"Got it," Mom says as she steps out of the RV. She's holding the beat-up San Francisco Giants hat we've been using to collect votes for as long as I can remember. "And here's the paper and a pen." She hands a sheet of notebook paper to Jeff, along with a crappy Bic that's missing a cap. "So, do we take Dessa to Santa Fe?"

The paper travels from person to person, everyone ripping off a piece. Then we pass the hat and pen around. We all avert our eyes as each person decides what to do with their paper—*Y* for "yea," *N* for "nay," or blank if you don't want to decide one way or the other. Even Rodney and the twins get a vote, though I'm pretty sure the girls have no clue what's going on. I stand at the end of the line, bouncing up and down on the balls of my feet as I wait for my turn.

But when Dad hands the pen to me, I hesitate. Yesterday I would have cast my vote without a second thought. This internship is the universe's way of giving me a second chance. Not at college, but at finding a way to make a new life for myself. A life of mixing pigments and staying up all night to capture the exact color of the moon at two in the morning. A life of color and light and texture. A life of my own, where I call the shots, instead of just being along for the ride.

But looking at my dad, I'm suddenly not sure. Going to Santa Fe will cost us money for gas and food, plus whatever we have to pay to park the RV overnight along the way. If Dad's struggling with money like I suspect, moving is the last thing we should be doing. Am I being selfish by demanding that we go?

"Go on," Dad says. He's looking right at me, which is against the rules since I haven't cast my vote yet. "It's okay, Dess."

I mark my paper with a *Y* for "yea," then drop it into the hat. Mom takes it from me, and shuffles through the papers. I watch her closely, my hands practically shaking with nerves. I know how Jeff voted, but what about my dad? What if he voted to stay? What if the McAlisters don't feel like visiting Santa Fe? If the vote comes out in favor of staying here, then that's it. My family would never leave the group behind. My heart compresses in my chest. I'd have to tell Fiona Velarde I'm not coming.

I feel Cyrus reach for my hand. I let him hold it.

"Okay," Mom says, dropping the slips of paper back into the hat.

"So?" I say. "Are we going?"

"Eight yea against two nay. Looks like we're going to New Mexico!"

"Yes!" I yell, throwing my hands up in the air. Jeff mutters something and walks away toward his RV to pack. I stick out my tongue after him.

"Dessa . . . ," Dad warns, but he's finally smiling.

"We better hit the road if we're going to make it in time," Mr. McAlister yells from the doorway to his RV.

"Everybody pack up." Mom kisses me on the forehead. "I knew it would work out," she whispers.

We pile into the RV to batten down the hatches. It's been a while since I've loved this lifestyle, but one great thing about being nomadic is that we don't have to do much before traveling—we don't have to put a hold on our mail, ask the neighbors to house-sit, or dig our suitcases out of the attic. Everything we need, everything we *own*, is already in the RV. All we have to do is make sure our stuff is locked away in the cabinets and off the floor so it doesn't roll around while we drive. Sometimes I make my bed before we travel, but since I promised Rodney he could hang out up there, I settle for climbing the ladder to straighten my comforter and lock the storage compartment by my bed. I may have agreed to let him up here, but that doesn't mean I want him messing with my stuff.

I'm about to climb down when I see the Greek prayer beads YiaYia gave me when I was Rodney's age. It didn't occur to me until just now, but if we're going to Santa Fe, we're going to see YiaYia. Stay with her, even. I grip the prayer beads tightly. Of all the people in my life, YiaYia is the only one who really understands why I want to go to art school so badly. She also totally gets why I'm tired of camping in the desert, or taking yet another detour down a random dirt road. Cyrus pretends to commiserate when I complain about not having a room of my own, but I can tell he secretly loves sleeping in his foldaway bed against the window, gazing up at the stars.

But none of that matters for the next two weeks. All that matters is that I kick this internship's ass.

"Buckle up!" Mom says from the front seat.

I jump off the ladder and shout, "Never stop moving!"

We break for gas outside Asheville. The three RVs in our caravan take up more than half the open pumps, earning us dirty looks from a few drivers, but we ignore them as usual. While Dad fills up the tank, I run over to Cy's RV and pull open the door. He's standing on the other side, a pile of clean laundry in his arms. A local hip hop station is playing quietly in the background, the DJ's voice barely more than a murmur. "Hey, what's up?" Cy asks.

"I thought I'd ride with you for a few hours so I can grill you about that unauthorized application you sent in."

"Sure," he says, stepping aside to let me in. "But you have to help me fold these."

My dad honks the RV horn, and moments later we start to move. Cy and I grab a seat on the foldout sleeper, the laundry between us. I sit on the edge, ignoring the fact that in a few hours he'll be lying here in nothing but his boxers, eyes closed as the moonlight pools on his skin. . . .

"Are you excited?" Cy asks.

"What?" I say, my cheeks flushing. "I mean, yes! But it's all happening so fast—I've barely had a chance to think."

"Don't think," he says, picking up a wrinkled T-shirt and handing it to me. "Do."

Cy turns up the radio, and we get to work folding clothes to the beat of old-school A Tribe Called Quest. It takes twice as long as necessary because I have to fix almost every shirt he folds.

"So which piece did you send Fiona?" I ask. "Was it the still life? Or the abstract?"

"Neither."

"Oh no," I say. "You didn't send—"

"The sunburst? Hell yeah, I did."

"Cyrus!" I grab a shirt and throw it at him. "That wasn't even in my portfolio."

"I know, but it's the best one. She said to send her something full of passion, and that one definitely is. So I took a picture of it with my phone—don't worry, I made sure it got good light and everything—and sent it to her."

I lie back on the couch, my head resting on some of the laundry. "She probably thought it was so juvenile," I groan. "The brushstrokes are messy and I completely disregarded what I learned last summer—"

"You already got the gig. Stop worrying."

"Yeah . . ." I sit back up, but my stomach is in knots. I never would have picked that painting. Not in a million years. Fiona is a serious artist, with shows all over the world. Sending her my sunburst painting is like sending J. K. Rowling my third-grade English homework and expecting her to be impressed I got an A.

But Fiona still chose it. Does that mean Cy was right, and if I had used that painting in my portfolio, I would have gotten into college? Or is this just a fluke? Did Fiona make a mistake?

"I wonder what kind of stuff she's going to have you do," Cyrus says, scrunching a pair of jeans into a ball and throwing them back on the couch. "Aren't most internships about getting people coffee and making photocopies?"

I pick up the jeans he threw, fold them in half lengthwise, then again three more times until they're a tight square. "She wants someone to help her prep for an upcoming show in Santa Fe. I'll probably be helping pack up her art so it can be moved safely, making a few phone calls, managing her calendar, stuff like that. And, you know . . . actual art classes." I grin at the thought. Me, taking art classes one-on-one with a *real* artist. It's been a while since I've sketched or painted anything, but working with Fiona will definitely help me find my muse again. I've just needed some good news, that's all.

"Right." Cyrus looks out the window. The recently rain-soaked North Carolina landscape whips past, a blur of green and brown I'd love to capture in paint. "So . . . there's one thing I forgot to tell you," Cy says. "But you have to promise not to freak out."

I pause, the T-shirt in my hands half-folded. "What is it?"

"I didn't think it was a big deal when I first applied for you, and I'm sure it's *still* not, but . . ."

"Cyrus. Tell me."

"There was a little note at the bottom of the application." He clears his throat. "It said she was only looking for 'college-bound' seniors."

My heart drops into my stomach, taking my breath with it.

"But you're still college-bound, right?" Cy asks. "You just haven't gotten in anywhere yet."

I look out the window.

"Dessa? It's okay, right?"

I sigh, but don't turn away from the window. I have to tell him the truth, but that doesn't mean I have to see the disappointment on his face when I do it. "UCLA was the last school. So, no. It might not be okay."

Cy lets out a long whistle. "What do you want to do?"

I lean my forehead against the window and watch the pavement streak by beneath us. This was supposed to be my second chance, not another reminder that I don't have what it takes. "I don't know."

CHAPTER 4

Graceland RV Park looks like every other RV park we've stayed in. Short, leafy trees planted in an attempt to make it feel homey, hookup sites to dump waste, 30/50 amp service to recharge. The only difference is that it's on Elvis Presley Boulevard behind Elvis Presley's Heartbreak Hotel, and there's a group of Elvis impersonators staying in the site next to ours. It's not even eight p.m. and they're already drinking hard. No fewer than thirty six-packs are stacked on a picnic table, and a middle-aged Elvis is busy unloading a cooler full of booze.

"These were the only spots available," Mom says.

"Let me guess," I say, tapping my finger against my chin. "Peanut butter and banana convention?"

As if he'd been waiting in the wings for his cue, a tall Elvis with a red face steps out of his trailer. "Hey, ladies! You ready to shake, rattle, and roll, or what?"

Mom and I look at each other. "I'm going to take a walk," I say.

"Okay, but keep an eye out for these guys," she says, nodding toward the Elvises. "All of them."

"Got it."

I leave our site, careful not to make eye contact with our drunk neighbors, and take a right. The first thing Cy and I usually do when we arrive in a new RV park is stretch our legs and figure out if there's anyone our age in the area. Being on the road all the time can be lonely, even if you're constantly meeting new people, and are surrounded by family. *Especially* when you're surrounded by family. But Cyrus had promised his dad he'd do some preliminary research on the Santa Fe motorcycle scene, so tonight I'm on my own, wandering around an RV park like a loser. If it was up to me, we'd still be on the road, driving straight through to Santa Fe. But it's not up to me, or even my dad. It's up to the families, so here we are, stopped for the night.

I turn down Heartbreak Lane, taking in the sights. Elvis impersonators occupy most of the park, but only some of the Elvises—Elvi?—brought their A game. Most have shitty costumes, but a few look like professionals making a pit stop on the way to Vegas. Outside a Travel Trailer fitted with Barbie-pink spinning rims, a woman with Dolly Parton hair squints against the setting sun as her husband waits impatiently for her to dab at the fake tan spray running down his neck and onto his rolled-sleeve white T-shirt. Past them, two Elvises in motorcycle jackets, black jeans, and synthetic wigs sit outside a rickety, silver Airstream trailer. When they spot me, the one on the right raises his eyebrows and holds up a joint, but I shake my head and keep walking. My mom may be a tree-hugging hippie, but that doesn't mean she won't skin me alive if I come home smelling like pot.

I make a right onto Hound Dog Way, and my thoughts turn to my internship. Maybe I don't have to tell Fiona Velarde about the whole college thing. The internship is only for two weeks— long enough for me to say that I'm still waiting to hear back from schools. By the time it's over, she'll probably have forgotten all about it.

I approach a crowd of Elvises standing around a junky-looking trailer with floral curtains, watching something just out of view. "Hound Dog" blares out of somebody's RV speakers and a guy calls out, "a-five, six, seven, eight!"

A trio of Elvises start to dance. They're all wearing the King's signature white pantsuit, with the exception of the Elvis in the middle, whose jumpsuit is covered in sparkly pink rhinestones. As he thrusts, the sun bounces off the glittery plastic and throws pink light all over the side of the RV.

"No no *no!*" yells a short man standing off to the side. His styled hair is jet black and shiny, as if he and Elvis once shared a hairdresser. "Jimmy, you're still thrusting out of time," he says, glaring at the pink Elvis.

I stifle a laugh and pull out my phone.

Just saw dancing Elvises. You're missing out.

Cy's response comes fast. **You join in? You'd look cute in a white jumpsuit.**

A warm blush spreads across my cheeks, but I don't respond. He flirts with everyone.

I do a few more laps of the park, stopping more than once to watch an Elvis rehearse for an impersonation competition, or fix another Elvis' hair. By the time I get back to the RVs, the sewage tanks are empty and the dead bugs have been cleaned off the front windows. Mom stands over a picnic table, setting out plates and napkins, while Dad fiddles with the site's barbecue. Jeff, Cy, and the McAlisters are seated at the picnic table on the other side of the scraggly shrub separating our parking spots. I wave, but stay on our side of the foliage. Sometimes it's nice to have nuclear-family time.

"Oh good, you're back," Mom says. "Soy dogs for dinner. Chicago-style. Grab the pickles."

Dad hands out the food, and we each take a seat under the awning that slides out of our RV. I sniff the soy dog, then force myself to swallow one bite, then another, before setting my plastic plate on the bench next to me. I'd rather go to bed hungry than choke down another bite of these meatless monstrosities.

"I know soy isn't your favorite," Mom says, "but you know how I feel about processed meats."

"They're fine, Mom." I pick up my hot dog and take another bite. "See?"

On the other side of the shrub, the McAlisters, Jeff, and Cy talk and laugh, but I'm too focused on this whole internship dilemma to be very chatty. I notice Dad's distracted too. He keeps offering me ketchup even though I don't like it on hot dogs, and when Rodney does an impression of the Elvises' horrible singing, Dad doesn't laugh. He stares right through him, like my brother's not even there.

After dinner I help Mom carry the dishes inside to the kitchen while Rodney works on his homework outside. Dad disappears, but I figure he's walking off his food. Mom hands me the dirty plates just as my cell phone rings in my pocket, the Beatles crooning through the fabric. Cyrus' ringtone.

I hold up the phone in my free hand. "Can I—?"

"Go ahead," she says with a sigh, taking the dirty dishes back. "You can use our bedroom. But don't be long. We're getting an early start tomorrow."

I go into the back and close the door behind me. "Hey," I say, collapsing onto the Murphy bed. I can see the side of Cy's RV out the window. "What's up?"

"I finally finished researching our Santa Fe options. There are a couple of bikes for sale on Craigslist. When Dad gets back from the McAlisters', I'm going to show him the one I think we can fix up in two or three weeks."

The sound of his voice makes my fingers itch with the desire to touch him, even though I wouldn't do it even if he was sitting right next to me. "That'll keep you busy."

"For sure."

The line goes quiet. I grip the phone, imagining all the things he could be thinking and not saying.

"I got a weird email," he says at last. "Do you remember Rachel?"

Roscoes and Rebeccas and Roberts and Rashidas flash before my eyes, but no Rachels come to mind. "No, should I?"

"I guess not. She was the girl who worked at the coffee shop in Dallas."

"The one with the lip ring?"

"Yeah, that's her. She's thinking about buying a bike, and she wanted my opinion."

"Oh."

"Anyway, I told her we're going to be in Oklahoma City tomorrow night, and she offered to drive up and meet me. I guess there's a show she wants to see anyway, so we're gonna go together."

I sit in silence, waiting for him to invite me. But the silence stretches on.

"Anyway, I just thought that was a weird coincidence," he says. "What are the chances, right?"

I stare up at the ceiling of the RV. My chest is so tight I'm not even sure if I'm breathing.

"So," Cyrus continues, "your dad didn't seem too excited about driving to Santa Fe. You think he's mad at me for springing the internship on everyone?"

"He's not mad."

"So everything's fine?"

"Well . . . he *did* try to give me ketchup at dinner."

"You hate ketchup."

I laugh, but it sounds raw. Fake. "Exactly."

A door shuts on Cy's end. "Dad's here. I gotta show him what I found."

I hesitate, wanting so badly to tell him not to go out with Rachel. But even as I think it, a little voice in the back of my head reminds me that there's no point.

"See you in the morning?" he asks.

I pull in a shaky breath. "Okay. Bye."

The phone clicks, and he's gone.

I lie there for a second, staring into the darkness outside the window. I always told myself he wasn't interested in me, but deep down, I thought . . . maybe. Maybe he felt the same way, but was better at hiding it than me. Maybe he wanted me to kiss him that day in the rain, just like I wanted to. But I'm kidding myself by even considering the possibility of us being together. We can't date. Not as long as we're travelers. Not as long as we're family. It's too big a risk. Even if our parents were fine with it—they'd tease us, for sure—what if it didn't work out? It'd be chaos. Hurt feelings, fighting between the families. And it'd be all our fault. All *my* fault.

In the space next to ours, the Elvises begin a raucous rendition of "Viva Las Vegas," complete with a loud instrumental track to back them up. I hear Mr. McAlister yell, *"Keep it down!"* but they just keep singing.

CHAPTER 5

The RV bumps along a side street, the headlights casting a yellow-white glow on the asphalt ahead. Mom strains to make out the street signs, but apparently, signage wasn't a priority when they built this Oklahoma City suburb. "When Jeff said the lot was off the beaten path," she says, "I didn't think he meant we'd have to drive around in the dark for thirty minutes, searching for an invisible sign."

"Maybe we should go back the other way," I suggest from the passenger's seat. The other RVs stopped for gas about ten minutes ago, but we foolishly volunteered to scout the lot. "Maybe it was—" A handwritten sign flies by my window. "Wait—stop!"

Mom slams on the breaks and we both crane our necks to see behind us. Leafy trees loom overhead. "Was there a road back there?" she asks.

"I think so. Back up."

Mom slowly reverses. The crooked white sign comes into view. "It says 'Parking for Greeks Only,' and there's a really bad drawing of the Parthenon." I turn back to look at her. "It's gotta be the one."

"Yep." She turns down a short gravel driveway and into a dirt lot, throwing the RV into park at the first opportunity. "Home sweet home," she says, stretching her arms overhead.

I roll down the window, and we listen to the sounds of the night outside. Crickets, distant traffic, the wind whistling through the trees surrounding the lot. I breathe deeply. Mom and I spent the last ten hours sitting side by side, and somehow I filled that space with everything but the one thing I have to tell her, but can't bring myself to say: I didn't get into college. There were opportunities—plenty of them—but each time I opened my mouth to tell her about UCLA and all the other schools I didn't get into, the future I let slip through my fingers, it felt like my throat was closing up. It also didn't help that Mom kept saying how proud she was of me. So instead, I said nothing.

Dad comes out of the bedroom, where he's been looking for freelance work on his laptop using a personal hotspot thingy he bought when we first started traveling. I try not to wonder how badly our family needs that work.

"Found the lot?" Dad asks.

Mom nods. "Finally."

Rodney jumps off my bed and lands with a thud in the middle of the aisle. "I want to go outside," he says. "Can I?"

Mom shrugs, but Dad shakes his head. "It's bedtime."

"It's only nine thirty," Rodney whines. "I still have an hour left."

"We're leaving early again," Dad says. "Brush your teeth. You can have the bathroom first."

Rodney groans, but there's no point in arguing with Dad on travel days. We either stick to the rules, or he'll put us on windshield duty—a particularly gross job when we're driving across the country, since there are so many bugs just waiting to splatter across the front of the RV. I learned that lesson the hard way.

But then again, I was a kid when that happened, like Rodney is now. "Dad, I'm going for a quick walk to stretch my legs."

Dad raises an eyebrow. "You heard what I told your brother."

"Right, but I'm seventeen, not ten."

"Seventeen is still a kid."

"But Cyrus went out—"

"Cyrus is eighteen, and Jeff's kid, not mine." He rests a hand on my head for a second, then ruffles my hair. "Get some rest."

Dad opens the door and steps outside. Where is *he* going? It's not like there's a convenience store or something nearby— the closest street light is half a mile away. I shut the door behind him, and lean against it. I'm used to how quiet he is, to how he'll listen to an argument for ten minutes before offering his opinion. But he's always here. Not like the last few days—his mind seems to be anywhere and everywhere else.

I close the door behind him, but not before I hear the click of his lighter, and catch a whiff of cigarette smoke. *Shit.*

The bathroom door opens and Rodney comes out. I go in, put down the toilet seat, and sit. But instead of enjoying my few minutes of solitude, I imagine my dad, standing out there in the dark, smoking. I take a deep breath and exhale slowly, trying to relax, but I feel trapped in the cramped bathroom. It reminds me of how close I came to getting out of here, to having the sort of life where I could take a walk just because I felt like it. Applying to colleges was scary, but it felt so good to know the end was near. Now I don't even have *that* to look forward to.

At least I have the internship . . . for now, anyway. That'll have to be enough.

I turn on the sink and splash my face with cool water. We've been driving for hours, but I'm not tired. My muscles are coiled and buzzing with unspent energy. Any minute now, Cyrus and Rachel will meet for the first time in almost a year. They'll hug hello, say how good the other looks, laugh at some dumb joke. I groan and rest my head against the mirror. I should have stayed with him in the rain. I should have pressed my body against his, and told him the truth I've carried since that hot day in Mississippi when our parents introduced us—

There's a knock on the bathroom door. "Dessa?" Mom calls. "You almost done?"

"Almost," I say, flushing the toilet even though I didn't use it. I turn on the faucet again, and stare at myself in the mirror. *I am not afraid of the future,* I tell my reflection. *I am not afraid of tomorrow, or the day after that. I am not afraid of spending every hour of every day with my family until I die, curled up in my bed like a mummy in a too-small sarcophagus.*

"Dessa," she calls again. "Your brother forgot to wash his face. You need to hurry up."

I wipe my hands on a towel and then open the door. "All yours," I tell Rodney, who's standing there, glaring at Mom.

"You'll thank me when you don't get acne at eleven," she says.

Rodney locks himself inside the bathroom, leaving Mom and me standing alone in the galley kitchen. I look around for Dad, but he's still not back.

"Hey, Mom?"

"Hmm?"

"Is Dad . . . is he smoking again?"

"Of *course* not," she says, her voice ticking up an octave. "Why would you say that?"

"He seems stressed, and he's been gone awhile. Is everything okay?"

Mom picks up a towel and twists it around in her hands. She's going to tell me the truth. She has to. She'll tell me that Dad's smoking, that he's struggling to support us financially. She has no choice.

"I'm going to bed." She drops the towel on the stove. "Night."

Anger bubbles inside of me as I watch her shut the bedroom door behind her. But there's nothing to say, nothing to do. That's the irony of living in a mobile home. You can travel anywhere you want, but as soon as you need space, there's nowhere to go.

I climb up the ladder to my bed and pull out my cell phone.

My finger hovers between Twitter and Facebook—do I want to live vicariously through strangers, or old friends I never talk to anymore? I settle on Facebook, and within seconds I'm scrolling through a mix of spring break photos and emoji-studded political rants. Then something new catches my eye: Charlotte Rosenberg's smiling face.

Charlotte was my best friend from the moment we met in second-grade art class. We played video games and rode our bikes, and she was the first person that noticed I could draw. I thought we'd stay best friends, even when I moved away. And for a while, we did. We talked on the phone every night, and I sent her postcards whenever we stopped somewhere new. But then she made new friends, and started telling me stories about people I didn't know. Who I didn't *want* to know. I'm not sure who stopped calling who first, but in my heart of hearts, I think it might have been me.

But here she is, Charlotte Rosenberg, staring up at me from my phone with a smile so big it's practically leaping off the screen. She's holding a piece of paper. I try to read it, but the type's too small, so I read the caption instead.

Just got the news! University of Southern California said YES. Film school here I come!!!

I stare at the screen, Charlotte's face blurring into colorful pixels. Charlotte is going to college. I squeeze my eyes shut, and try to breathe. I shouldn't be surprised. Charlotte was always a good student, and I remember seeing a post about the film club she started her sophomore year. She worked hard. She deserves this. But that doesn't make the truth of the situation hurt any less: Charlotte's going to college, to live the life I want so badly that I can taste it in the back of my mouth. And I'm staying right here.

The RV door opens, and Dad comes back inside. As he walks by my bed, I catch a whiff of something stale and burning—cigarettes. I grip my phone. First Charlotte, now this. There are so many things I want to say. I want to shout and cry and beg Dad to stop, but he's heard it all before. Nothing makes a difference once he starts, not even the cancer scare YiaYia had a few years ago. She quit, but it took him months to finally kick the habit. And now it's back.

"Everyone's parked. You should get ready for bed," he says, gesturing at the boots I'm still wearing. "Early start tomorrow."

I glare at him, but he just nods and pats my knee. "Chuff, chuff," he says with a tired smile. "See you in the morning."

I don't answer.

Below me, Rodney curls up on his pullout bed, and Dad turns out the lights. "Good night," he whispers, then goes into his bedroom and shuts the door, leaving Rodney and me alone, cocooned in darkness. I let the sounds of nighttime wrap around me. Mom snoring in the other room. The creak of the RV's suspension. Rodney tossing and turning in his bed, making little noises as he battles whatever monsters populate the dreams of ten-year-old boys. I pull my pillow over my head, humming to drown out the noise. Instead, my mind returns to

Charlotte's radiant smile, and to the hateful, hateful message on the UCLA website.

Application Status: Enrollment Denied.

What will Fiona say when she finds out I'm not going to college? Will she kick me out of her studio for being a liar, for wasting her time? I groan, and rub my eyes. I have to focus on something else. On *anything* else. I reach for my cell phone again. Whenever I can't fall asleep, I text Cyrus. He's got a touch of insomnia, so there's usually a good chance he's still awake, reading an auto magazine, or researching the music scene wherever we're living. Sometimes we talk about what we're doing the next day, and sometimes we just send goofy selfies back and forth until we're laughing so hard we wake our parents. I start typing a message to him—then stop.

He can't talk right now, because he's not home. He's on a date. With Rachel.

I throw my pillow at the wall. "Damn it."

Rodney turns over in his sleep. I freeze, counting slowly to ten before I let myself move.

The earthy smell of Oklahoma dirt drifts into the RV through the open windows. Cyrus is out there somewhere, having fun. I bet Charlotte is too. Why should I be stuck in here? I always follow the rules, always do what I'm told. I aced the SATs, busted my ass in my home school classes. And for what? All my good behavior has ever gotten me is a stomach full of disappointment. Maybe it's time to try being the laid-back traveler kid my parents always wanted me to be, instead of an uptight artist with a freaking pipe dream.

Before I lose my nerve, I climb down the ladder, careful to skip the squeaky third step. When I reach the bottom, I grab my purse with one hand and open the door of the RV with the other. It's warm and humid, so I pull off my sweatshirt and stuff it into my bag. I can't believe I'm doing this. I've explored the nighttime world with Cy a million times, but I've never snuck out alone. Just the thought of it sends a shiver down my spine.

As soon as I reach the main street, I pull out my cell phone and open the map. Usually Cy and I waste at least ten minutes arguing about how to spend the first night in a new place—wander around downtown? Dollar movie night? Catch up on laundry?—but tonight the decision is all mine. I'm not too far from downtown Oklahoma City, so I figure I'll start there. I use my phone to find out which bus will take me, then set off in the direction of the nearest bus stop.

Walking alone with no one asking anything of me, no one telling me what to do or where to go or who to be . . . it's incredible. As freeing as traveling the country can be, it's not often I get to do exactly what I want to exactly when I want to. I grin into the darkness, punctuated only by the winking bodies of the fireflies hovering around me, their soft light pulsing their hello.

When I reach the bus stop, I take out my phone and see a text from Cyrus. **This place is packed. Rachel says hi.**

I clench my teeth. Is he trying to torture me? My fingers

itch to answer him. I want to tell him what I'm doing. Maybe it'll make him wish he was with me instead of with Rachel. It would serve him right.

I shake my head and drop my phone into my purse. I'm not going to spend my one night of freedom worrying about Cyrus. He can hear about it tomorrow. Tonight is for me.

The bus pulls up to the curb, and I get on. The driver barely looks at me, and he takes off with a lurch as soon I drop my coins into the machine. I make my way down the aisle, holding on to the backs of seats even though I'm used to walking while a vehicle's moving—nothing like living in an RV to give you sea legs. I catch a glimpse of my reflection in the window. I'm smiling like I've never been on a bus before. I try to stop, but I can't help it.

There are only two other passengers on the bus. An old man, slumped over in his seat, his hat pulled down to cover his eyes. And a girl around my age wearing a cropped leather jacket despite the heat. I take a seat across the aisle from her and look out the window. The bus is the brightest thing in this neighborhood, its yellow headlights illuminating the sleeping lawns as we pass. I imagine my bed, the sheets holding the shape of me even though I'm not there, my worries pressing down on the fabric in my absence. I'm glad to be out here, speeding through the night, on my way to nowhere in particular.

The quiet neighborhood slowly gives way to lively city streets. The *ding* of a passenger requesting a stop rings out, and

I turn to see the old man using the back of the seat in front of him to pull himself up. When the bus stops in front of a convenience store, the old man gets off, leaving just the girl and me. I wonder where she's going. A friend's apartment? Maybe to a late-night job? She glances at me, and I look away, but a second later I'm staring at her again. Her red hair is pulled back tight against her head in a ponytail, and her eyeliner is razor thin. She'd look severe, but there's something about the way her lips are curled up at the sides that makes it look like she's about to smile at any moment.

"Can I help you?" she says.

I jump in my seat. She's the one staring at me now, an expectant look on her face. "Sorry," I say. "You just remind me of someone."

It's a bad excuse, but then she smirks and I realize it's true—she really *does* remind me of someone. The way her head is tipped to the side as she waits for me to answer, how she's squeezing her knees to her chest while her cowboy boots tap against the back of the seat in front of her—it's *exactly* how Charlotte used to sit on the bus ride home from school, back when my family still lived in Chattanooga in the Pre-Nomad days.

"I get that a lot," she says. "What's your name?"

"Dessa. You?"

"I'm Taryn."

"Where are you headed?"

She looks at me funny, and I remember that non-travelers feel uncomfortable when a stranger asks them where they're going. "Sorry," I say. "You don't have to tell me."

She shrugs. "I'm going to the Little Red Rooster. You heard of it?"

"No, sorry."

She turns in her seat to face me, her legs sticking out across the aisle. "What about you? Where are you going?"

"I'm not really sure," I admit. "I'm only in town for one night, so I thought I'd walk around for a while."

"You're traveling alone?"

"No, with my family. We're going to Santa Fe so I can start an internship. But I needed a break."

She laughs. "I know that feeling."

The bus stops at a red light, and a pregnant woman gets on. When the bus moves again, Taryn scoots across the aisle into the open seat in front of me. Her green eyes stare straight into mine.

She folds her arms over the back of the seat. "Where's your family? In a hotel?"

I shake my head. "RV."

"And they just let you go out?"

"Actually . . . I snuck out."

"No shit? Well, you should probably make sure it's really worth it."

I consider this. "I've never been to downtown Oklahoma City before. Do you have any suggestions?"

She smiles, her lips curving up like the Cheshire Cat's. "Yeah. You should come with me."

"With . . . you?"

"Yeah!" Taryn says. "Why not? But I should warn you . . . there will be dancing."

I chew on the inside of my cheek, considering. The old Dessa would have said no—roaming around in the middle of the night with a stranger was definitely not part of The Plan to get into college. But the old Dessa wouldn't have snuck out in the first place. Taryn could turn out to be totally bananas, but she could also be a lot of fun. Probably both. After the day I've had, this might be exactly the kind of night I need. "I'm in."

Her smile stretches into a full grin. "Sweet. We'll get off at the next stop."

Before long, Taryn is leading us down a residential block. It's so quiet that I can hear myself breathing. I glance over at her, but she's looking straight ahead. I should say something. Make conversation. I swallow hard. "Are we close?"

"It's just around this corner," she says.

We turn left and a single-story building comes into view at the end of the street, a blue fluorescent sign blinking from the roof.

It's a bar.

I stop walking. "Shit. I'm not twenty-one."

"Oh, that's okay. Neither am I."

"Do you have a fake ID?"

"Nah. I used to date one of the bartenders, so they know me." She shrugs. "Come on, the band goes on in ten minutes."

We start walking again, Taryn a few steps ahead. I look down at myself—plain white shirt, ripped thrift store shorts, scuffed ankle boots, sweatshirt hanging out of my bag. No way do I look cool enough to hang out with the bartender's ex-girlfriend.

We stop in front of the Little Red Rooster, which squats between two houses. I shield my eyes from the glare of the sign.

Taryn rolls her shoulders. "Ready?"

The tiniest bit of apprehension rises inside me, but I shove it back down. For once, tonight isn't about thinking or worrying or planning. It's about throwing myself in headfirst, consequences be damned.

"I'm ready."

CHAPTER 6

Taryn strides up to the front door, past a short line of people waiting to get in. Everyone looks so much older than me, so much cooler. I follow her, my palms sweating at the thought of going into a bar for the first time. But when I catch the dirty looks I'm getting for cutting, I hang back.

"Hey, Eddie!" Taryn calls. "Miss me?"

"There she is!" A bouncer dressed in black pants and a black T-shirt wraps Taryn in a tight hug, lifting her a few inches off the ground. "I wondered if I'd be seeing you tonight."

Taryn beckons me forward.

"Sorry," I mutter as I pass the people waiting. A guy in an orange OSU hat throws his hands up into the air, but doesn't say anything.

When I reach the front of the line, Taryn takes my hand and says, "This is my friend Dessa. We're here to dance."

"Dessa, huh?" Eddie narrows his eyes, but his lips quirk into a smile. "You gonna behave yourself in there, Miss Dessa?"

I can feel the whole line watching us. "Yes, sir," I say, nodding. "I promise."

"Sir!" He laughs and smacks his leg. "Taryn, this girl is way too polite for your rude ass."

Taryn pretends to look hurt. "Well, I *never.*"

The guy in the OSU hat steps out of line. "Hey, man! The band is going to start soon. Can we move this reunion along?"

Eddie points at him. "Stay in line or you ain't getting in."

OSU-hat groans, but steps back into line.

"Now, you two behave," Eddie says as he pushes open the door to the bar. "Don't make me call your brother again, Taryn."

"I won't," Taryn says over her shoulder as she pulls me inside. Country music and cigarette smoke immediately battle for my attention. I cough, and Taryn laughs. "Gross, right?" she yells. "I always shower as soon as I get home."

"What did he mean, 'don't make me call your brother?'" I yell back. "What happened?"

Taryn shrugs. "I had a little too much to drink a few weeks ago after a fight with my ex. But it's no big deal. Come on!"

Before I have a chance to ask how much is *too* much, she leads me deeper into the crowded room, keeping a tight hold on my hand so we don't get separated. All around us, people are laughing and drinking, forced to yell over the music to be heard even though they're standing right next to each other. I'm still a little unnerved by what Eddie said, but I push the feelings away.

"Is it always this busy?" I yell.

Taryn shakes her head. "Only when there's a band!"

We keep pressing forward, Taryn squeezing between

people when she can, tapping them on the shoulder and asking
them to move when she can't. I follow her, pulling my hair out
of its ponytail and tugging on my tank top so it looks purposefully disheveled instead of just stretched out from wearing it all
the time.

We finally reach an old-fashioned jukebox. Taryn presses
her back against it so I can squeeze in next to her. "Fun, right?"
she says, her cheeks flushed. "I'm going to get a drink. Want
anything?"

"Water?"

Taryn looks disappointed. "Be back in a minute—don't
move."

She lets go of my hand, and I lose sight of her almost immediately. I take a step into the crowd and stand on my tiptoes,
looking for her red hair in the sea of blondes and brunettes. I
shouldn't have stayed behind. What if it gets so crowded that she
can't find me again? Or what if the band starts and she forgets
I'm here? What if I wait for her for hours, and then everyone
leaves, and I'm stuck here alone, and—

A splash of something cold and wet runs down the back of
my shirt.

"Hey!" I say, spinning around.

A tall guy in a button-down shirt and a cowboy hat looks
back at me, his eyes so blue they shine in the dim light. "I'm
so sorry about that!" he says in a voice with just a hint of a
Southern accent. "I was trying to get through this crowd, but

someone bumped into me." He takes off his hat and holds it to his chest. He shakes his head, and a lock of messy blond hair falls into his eyes. "But I shouldn't be making excuses. Are you all right?"

A warm blush creeps up my neck. "I'm okay."

He leans to the side so he can see my back. "Oh, man. I really got you. I'm so sorry."

"It's okay. Really."

"Well, can I buy you a drink to make it up to you? It's the least I can do."

A woman steps between us, forcing me back against the juke-box. When she's gone, the cowboy steps close enough that I can smell his spicy cologne. I tip my head back so I can still see his face.

"My friend is bringing me a drink," I say.

"Your friend?"

His smile falters, and I realize my mistake—he thinks I'm not interested. *Crap.* "But . . . maybe later?"

He grins again, so big and goofy this time that my nervousness starts to melt away. "Later it is. I'll find you."

He disappears into the crowd, hat back on his head. I'm only alone for a few seconds before Taryn appears beside me. "Were you talking to someone?" she says, handing me a plastic cup of water. I guess people drop a lot of glasses in this bar. "All I could see was a cowboy hat."

"It was no one, really. He just spilled some beer on me, and then he offered to buy me a drink."

"Did you say yes?"

"Um . . . I said you were already getting me one, actually."

She rolls her eyes. "Oh, Dessa."

A guy in a plaid shirt steps onto the low stage at the back of the room. "Hello, Oklahoma City! Are you ready to dance?"

The crowd cheers. Beside me, Taryn takes a gulp of beer, then wipes her mouth with the back of her hand. I remember what she said about drinking too much, but one beer is nothing to worry about. It's not like she's driving. I take a sip of water.

"We've got a special guest tonight. All the way from Memphis . . . it's Ben Mathers!"

"Oh my god!" Taryn yells, jumping up and down. Her beer sloshes out of her red Solo cup, narrowly missing my foot. "I didn't know he was coming! I cannot believe this. I cannot freaking believe this."

"Who's Ben Mathers?" I ask, peering up at the stage to see if I can get a glimpse of him.

Taryn stares at me wide-eyed. "You've never heard of Ben Mathers? Holy crap, Dessa, you haven't *lived* until you've heard him sing 'One Night Only.' This is going to be *amazing*."

The guy onstage motions for everyone to quiet down. "Now, before we start—let's go over the rules."

Everyone cheers, and the guy with the mic grins.

"Rules?" I say to Taryn, but she only laughs.

Mic guy holds up his hands to get everyone's attention again. "Rule number one," he says. "If you're going to sing—"

"Don't spill your beer!" the crowd responds, their voices rising as one.

I laugh, and Taryn throws her arm around me.

The mic guy nods. "Very good. Rule number two. If you're going to dance—"

Taryn holds up her cup. "Don't spill your beer!" she yells with everyone else.

"Exactly," mic guy says as he walks across the stage. "And finally, the third rule. The most important rule."

The room goes quiet—or as quiet as two hundred people packed into a smoky room can get.

"If you finish your drink . . ." he says, his voice low now, "and you're thinking of going home . . ."

I raise my glass—I can see where this is going. "Have another beer!"

The crowd explodes with cheers and shouts and whistles, and I join them. In all the time I've spent traveling with the families, I've never been anywhere like this. Not without parental supervision anyway. All around us people tap their beers against one another and throw back their drinks. Beside me, Taryn swallows hers in one gulp.

"Do you want one?" she asks when she sees me looking at her empty cup. "I'm going to have another."

I bite my lip. If I have one now, and then the cowboy brings me another, that'll be two beers and no food since I ate a peanut butter and jelly sandwich for dinner hours ago. But then again, when's the last time I did anything fun like this? And when will I get the chance again?

"What the hell," I say. "I'll have whatever you're having."

"Atta girl! Be right back." Taryn wades into the crowd, leaving me to slide back against the wall, the trusty jukebox on my right. All around me, people are staring up at the now-empty stage, eagerly awaiting the famous Ben Mathers. I pull out my phone to Google him and notice I have a text from Cyrus.

You asleep already?

I'm still staring at his message when Taryn appears beside me. "For you," she says, handing me a cup full to the brim with beer.

"Thanks." I take a sip and feel the cold bubbles slide down my throat. I grimace a little at the bitterness, but swallow another big gulp anyway.

"Boyfriend?" she asks, nodding to my phone.

"Just a friend."

"Hmmm. Your face says you wish he was more.'"

I take another swig of beer. "Something like that."

"Well, forget him. You've got a cowboy waiting out there, and you're about to hear Ben sing for the first time. We don't need any stupid not-boyfriends in our lives!"

I look down at my phone. Taryn's right. I'm still hanging on to every word Cyrus says. Enough worrying about him and his date. Enough worrying about *everything*. I hold down the button on the side until the phone turns off, then drop it into my bag.

"Yes!" Taryn chugs the rest of her beer, then grabs my arm. "Come on. Let's get a spot near the front. I've seen Ben ten times but I always end up getting stuck at the back."

We push our way onto the dance floor, me holding my beer above my head. This time I make my own way to the front instead of following in Taryn's wake. It takes a lot of "excuse me's" and a few gentle shoves, but within minutes we're right up against the stage, inches from the mic.

The guy in plaid walks back out. "Okay, Oklahoma City. Put your hands together for the one and only Ben Mathers!"

Taryn screams, and I join her. Ben walks out, and I immediately see at least *part* of why she likes him so much. He's got wavy brown hair and high cheekbones, and his guitar is slung across his back like he was born with it. But even as he steps up to the mic, I can't help but notice he isn't as good-looking as the cowboy who offered me a drink earlier, and nowhere near as hot as Cy. I chug my entire beer, then place the empty glass on the floor. The sooner I'm not holding one, the sooner that cowboy will come by with another.

"Hello, Oklahoma City," Ben says, his smooth voice barely more than a whisper. It sends a little thrill through me. All around us, people stomp their boots and call out. A big guy at the edge of the stage blows a loud wolf whistle. Only Taryn is standing quietly, her eyes fixed on Ben.

Ben pulls his guitar around to his chest, then leans into the mic. "This first song is called 'Home for Good.'"

He closes his eyes and begins to play. His singing voice is great—a little gravely, a little soulful, and a lot country. I look over at Taryn, but she's swaying back and forth, singing along.

The song ends and Ben says, "Now, I know y'all didn't come out just to hear me sing."

"We wanna dance!" a woman in the back yells.

Ben laughs. "I think you'll all recognize this next song. It's by the one and only Garth Brooks, and it's one of my favorites." He takes off his guitar and grabs another from the guy standing at the edge of the stage. It's older-looking, and sort of plain. But from the way he cradles it carefully in his arms, I can tell he likes it much more than the other one.

"This," Ben says, "is 'Friends in Low Places.'"

He strums the opening notes, and the crowd goes wild. People quickly form four lines, all facing the stage. Taryn grabs my hand. "Come on—let's dance."

Panic sweeps through me. I knew we were going to dance, but I didn't realize it would be *line* dancing. "I don't know how."

But Taryn's already joined the middle of the line closest to us, her thumbs hooked into the belt loops of her jeans. Just as Ben reaches the chorus, people start to move. Somehow they all seem to know the steps. I watch carefully, trying to pick it up, but they dance so fast it's hard. They turn to face the right side of the bar instead of the front, and I realize they're repeating some of the same moves. I keep watching, and sure enough, they face the front of the bar, and the choreography begins again.

When the song ends, everyone turns to the stage and cheers. I expect Taryn to come back and join me, but Ben strikes up a new song I don't recognize, and everyone begins dancing again. I watch for a minute, wondering if maybe this song has different steps, but after a few seconds I realize everyone's still doing the same choreography from before.

"Don't be a wuss," I whisper to myself, before running forward to squeeze between Taryn and a pretty blonde who winks at me. I manage to work my way through the entire chorus. It feels fantastic—I follow the steps, clap in time with the music, and let Ben's voice drown out my own. We move as one, like we're part of something bigger than just ourselves. The night slips away, taking my fear and sadness with it.

When I finally take a break after a few more songs, I notice the cowboy grinning at me from off to the side of the dance floor.

"You're not bad," he says, walking over.

"Thanks." I swipe the back of my hand across my forehead. Not too sweaty, thankfully.

"So, how about that drink?"

I look around for Taryn, but she's deep in conversation with the blonde from the dance floor, their fingers intertwined. I take a deep breath, and smile up at him.

"What the hell," I say. "Lead the way."

CHAPTER 7

"I never asked your name," the cowboy says as we grab a spot at the bar.

"No, you didn't." I reach across him for a napkin, taking the opportunity to lean into him a little, my hip against his. I blush at my own bravado. So *this* is why people call beer "liquid courage." "Do you want to?"

He grins. "I do."

"Dessa Rhodes."

"Roads, like traveling? That name's begging to have a country song written about it."

"No, Rhodes, like—"

"Just a second." He flags down the bartender—a guy with a look on his face that says he knows all your secrets, especially the dirty ones. I wonder for a second if he is Taryn's ex, but based on how obsessed she was with adorable Ben Mathers, this guy doesn't really seem like her type.

"What'll you have?" the bartender asks me.

"Beer."

The cowboy laughs. "Any preference?"

"Oh." I look at the row of taps. "Uh . . . Stella?"

"Make that two, Mike," he tells the bartender, who walks away to get our drinks. "I'm Luke, by the way."

I reach out my hand. "Nice to meet you, Luke."

We shake, both of us smiling like idiots.

Mike returns with our drinks. I notice him frown a little but then Luke hands me a beer and taps his glass against mine. "To you, Dessa Roads."

I smile into my beer, and take a sip. It's better than whatever I had before—not as bitter. I drink more.

"Whoa," he says. "Thirsty?"

"From dancing," I say, reluctantly putting the glass down. "I've never done that before."

"You must not be from around here."

"Nope." I shake my head, and the motion makes me dizzy. I lean against the bar.

Across the room, Ben says, "This next song is called 'One Night Only,' and it's a slow one. So partner up, lovebirds."

"This is my friend's favorite song," I say.

"It's a good one," Luke agrees. He gestures toward the dance floor, leaving our half-finished drinks behind. "Do you wanna—?"

I nod, and he takes my hand and leads me onto the dance floor. Luke slides his arm around my waist. I breathe in his cologne, the smell of his hair. The song is romantic, the kind that makes you want to dance forever.

He puts his hand under my chin and tilts my face up toward his. Just an inch closer, and our lips would be touching. "Where in the world did you come from, Dessa Roads?"

I laugh. "You keep saying my name." Sort of.

"Well, it's pretty. Like you." He wraps his hand around the back of my neck, and brushes the tip of his nose against mine. "Can I kiss you, Dessa Roads?"

My heart pounds in my chest. "Yes."

He presses his lips to mine. They're warm and soft. The noisy bar fades away as we kiss, slow and gentle. He tastes like beer, or maybe it's me—I don't know, but I like it. I reach up and wrap my arms around his neck, so I'm pressed up against him. The kiss deepens, and I feel everything I've been worried about slipping away. All that matters is the way our lips move together, pulling me under.

"We have to go," a voice says into my ear. "Now."

I pull back from Luke, but I've barely had a chance to smile at him when Taryn grabs my arm and yanks me off the dance floor. "What are you doing?" I demand.

"We're leaving."

Up onstage, Ben Mathers switches to a new song. I try to catch sight of Luke, but he's lost in a sea of people on the dance floor. I pull my arm away from Taryn. "I want to stay for one more song."

She shakes her head, her eyes wide and pleading. "No, we have to go *now*."

"What's wrong? Did something happen with that blond girl?"

Luke appears beside me, but he's not smiling anymore. He takes my hand. "Taryn, why don't you run along now."

"Wait," I say. "You guys know each other?"

He smirks, and I take a step back, letting go of his hand. Beside me, Taryn's eyes are starting to fill with tears. "Remember how I told you I used to date the bartender?" she asks, holding her arms out as if presenting Luke to me. "Meet the shittiest whiskey sour maker in Oklahoma."

"*What?*" I stare at Luke. "Did you know I was here with her this whole time?"

He shrugs. "Maybe."

Taryn tugs on my arm again. "Dessa, please. Let's go. It's almost one and the buses stop running soon."

"Shit."

"Don't leave," Luke says, his hand snaking around my waist again. "Forget her."

I push him away. "You're a jerk."

"You didn't think that a minute ago," he says, running his thumb along his lips. "And neither did the last girl I kissed to piss Taryn off."

His words hit me hard. Any possibility that he actually liked me goes flying out the window. I finally meet someone new, and it all turns out to be a big joke.

"You know what?" I grab a stranger's beer off a nearby table. "Go to hell."

Then I throw the beer in his face.

It's like the world around us freezes. The music stops, the people disappear. It's just Taryn, Luke, and me, staring at one another. I should be worried that making a scene will get me busted for underage drinking. I should be scared that Luke is going to hurt me or Taryn. But all I feel is satisfaction as I watch the beer running down his handsome face and off his chin.

Then Taryn takes my hand, and the music blares back to life. "Come on," she says. We dive into the safety of the crowd. Behind us, I hear Luke yell, "Stop!"

I glance over my shoulder to see if he's following us, but there are twice as many people here as when we arrived, and I can't see him. Taryn and I don't slow down. We move forward together, practically shoving drunks out of our way. Twice I have to yank my arm away when guys try to pull me toward them, and I almost trip over a barstool in my hurry to escape.

We finally make it to the front of the bar. Taryn throws open the door and we burst out onto the sidewalk.

"Whoa!" Eddie says. "Where's the fire?"

"Luke," Taryn pants. "He's coming."

Eddie's face hardens. "What happened?"

"It was my fault," I say, stepping forward. "I kissed him."

"She didn't know who he was," Taryn says. "And then she . . . well . . ." She looks at me helplessly.

"I threw my beer in his face."

Eddie's eyes go wide. "You did *what*?"

The door flies open.

"What the fuck was that?" Luke yells. His shirt is soaking wet. "You bitches!"

Eddie steps between Luke and us, his arms crossed over his chest. "Go back inside."

"Hell no," Luke says.

"They don't want to talk to you," Eddie says. "Now go back inside."

Luke narrows his eyes. "Shut up, Eddie. You have nothing to do with this."

He tries to push past, but it's like trying to move a mountain. "Get out of my way, damn it."

Beside me, Taryn whimpers. She looks so small, nothing like the fearless girl who led me through the bar and onto the dance floor.

"Taryn, why don't you and your friend head on home," Eddie says, not taking his eyes off Luke. "Me and this fool are gonna have a little talk."

Luke takes a step back. "Listen, man, I just want to talk to my girlfriend. That's all."

"I'm not your girlfriend!" Taryn says. I squeeze her hand, trying to tell her to keep quiet, but she doesn't take the hint. "We broke up."

I tug at Taryn's hand. She resists, but I pull harder. Luke tries to follow us, but Eddie blocks him.

"Come on," I say, dragging Taryn down the street.

The night feels colder than when we arrived. I reach for my hoodie, but it's gone—I must have lost it in the bar. I wrap my arms around myself. This night hasn't turned out at all like I expected. I glance over at Taryn. She's walking in silence, her eyes glossy with tears. "I'm really sorry," I say.

She stops walking. "If it's anyone's fault, it's mine. I shouldn't have left you before. I knew he was going to be here tonight." She hiccups, and laughs. "I can't believe you threw a beer in his face."

The rush of the moment sweeps through me all over again. "I shouldn't be allowed to drink."

"Technically, I don't think you are."

We burst out laughing, and Taryn links her arm in mine. "At least one good thing came out of this night."

"Oh yeah?"

She shows me her phone. "I got that girl's number."

"Nice!"

We keep walking, our conversation turning to line dancing and Ben Mathers, but when we reach the bus stop, Taryn turns to me and frowns. "Do you know how to get back home?"

"Aren't you coming with me?"

She shakes her head. "This bus doesn't go to my house. I have to get the twenty-four."

"Oh, okay. Well . . ." We stand there for a second, looking at each other. "It was nice to meet you."

"Wait," she says, pulling out her phone. "We need to swap numbers. I want to keep in touch."

"Really?"

Taryn hands me her phone. "Yes, really. Why wouldn't I?"

I reach into my purse and pull out my cell, which is still turned off. While I wait for it to turn on, I plug my number into her phone. I can't remember the last time I bothered to exchange information with someone on the road. I rarely hear from anyone for more than a week or two after we meet, so eventually I just stopped trying to stay in touch. I figured if I ever wanted to see them again, I could find them on Instagram.

"Your phone's back on," she says.

"Thanks." I give her phone back, then quickly type my password into mine. "Make sure you save your name under 'Taryn OKC,'" I say, handing the phone over.

It immediately buzzes in her hand. "Dude . . . you have a ton of text messages. And missed calls."

"Oh, no." I grab the phone back. She's right. My mom has called me four times, and so has my dad. There's even a missed call from Cyrus and Mrs. McAlister. Not to mention all the text messages. "Shit. *Shit.*"

"Should you call home?" Taryn asks.

"Yeah . . ." I try to dial, but my hands are shaking.

"Let me help." She takes the phone from me and selects my mom's number. Then she hands it back. "Just stay calm."

Mom picks up on the first ring. "Dessa! Are you okay?"

I cringe. "Hi, Mom. I'm fine."

"Peter! It's her."

"Thank god," my dad says in the background. "Is she okay? Where is she?"

"I'm fine," I say again, trying to keep my voice steady. "I'm near downtown."

"Why?" she demands, her voice losing its worried edge. Now she just sounds pissed. "Why aren't you *here*, where you're supposed to be?"

"I went out for a little while," I say, "and I lost track of time—"

"It's almost one thirty!" Mom yells. I have never, in my entire *life*, heard her this angry. "Do you have any idea how scared I've been? I was just about to call the police. You *know* how I feel about them."

"I'm sorry, Mom. I didn't mean to—"

Dad picks up the phone. "Where are you exactly?" he says, his voice gruff.

I look up at the sign for the bus and tell him where I am. A few blocks away, a number twenty-four bus turns onto our street. Taryn barely glances at it.

"Dad . . . I'm really sorry," I whisper. "I didn't mean for this to happen."

"We'll be there soon. Don't move."

"Okay. Bye." I hang up.

"Are they coming?" Taryn asks. She looks almost as freaked out as I feel.

"Yeah." I comb my fingers through my hair in an attempt to

make it look more presentable, but it's hopelessly tangled and sweaty.

Taryn bites her lip and looks down the street at the approaching bus. It's only a block away now. "Okay. I'll wait with you."

"No . . . you should go."

"I shouldn't leave you out here alone. It's late and your parents—"

"They'll be here soon." The bus pulls up and the door opens. "Go." I give her a quick hug and then push her toward the bus.

"Are you sure?" she says, stopping in the doorway. "Because I can wait for the next one."

"Are you getting on or not?" the driver says.

"She's getting on," I call back.

"I'll text you," Taryn says. "And sorry, again. About tonight."

The doors close. I sink down to the curb and watch the bus drive away. I can't believe I missed those calls. I can't believe I was stupid enough to turn off my phone. I can't believe I kissed a guy I barely knew, and then threw beer in his face.

But as I sit on the curb, listening to the crickets, I can't help but smile.

The night might have been a disaster, but I had a great fucking time.

CHAPTER 8

"Get up."

I open my eyes just as Mom walks away from my bed. I push myself to a sitting position, grimacing when my stomach gives a nasty lurch. My head is foggy and heavy, and my mouth tastes like sour milk. The night rushes back to me, like a Mack truck headed straight for my face. I groan and lie down again. This is what I get for being spontaneous.

"Up!" Mom calls.

"Okay, okay." I take a sip of water from the bottle stashed between my bed and the wall, then climb down the ladder. I'm still wearing my beer-soaked shirt from last night, though I changed into a pair of pajama pants in the few seconds before my parents turned off the lights. I had expected an argument after being picked up, or at least a serious lecture, but instead they pulled the RV into a parking lot, turned off the engine, and walked straight back to their room.

I was too hyped up to notice where we parked last night, but one look at the giant blue building outside tells me we're at Walmart. It's only seven, which means I got less than five hours of sleep. I want coffee, but instead I sit at the table. And wait. I don't know where Mom went. She might be avoiding me, but there's no way Dad's going to let last night go entirely. Maybe they'll ground me—it'll be the first time since I was twelve, when Cyrus and I decided the long stretch of grass along a Mississippi highway was the perfect place to play tag.

The side door opens and my dad steps inside.

"Hey," I say, my voice raw. I clear my throat. "I'm really sorry."

Rodney pushes past him into the RV. "Dad says you snuck out. Where did you go?"

Dad's eyebrows rise a fraction of an inch, but he doesn't say anything. In fact, he doesn't even wait for my answer. He walks to the front of the RV and sits down in the driver's seat, his back to me.

His message is loud and clear: *I have nothing to say to you, and you have nothing to say that I want to hear.*

"Well?" Rodney asks. "Where were you?"

I rub my temples. "Go away."

"Dad is really mad."

"No shit."

"Don't cuss at your brother," Mom says as she comes out of the back. I pull my knees up to my chest so she can walk by the table, and rest my chin on my folded arms.

"We need to talk about last night," she says quietly. The skin around her eyes is a little yellow and puffy, like she got even less sleep than I did.

"Okay," I say. "Now?"

"No," Dad says from the front seat, his voice harsh in the morning air. "Later. You may have forgotten, but we're all trying to get to Santa Fe in time so *you* can start an internship."

I sink back into the booth, his words washing over me. Mom looks at me, and for a second I think she's going to reassure me that everything is okay. Instead, she turns to my brother. "Rodney, please sit down. We're leaving."

Dad pulls the RV onto Interstate 40 West. There aren't too many cars on the road since it's so early. Mostly big trucks and a few delivery vans, probably full of milk and eggs from local farms. I stare out the window, my head resting against the glass, and count license plates. Oklahoma, California, Oklahoma, Oklahoma, Texas, Florida, Oklahoma, New Mexico. It takes almost fifty license plates before I see a state I haven't visited.

My phone buzzes in my pocket during hour two. I pull it out and see a text message from Taryn. **How bad is it?**

Bad, I write back.

A second later, she replies, **Silent treatment or screaming?**

So far mostly ST + disappointed head shaking, I reply. **Real punishment is still coming.**

Bummer. Text me later.

As shitty as I feel, I still smile. Maybe Taryn really does want to keep in touch. It wouldn't be the worst thing in the world to have a friend other than Cyrus. Especially one as fearless as Taryn.

Eight grueling hours later, we arrive in Santa Fe. The other families ditched us for Albuquerque almost an hour ago. Dad says it's because they wanted to check out some restaurant called Sophia's that makes duck enchiladas, but the real reason is that they don't want to be around when my mom finally snaps. Cyrus texted a few times, apologizing for ditching us, but I told him I didn't blame them for steering clear of the cold war going on in our RV. He tried to swap stories about our nights but the last thing I want is to hear how his stupid date with Rachel went, especially after the way things turned out with Luke, so I turned off my phone.

We pull into YiaYia's driveway around three, right in the middle of her weekly hair appointment. We let ourselves into her single-story adobe house with the key she keeps hidden under a flowerpot in the back. I wander around, flipping switches, flooding the colorful home with light. When I finish, I run my fingers against the orange accent wall in the living room. Even though it's a dry eighty degrees outside, the combination of the air conditioning and the stucco walls keep the inside of the house comfortable. I walk between the couches in the middle of the sunken living room and stop in front of YiaYia's wood-burning fireplace. It would be intimidating if not for the painting of yellow yucca flowers—the very one that inspired me to paint my own—hanging in the center of the wall.

Mom appears in the doorway. "Get unpacked, Dessa. You

know how your grandma feels about us sleeping in the RV when we visit."

I pull my seldom-used suitcase into the guest room that Rodney and I share. YiaYia hates the idea of us all cooped up outside when we could be in the house with her, which is more than fine with me. I'm eager to sleep in a normal-size bed in a normal-size room, beneath one of YiaYia's hand-knit afghan blankets. I prop my suitcase up on the dresser and unzip it. A framed photo of Patras—the coastal city in Greece where YiaYia was born—hangs crooked on the wall in front of me. I tip it back into place. Someday YiaYia will take me there, and we'll spend our days swimming in the warm Mediterranean, and our evenings drinking wine and eating flaming saganaki. Someday.

When I'm finished unpacking, I turn around to find Rodney splayed out on his twin bed reading a beat-up book called *Poop Jokes for the Easily Amused*. I don't know where he got it, but I have a feeling my dad's name might be scrawled in messy kid handwriting on the inside cover.

I creep over to Rodney's bed and snatch the book out of his hands. He shouts in protest and grabs for it, but I hold it out of reach, backing away from the bed so he can't jump on me. I open the front flap, and sure enough it reads, *Property of Peter Rhodes*.

"Give it back, Dessa," Rodney demands.

"Nope. It'll rot your brain."

"It's a book!"

"A book about poop. That doesn't count."

Rodney gives me the finger.

"I am *so* telling Mom you did that."

He crosses his arms. "That's tattling. Plus, Mom is so mad at you she won't even care."

"True," I say, the levity from a moment ago disappearing entirely. I toss the book back to him and he catches it. "Tell me a joke."

Rodney's face lights up. "What do you call taking a poop after you eat alphabet soup?"

"What?"

"A vowel movement!"

Rodney collapses onto the bed in a fit of laughter. I groan and smack him on the leg. "You're gross."

A car pulls into the gravel driveway outside our window. I race down the hall to the entryway. The front door opens just as I arrive, revealing a harassed-looking cab driver and a grumpy, crutch-leaning, sparkly blue jumpsuit–wearing YiaYia.

"Dessa?" she gasps.

I throw my arms around her neck. She smells like oregano and Chanel No. 5. I hug her tighter.

"I can't believe you're here," she says. "What a lovely surprise!"

I let go, only to have Rodney squeeze his way between

us. He hugs YiaYia just as tightly as I did, making her laugh. "Sweetheart—you're strangling me."

"Here's her purse," the cab driver says, handing it to me before stalking back to his car.

We file into the kitchen, YiaYia cursing softly in Greek when she bumps into the doorframe. She's got a bulky white cast on one foot and a slim blue Tom on the other. I slip my arm around her waist and help her forward.

Dad picks up YiaYia in a giant hug, letting her crutches fall to the floor. "You should have told us you broke your foot!" he says, spinning her around in a circle.

"Peter Dimitris Rhodes!" YiaYia cries out, "you put me down or I will kick you with my big heavy foot."

He sets her down carefully and she slides into a creaky chair at the kitchen table. "Bully," she says, winking.

Mom walks around the counter and embraces YiaYia. "Dessa has some good news."

YiaYia turns to me. "College?"

I shake my head. *Please don't ask me anything more, not in front of everyone,* I plead with my eyes. *Please.*

"Dessa got an internship with an artist here in Santa Fe," Mom answers. "It starts tomorrow."

"That's wonderful!" YiaYia says. "I didn't even know you'd applied."

"Cyrus did it," I say. "It was a surprise."

"Oh, that sweet boy."

When I don't agree, YiaYia narrows her eyes. "I'd like to lie down for a bit. Help me to my room, Dessa?"

I hand her the crutches, then slip my arm under hers to help her up. It takes us a second to navigate around the table, but then we're out in the hall, everyone else left behind.

"How have you been?" she asks as we enter her bedroom. The lights are off, but I can still make out the framed photograph of Rodney and me on her dresser. I help her sit on the bed.

"We stayed in North Carolina for a few days, and before that—"

"I didn't ask *where* you've been, I asked *how* you've been. It's about time you heard back from UCLA, isn't it?"

I try to keep a straight face, but her question is like a knife in my heart.

YiaYia's face crumples. "Oh, psihi mou. I'm so sorry."

The sight of disappointment on her face is too much—all the feelings I tried to drown last night return, and my eyes fill with tears.

"No, no, no," she says. "Don't cry."

"I'm sorry. I don't know how this happened." I push the heels of my hands against my eyes, but the tears keep coming. "I did everything I was supposed to do. I studied. I practiced my technique. I've been over it in my head, and I just . . . I don't understand. What did I do wrong?"

YiaYia makes a noise in the back of her throat. "You did nothing wrong," she says. "Come sit with me."

I prop the crutches against the wall and perch on the edge of the bed next to her. "There's something else. Last night, I snuck out and . . . got a little drunk." Before she can scold me, I continue, "I was upset, and then Cy went out with Rachel, and I just—"

YiaYia holds up her hands. "Wait a minute. Cyrus went out with another girl? A girl who isn't you?" She shakes her head. "That boy loves you, and you love him. The two of you were made for each other."

I moan, and she lifts her chin and stares down her nose at me. "Are you doubting my years and years of experience?"

"No, YiaYia." I wrap my arm around her shoulders. "I'd never doubt your years and years and years and years—"

"That's enough!" she says, laughing.

We lie back on the bed, our heads tipped toward each other. I breathe in the smell of her face cream and of the heavy quilt on her bed, and I feel the tension in my body start to melt away. Something about being here, about being with her, always makes me feel like I can finally and truly relax in a way I never can on the road.

YiaYia throws a blanket over us, arranging it carefully to make sure it covers everything from our toes to our waists. I feel a surge of love for her, and I slip my hand into hers. She squeezes back softly.

"My parents don't know yet," I say.

"We don't know *what*?"

Mom and Dad are standing in the doorway, both wearing identical masks of suspicion. I cringe and bury my face in YiaYia's shoulder.

"Dessa?" Mom says. "What's wrong? Is this about last night?"

"No," I say, my voice muffled. I glance up at my parents. They look worried now, like they're afraid I'm about to tell them something horrible.

I take a deep breath and sit up. If I see even the tiniest hint that they're disappointed in me, I'll fall apart. But I don't have a choice. "I know you're angry about last night—"

"You're damn right we are," Dad says. "You could have been hurt!"

I wince. "I know. But I was really upset, and I just needed to get out."

"Upset about what?" Mom asks.

I hesitate, but YiaYia pats my hand beneath the blanket. "Go on," she whispers.

I take a steadying breath. "I've been waiting to hear back from colleges, right?" My voice cracks, but I force myself to continue. "Well, a few days ago I found out I didn't get into UCLA or . . . anywhere else."

"Oh, honey, I'm sorry to hear that," Dad says, his voice softer than before. He rests his hand on the side of my head, and I lean into the warmth of his palm. "But Dessa, there's no excuse for disappearing in the middle of the night. That's no way to handle life's problems. You know that, right?"

I swallow hard. I know he's waiting for me to promise that last night isn't ever going to happen again. But I can't. I *needed* the freedom of last night, even if the bar was a bad idea.

"What I did was reckless and dumb," I finally say. "I'm sorry."

"Oh, sweetheart." Mom hurries forward and kisses me on the forehead. "It's going to be okay."

She wraps her arms around me, pulling me to her chest. My heart leaps into my throat, and I hug her back. Maybe she *does* get it. "I'm just so disappointed," I say, my voice muffled by her shirt. "I wanted to go to college so badly."

"I know, sweetheart. I know."

I look up, expecting to see my sadness reflected on her face. But instead of sympathy, she looks . . . *relieved.*

"Applying to art school was very brave," she says. "But you don't belong in a building full of old white men and students desperate to impress them. You belong with your family, not in a stuffy classroom."

I pull back, my eyes filling with tears. "But Mom—"

"I understand, I promise I do," she says, hushing me. "But you've done everything you can. Now it's time to hold your head high and move on."

A burning mixture of anger and hurt courses through me. It's easy for her to say I don't belong in art school—she's always felt right at home on the road, even before she and Dad bought the RV five years ago. But the only place I've felt truly happy was hunched over a pad of drawing paper, or standing in front of a fresh piece of canvas. Even Dad says I'm the most myself when I'm covered in paint, and he didn't want me to apply to art school either. Too expensive, not practical. Says the man who travels the country in a gas-guzzling RV.

But maybe . . . maybe she's right. I *don't* belong in art school. Not according to half the schools in the country, anyway.

"The good news is that you have your internship, and you have us," Dad says, ruffling my hair like I've fallen off my bike. Like failing at the most important thing in my entire life is no big deal.

"That's right," Mom says. "You'll always have the families. And we have lots of adventures ahead of us. Now, let's all go into the kitchen and start dinner. Maybe your Dad can show you how to make keftedes," Mom says, helping me to my feet. "You'll feel better in no time."

I glance back at YiaYia, still sitting on the bed, just before my mom pulls me through the door and into the hall. Her face is pinched up, like she's fighting off tears. She understands this isn't the beginning of a new adventure. It's the end of one.

Cyrus, Jeff, and the McAlisters arrive late. I meet them a few streets away from YiaYia's house, where they've parked on the side of a dirt road. Cyrus jumps out of the RV.

"Hey," he calls, and jogs across the street to where I'm waiting. "What are you doing out here? Not sneaking off again, are you?"

I smile for the first time in hours. "Wanna take a walk?"

We walk in silence, leaving the yellow glow of the streetlight behind us. Our shadows stretch out in front of us, leading the way.

"How pissed are your parents about last night?" Cy asks.

"They're more *disappointed*."

"Oh man, that's way worse."

I shake my head. "Tell me about it. At least it looks like I'm going to get off without a punishment."

We reach an alleyway, and he stops. "Why'd you sneak out, anyway?"

I look down at my beat-up Converse. The canvas is peeling away from the rubber on one side, and the laces are gray. "Oh, you know . . . I was too cooped up in the RV."

"That's it?" he asks, his voice skeptical.

"And . . . I felt bad for myself."

"Why?"

I look up at him. His forehead is creased, and his eyes look worried. I take a deep breath, and say the one thing I never thought I would.

"Honestly? You and Rachel were on a date, and I was jealous."

"Are you serious?" He runs his hands over his head and groans. "That wasn't a date. We're just friends."

I cross my arms. "Well how was I supposed to know that?"

"How were you—Dessa, there's only one person I want to be with."

Cy takes my hand, holding it palm up. He makes a circle with his finger, then a dot in the middle. It's something he's been doing since we were kids, back when we used to camp and I was afraid of the dark. He'd draw circle after circle, until the fear drained away and all I could feel was his warm fingers on my skin.

But tonight his touch doesn't calm me. It's electric.

His hand travels up my arm, until his palm presses against my neck. His fingers curl into my hair.

"It's you, Dess. It's always been you."

My breath hitches as I stare into his brown eyes. He pulls me close, and my lips part, hungry for his.

"What are you kids doing out there?" Jeff calls down the block.

We jerk apart.

"Nothing!" I yelp.

Jeff is standing outside their RV, a trash bag in his hand. He holds it up. "Cyrus, come get this. It's stinking up the whole kitchen."

Cy grimaces. "I'll be there in a second, Dad."

"No, come get it now."

Cyrus turns to me, his eyes full of apology.

"It's okay," I say. My chest is heaving like I've just run five miles. "Go. I'll see you tomorrow after my internship."

Cy starts back down the block. "I'll call you. We'll . . . figure this out. Right?"

I nod, even as my heart rebels against the idea of waiting even a second longer to kiss him. "Yes. Definitely."

CHAPTER 9

The outside of Fiona's studio looks like a post office—adobe and concrete, a drooping US flag, and a few people hanging around near a scraggly bush. It's only nine a.m., but already the sun is beating down on my head, a welcome change from the rain in Asheville and the chill night air in Oklahoma. I ring the bell, my fingers shaking a little.

A minute passes and Fiona doesn't answer the door. I knock, lightly at first, and then not so lightly. I'm starting to sweat, and my tank top is sticking to my stomach. I take a step back from the door and peer up at the windows on the second floor, but they're covered in newspaper or cardboard or something, so I can't tell if the lights are on inside.

I grab a piece of paper that's stuck halfway under the door and use it to fan myself. I'm not early, and I triple-checked the address. Definitely in the right place at the right time. Maybe this is a test. Maybe she wants me to prove to her how badly I want this, and the only way I can do that is to stand here, baking in the sun, fanning myself with a piece of trash.

I ring the bell again, then look down at the piece of paper

in my hand just to pass the time. There's a bit of tape on the end, as if it had been stuck to the door. I turn it over and see the handwriting on the other side.

Dessa, come to art fair! –F

Shit. I flip the paper over again, hoping there's more to her note, but that's it—"come to the art fair." Except I have no idea where this art fair is and even if I did, it's not like I have a car. I pull my cell phone out and check the time. I've already been standing here for almost five minutes, which means at the very least I'm running five minutes late to a location I've never heard of. *Double shit.*

I Google "Santa Fe art fair," and about twenty million results come up, so I add today's date. There's an outdoor art fair today near the Santa Fe plaza, which is only a few blocks away. I take off running, Fiona's note clutched in my shaking hand. This is *not* how I wanted to begin my first day.

By the time I reach the plaza, I'm a sweaty, disgusting mess; my hair is frizzy and falling out of its ponytail, and my heart is pounding in the back of my throat. I stop and bend over, my breath coming hard and fast. It's Monday, but the plaza is full of people. Parents crouch in front of their children, wiping ice cream off their mouths. Two old men lean over a card table they've set up in the shade of a tree, a chessboard between them. And directly to my right is a bench where a couple my age is in the middle of a *very* passionate kiss. The handsy kind that makes people yell *get a room!* The guy cups the back of the girl's head, and I notice a thick leather cuff around his wrist just like the one Cy always wears. I feel of tug of longing, but I don't have time for this. I cross the plaza and keep walking.

I catch sight of an outdoor market set up next to the Cathedral Basilica of St. Francis of Assisi. There are tons of vendors, many selling plastic keychains, silly tchotchkes for kids, paper masks, and *Welcome to Santa Fe* postcards. But there are lots of artisans, too. Vibrant kachina dolls line tables, accompanied by little cards explaining their Hopi roots, and I spot a stall full of intricate turquoise jewelry and painted pottery. I look at Fiona's crumpled note again, but she didn't give me any hints about where to go once I got here. I'm on my own.

I wander through the stalls, keeping my eyes peeled for someone who looks like the picture of Fiona on her website, but there's no sign of her. I don't see any art that looks like it could belong to her either. I see plenty of amazing stuff—I'm particularly intrigued by the glass blowers—but no found art sculptures like the ones Fiona is known for. I'm about to accept that whatever this test is, I've failed it, when I hear a snatch of conversation behind me.

"—she made them out of *trash*, can you believe that?"

"They looked so real."

Two women are standing off to the side, both in matching purple T-shirts that read KNIT FIRST, ASK QUESTIONS LATER. The taller of the two is wearing a neon yellow fanny pack around her waist.

"Excuse me," I say, taking a step toward them. "Did you say you saw something made out of trash?"

"Yes!" exclaims the one with the fanny pack. "It was incredible. The artist says she spent a month collecting bottles from around town so she could use the glass. She means it to be a protest of pollution, I'm sure. It's just horrible how everyone dumps their trash—"

"Where did you see her?"

The woman points back in the direction I just came from. "That way, then left, about ten stalls down."

"Thank you!"

I set off down the aisle, dodging tourists and small dogs as I go. When another aisle splits off to my left, I take it. It looks exactly like the rest of the art market, full of people leaning over tables, trying on handmade purses and silver jewelry, but a group of women is gathered to one side, and I recognize their vivid purple T-shirts.

Jackpot.

I hang back, not wanting to be pulled into the gaggle of tourists until I'm sure I'm in the right place. But then two ladies step away from the table, and I see her: Fiona Velarde. She's talking and smiling, her hands moving back and forth between her cash box, the display table, and her customers. She looks exactly like the picture on her website—long black hair hanging free around her tan shoulders, no makeup, save for cherry red lipstick. But she's wearing tons of jewelry. Her fingers are covered in rings, and a twisty gold bracelet curls around her upper arm, ending in a delicate arrow.

I step away from the table and take out my phone, using the camera as a mirror. My hair is plastered to my face and my cheeks are flushed. I fan myself, trying to cool down while Fiona helps her customers. But as they wander away, bags clutched in their hands, I hear the familiar voice in my head, whispering worries. *What if she doesn't like you? What if she finds out you're a fraud?*

The last customer hands over a twenty in exchange for a bag. Fiona waits until they walk away, then slumps back against the wall between her table and the next artist's. She blows out a puff of air, sending her black bangs flying away from her face.

I should go up to her, but I feel glued in place. Maybe I'll take another lap around the stalls—

"Dessa?"

Fiona is looking at me, her head tilted to the side, like she's not sure it's me. "Yeah?" I say. "I mean, yes! Hi!"

I hurry over, my hand held out to shake hers. But after a few steps, I realize I must look like a total lunatic with my arm stretched out as I walk, so I drop it down to my side. But then I'm at the table, and I offer it again. *Kill me now.*

Fiona takes my hand, but instead of shaking it, she pulls me into a hug across the table. "It's so wonderful to meet you. I've been looking forward to this for days."

"Me too," I say into her hair. She smells like wildflowers caught in a summer shower.

"I'm sorry I wasn't at the studio," she says, releasing me. "I do my best to engage with the local art scene, and I completely forgot there was a fair this week. But it seems you found my note."

"I did, yeah."

My gaze lands on the table between us, which I can now see is covered in perfect little glass flowers, each one a different color. They shine like jewels in the filtered sunlight. "Wow. They're beautiful."

Fiona twists her long hair up into a knot on the back of her head and fans her neck. "You're welcome to pick one up."

I choose a pale yellow flower that looks like an upside-down bell.

"Much of my work is made of things I find on the street, in dumpsters," Fiona says. "Some people like to call it mixed media, but I call it—"

"Found art," I say, turning the flower over in my hand, the petals catching the light. It looks just like the painting of the yellow flower hanging over YiaYia's fireplace. A yucca.

I gently place the delicate flower back on the table, and for the first time in days I remember the box of glass still sitting inside the RV, untouched and untransformed. I can't imagine ever turning it into something even half as beautiful as Fiona's flowers. Actually, I can't imagine *anything* of mine measuring up to Fiona's work.

"I'm not sure if you remember," I say, "but last year you

were at a gallery show in Houston, and you had a wolf sculpture made from pieces of a rubber tire. It was incredible."

She signals for me to wait a second while she ducks under the table. When she appears again, she has a thick binder. Inside are hundreds of photographs, each one depicting a different sculpture. She flips through a couple plastic-sheeted pages, then turns the binder to face me. "This one?" she asks, pointing at a photo on the bottom row.

"Yes!" The wolf howls up at me, almost as fierce in the picture as he was in person. I trace my finger along his arched back, the tiny threads of tire tread just barely visible. "So much movement in those lines," I whisper. "It's like he's alive."

"He's one of my favorites." She smiles down at the photograph. "He's on exhibit in Houston until next spring, but once I get him back, I'm going to retire him permanently. I like having him in the studio with me. He reminds me to be ferocious, to be brave. Sometimes I need that reminder."

She tucks the binder back under the table. "So, if I remember correctly, you're applying to art school." Fiona straightens the glass flowers on the table. "Have you decided where you're going yet?"

A million answers fly through my mind. *I'm still waiting to hear back. I'm weighing my options.* Anything so she keeps looking at me like I'm someone talented and worthy of this internship. Like the kind of person I so badly I want to be.

"I'm going to UCLA," I blurt.

A flood of hot shame crashes through me. I want to take my lie back as soon as the words leave my mouth, to shove it deep into the black hole where I hide the ugliest parts of myself.

"Wow," Fiona says. "That's a great school."

An old man wanders up to the table, his hands clasped behind his back. While Fiona shows him her work, I look down at the rows of flowers and swallow hard. The lie is out—now all I can do is prove to Fiona that I'm worthy of this chance. And hope she never figures out the truth.

Fiona and I stay at the fair for a few more hours, then she tells me to take a half-hour lunch break. Dad meets me in a nearby park, two paper bags clutched in his hand. Once we find a good spot beneath a tree, I spread the picnic blanket Fiona insisted I take on the ground, and lie down along one side. Dad takes a seat against the tree trunk.

"Your mom made sandwiches," he says, handing me a bag. "I think they're peanut butter and strawberry jelly."

I pull my sandwich out and peel back the thin plastic wrap. "I wish Mom would buy regular peanut butter once in a while," I say. "This low-fat stuff isn't as good."

Dad unwraps his sandwich and takes a big bite. "You know your mom," he says through a mouthful. He swallows. "She wants us all to live to be a hundred."

I pull out another baggie filled with potato chips. I don't have to count to know there are exactly ten chips inside. We figured out a long time ago that if we each eat no more than ten chips at a time, we can make a family-size bag last at least two weeks. It's little tricks like that, ways to save here and there, that make traveling possible on such a tight budget. That, and Dad's web design business.

"Dad, I need to ask you something."

"What's up, kid?"

I look across the park, unable to meet his gaze. "I was wondering if everything is okay. You know . . . with money?"

"Why do you ask?"

I can practically hear the frown in his voice. I force myself to make eye contact. I need him to take this seriously. "You seem more stressed than usual about the price of gas, and you got sort of upset at breakfast in Asheville when Jeff suggested—"

"I just didn't want you to worry," Dad says. "And gas *is* too expensive."

"But Rodney said he heard something. When you were on the phone."

Dad goes perfectly still. "What did he hear?"

"Something about Mark being an ass."

"Dessa—"

"He's your biggest client, so I've been worried. Are you still doing work for him?"

Dad waves this off, but I can tell he's shaken. This isn't nothing.

"Dad," I say quietly. "Please?"

We sit in silence for a few minutes, watching two kids chasing each other around in circles. I take a bite of my sandwich, but the bread is mush in my mouth.

"Damn it," Dad says at last, sagging back against the tree. "We're hemorrhaging money, and it's not like we had that much to begin with. That jackass Mark said he wasn't making enough to pay freelancers anymore, so we've been living on savings, and now our account is overdrawn."

It's like I've been sucker-punched in the stomach. The last time Mom and Dad's account was overdrawn was when they took out a bunch of money to buy new tires for the RV. But they've been careful with money since then. They even set up a spreadsheet with all their finances so they could keep track of what they were spending and when they needed to pay their credit card bills. "How long ago did Mark stop giving you work?"

"It's been two months since my last paycheck." He takes a deep breath. "You can't tell your mom."

My mouth drops open. "But . . . but she deserves to know."

He shakes his head. "Just let me handle it, okay?"

"Okay . . . ," I say, but I regret agreeing to this before the word is even out of my mouth. How am I supposed to keep something like this from her? It's bad enough the families don't know the truth. It goes against everything we believe to keep something this important a secret, especially since it affects everyone. But to not tell Mom? Just the thought makes my stomach hurt even worse.

But then I think of how I lied to Fiona this morning about getting into college, and I realize there's no way I can hold this against him when I'm just as guilty.

"Everything is going to be okay," Dad says. "I promise. Things are just hard right now."

He pulls a plastic bottle of water—one he's been reusing for weeks—out of his lunch bag and takes a long drink. His Adam's apple jumps up and down as he swallows, and it's like watching him try to wash away what he just told me.

"So," he says, putting the bottle down. "How's your first day going?"

"It's great," I say impatiently. "But Dad, what are you going to do about money? Maybe I can help—"

He shakes his head. "This is my problem and I'm going to fix it. I'll find a new client, pick up a few freelance jobs. Now tell me about your internship."

I know when a conversation is over, and this one is definitely over. For now.

"Fiona's going to keep me pretty busy," I say, picking up my baggie of chips again. I pull one out, but my appetite is gone.

"What's she having you do?" Dad asks. I notice he hasn't picked up his sandwich again either.

"A lot of stuff, but right now she wants me to come up with a schedule for the next two weeks leading up to the show. We're going to talk more about it tomorrow, at her studio. She also wants me to come with her to see the gallery space on Sunday.

That way I can envision where we're displaying her art as we figure out which ones to hang."

"Sunday?" Dad asks. "We were talking about going to Albuquerque that morning. It's the only day Jeff can spare from his auto shop gig. Can you go another day?"

"I just started, so I probably shouldn't be asking to take time off."

"But this is a weekend we're talking about. She can't expect you to work seven days a week, can she?"

"I get Saturdays off—"

Dad picks up his sandwich and tears off a piece of crust. "One day off a week is nuts. She's not even paying you."

"I know, but this is what I signed up for. I can't let her down."

Dad pops the crust in his mouth and chews. "Okay, I hear you. I still think she should be paying you, though."

I roll my eyes, but don't argue.

"Oh, before I forget," Dad says, "your mom and I came up with the perfect punishment for your disappearing act the other night."

"Seriously? You know how sorry I am about sneaking out—"

"Nice try, but we've already decided: You're going to clean out YiaYia's garage."

"By *myself*? That'll take forever!"

"Life's tough and then you die," he says with a shrug.

I shove a handful of chips into my mouth, chew them a

little, then open my mouth so he's forced to see the soggy, broken mess.

"Very nice," he says, laughing.

We finish lunch, and Dad walks me back to the plaza. I give him a hug, but as I turn to walk away, he says, "Dessa, wait a second."

"Yeah?"

"Your mother and I are proud of you for getting this internship. I know you're disappointed about college but you're still going after your dreams. No matter what happens, you're doing your best, and that's what counts."

I nod, even though I can't help thinking that he's wrong. Doing your best isn't what counts. It's just a consolation prize.

By the time we pack up Fiona's booth, she's sold almost five hundred dollars' worth of art, and ten people have asked for her card, promising to check out more of her work online. As we go our separate ways—Fiona back to her office, me toward the bus stop—a thought stops me dead in my tracks.

Mom was right when she said it was hard to get a job when we're always on the road, but I don't need a job to make money. I just need to sell something. And where better to do that than at an art fair? I run back down the block, texting Cy with one hand.

The plaza is still packed when I arrive. *Perfect.* Lots of people means lots of buyers. I wind my way through the throng, ignoring the bodies pushing against me, their skin warm against mine as they jostle for space.

Fifteen minutes later, Cy arrives with a canvas bag over his shoulder, his hand clutching it to his side so the contents don't bump into anyone. Under his other arm is my easel.

"You're the best!" I call, hurrying forward to help him.

"You sure about this?" he asks, looking over my shoulder at the sea of people roaming the stalls.

"Totally. Let's find a place to set up."

We need somewhere that gets lots of foot traffic, but isn't anywhere near the outside ring of stalls, just in case someone is keeping track of vendors. I'm not sure it's okay for me to sell my work since I'm not technically signed up to be part of the fair, but I'm hoping whoever organized this shindig will be too busy to notice. Unfortunately, my options are somewhat limited by how many vendors are still here. Some have booths, like Fiona, while others use tables or easels to display their work. A few rely on nothing more than a picnic blanket stretched across the ground. Since Fiona's booth has already been claimed by someone, we wander through the aisles, our eyes peeled for an empty space. We're on our third loop when Cy touches my arm and says, "That guy's leaving."

He points at a man with a green card table, packing up his work. It's not a big space, but I don't have much to sell anyway. I hang back, not wanting to hurry the guy, but Cy strides over to him.

"You leaving?" he asks.

"Yeah," the guy says, resigned. "I've been here since seven. Haven't sold a damn thing." He sweeps an arm at the space. "It's all yours."

I set my bag behind his table, where no one will step on it. "What are you selling?"

"Organic soap."

He tosses me a small package wrapped in brown paper, then starts folding his card table. I hold the soap to my nose. Lilac and vanilla. "How much?"

"Fifteen."

"For *soap*?" Cy says.

The guy laughs and takes back the soap, dropping it into his bag. "I'd say it's worth the money, but since no one has bought even a single bar, I might need to rethink my price point." He shrugs and slings his bag over his shoulder, then picks up the folded card table. "Good luck."

I set up my easel, then pull out the three paintings I asked Cy to bring, placing them carefully on the ground.

"Which one are you going to put on the easel?" Cy asks, examining my pieces. He worked in a pawnshop the summer before we started our freshman-year curriculum, so he's an expert at selling stuff, especially stuff that's not worth much in the first place.

I bend over next to him and study each painting carefully. But the smell of his skin, his shampoo, his leather jacket . . .

it's too much. I can't focus. The last time we were together, we almost kissed. Does he still want to?

I feel his fingers curl around mine. I let out a shaky breath. "Hi," I whisper, not trusting myself to look at him.

"Hi," he says back.

I swallow hard, forcing myself to remember what I'm here for. I'm going to sell a painting. I'm going to make money. And then I'm going to give that money to my family.

I focus on the paintings in front of me. I try to recall how each one made me feel as I created it. I start with *Blue*. I came down with a terrible flu the day I started it, but I refused to let go of the paintbrush even as my fever spiked over a hundred. The spirals of paint, rich indigo and brilliant turquoise coiling around one another against a backdrop of black—I was mesmerized. Mom had finally been forced to pull the brush out of my shaking fingers.

Next, I turn to the watercolor portrait of Rodney I made when he was seven. I painted it quickly, my brush flying over the canvas in an effort to capture him before he woke up from his nap. I only got about halfway through before he opened his eyes and ran off. I'd been pissed at the time, but something about the half-finished work was even better than my original plan. Like I'd captured him half-formed, half-grown, stuck before there and *not there*. It's one of my mom's favorites.

"The Rodney painting is probably the best piece here, but the Burgess Falls is probably the most commercial." I point at the third painting, which is a realistic depiction of a waterfall, done in acrylics. The blue and white paints battle for space, creating a sense of movement. It took days to get it just right, and every time I look at it, I remember the cold spray of the water hitting my face as Cyrus and I floated in the swimming hole at the base of the falls.

"Yeah, that's the one," Cy agrees.

I set the Burgess on the easel. I feel a pang of loss at the possibility that it might sell. That any of them might. But it doesn't matter how I feel. We need money more than I need these paintings.

Cy takes a piece of paper out of the canvas bag I thought was empty, and hands it to me. "What's that for?" I ask.

In answer, he folds it lengthwise, then pulls a pen out of his back pocket and writes ART BY DESSA.

I smile down at the little sign as he sets it on top of the easel. "Thanks for being here."

"Of course," he says, and gives my hand a quick squeeze that both calms my nerves and makes my heart race at the same time.

We set the other two paintings up at the bottom of the easel, then step out of the way so people can see. "Think anyone will buy one?" I ask as people stroll past us, their eyes flitting from piece to piece.

"Definitely, just gotta be patient."

We stand beside the easel, watching for signs of interest. I do my best to look unconcerned, but inside I'm panicking. If no one buys anything, not only will I have to carry all my unsold work home, but I'll have to do it in front of Cy.

An hour and a half later, Cyrus is asleep against the back of the booth, and I've had tons of visitors but no takers. One girl seemed interested in *Blue*, but then her boyfriend came over and pulled her away. No one has shown any interest whatsoever in the portrait of Rodney, which I try to convince myself is disappointing, but I can't help feeling relieved. I'm about ready to pack up my stuff and check out the other vendors, when a middle-aged woman wearing a Burberry scarf comes up to my table. "Are those the Burgess Falls?"

"Yeah, they are," I say, surprised. "You've been there?"

"My mom took me as a kid. We loved it."

"It's a beautiful place," I agree, my eyes traveling over the painting.

"When did you make this?" she asks me. "It must have been spring for the trees to be so green."

"It was May of last year," I say, nodding. "I was there with my family. Have you been lately?"

"Not since my mother died."

If Cy were awake, this is the point when he'd push the sale. He'd tell her how sorry he was, how she should take this painting home with her as a memento of her mother. But I can't do it. She looks too sad.

She leans forward and examines the bottom of the falls. "You really captured the way the water slides down that giant rock. How tall do you think that waterfall is?"

"Over a hundred feet. Actually, this is technically the last of four falls. If you measure from the top of the first one down to the bottom of this one, it's over two hundred fifty feet."

"Wow."

"Yeah."

She takes a closer look at the painting. I realize she's actually considering buying it. I scan for hints as to how much she's going to offer. Burberry scarf. Clean, new-looking shoes. Chip-free nail polish. Shiny hair. A bubble of excitement builds inside me. A hundred dollars, maybe?

She looks up at me. "How does twenty dollars sound?"

My stomach drops. Twenty dollars for a painting that took me *hours and hours* to finish. A painting I gave everything to. And all I'll get in return is enough money to buy my family less than half a tank of gas?

"That's . . . um . . . a lot less than I expected."

She cocks an eyebrow. "Oh?"

I glance down at Cy, wishing he'd wake up and help me haggle with this woman, but he's still asleep. I'm on my own. "I thought maybe . . . a hundred?"

"One hundred *dollars*?" the woman says, like I've just asked for her firstborn. "I'm sorry, but that's just not possible. But I'll tell you what: I'll give you forty dollars. That's twice my original offer."

I open my mouth to argue—the least she could give me is fifty—but she purses her lips and says, "It might be less than you were hoping for, but it's really the best I can do." She stares at me, a look of impatience on her face. "Do we have a deal?"

Forty dollars. If that's not Karma biting me in the ass for lying to Fiona, then I don't know what is. But it's better than nothing.

"Yeah," I say, forcing a smile. "We have a deal."

She pulls two twenties out of her wallet, which I notice is full of bills. She hands them to me, and in the moment before I shove the money into my back pocket, I notice a streak of purple marker across Jackson's head on one of the bills. Maybe she has kids. The thought makes me feel a little better about giving this painting away.

But just a little.

"I knew those falls as soon as I saw them," she says, her voice warm once more. "You really captured the magic of that place. It's a special piece."

She reaches for the painting, but all I can see is my mom's smiling face as she watched me paint for the first time, an over-size smock smothering my nine-year-old frame. The urge to give the money back to the woman is hard to resist.

"I'm going to hang this in my daughter's room," the woman says. "She never knew my mom, so . . ."

"That sounds nice."

"Good luck with the rest of the sale," she says, then walks away, painting held by her side, inches from swinging back-packs and sharp booth corners. I watch her back, trying to catch one last glimpse of the Falls, but then she crosses between two booths, and she's gone.

Next to me, Cyrus wakes up. "What I miss?" he asks, stretching.

"I sold the Burgess." I turn away from him and slide the rest of my work back into the canvas bag. Rodney's half-formed face slips out of view. "Let's get out of here."

CHAPTER 10

I step off the bus the next morning, my mom's jean jacket from the eighties pulled close around my shoulders, and breathe in the smell of pine trees. My cell phone rings as I cross the street away from the plaza and head toward the Gala Art District. Who the hell is calling me this early?

"Taryn?"

"Good morning!" she says, so loudly I have to hold the phone away from my ear.

"You on your way to class?"

"I haven't even gone to bed yet," she says, laughing. "I was out all night dancing at the Red Rooster."

I stop walking. "Wait, you went *back* to that bar? Luke works there!"

"Not anymore," she says, and I can practically hear the devilish grin in her voice. "Apparently, after we left he got in a big fight with Eddie—the bouncer, remember?—and Luke got kicked out. The next day he was fired. Isn't that great?"

There's a strange clicking sound, an inhale, and then a

bunch of coughing. "Are you *smoking*?" I ask, immediately thinking of my dad.

"Hell, no. That's my friend Mickey. He's giving me a ride home. That is, if he can stop giving himself cancer for a freaking *second* and pay attention to the road."

The wind blows, and I start walking again.

"So what's up with you?" Taryn asks. "Don't tell me I turned you bad in one night and you've been out too."

I laugh. "Nah, I'm on my way into work."

"Oh, your internship, right? How's that going?"

"It's . . . okay."

"Just okay?"

I take a deep breath, and tell Taryn what happened—about finding out Fiona wanted someone who's going to college, about lying to her, about how impressed she seemed when I said I was going to UCLA.

Taryn whistles long and slow when I finish. "I was kidding before about turning you bad, but . . . you know she could fire you, right? If she finds out the truth?"

"Yeah, I know."

It's still a few minutes till nine, so I sit on the curb outside the studio. The cool concrete sends a shiver up my back.

Taryn sighs. "You're not going to like this, but I think you have to tell her."

"You just said she could *fire* me!"

"That's exactly why you have to come clean. If she finds out on her own—and she will—it's going to be so much worse than if you tell her the truth."

"But what if she fires me anyway? What if she decides I don't deserve this after all?" I bury my head in my hands. "I'm scared," I say quietly.

"I know," she says. "But I think that's how you know it's the right thing to do."

I hear a male voice in the background—Mickey, I guess—and then Taryn says, "Dess, I'm sorry, but I gotta go."

I grip the phone. "Wait—should I do it now? Like, right when I go inside? Or should I wait?"

"I'd wait for the right moment. Just feel it out."

"But how will I—"

"Let me know how it goes, okay?"

I swallow hard. "Yeah. I will."

We say goodbye, and I pull out the key to Fiona's building that she gave me at the fair. My hands shake as I unlock the door and step inside the entryway. I'm immediately met with stale air and the sound of something thudding overhead at regular intervals, like a bowling ball being dropped on the floor again and again. I look around for a light switch but I can't find one, so I start climbing the rickety stairs.

Halfway up, the thudding is replaced with the sound of running footsteps, and a second later the door at the top of the landing flies open. "Hi!" Fiona says. "Come on up!"

She disappears into the studio, leaving the door open behind her. I hurry after her, trying my best to ignore the nerves twisting inside me.

I reach the open door and my mouth drops open. Fiona's studio takes up the entire second floor of this building, and the ceiling is at least twenty feet tall. The windows facing the street are indeed covered with newspapers, fluttering in the breeze from the industrial-size fan oscillating in the middle of the room. The back wall is lined with floor-to-ceiling arched windows overlooking a brilliantly green park filled with trees. Morning light streams into the room, pooling on every available surface, including the sawdust-covered floor and countless workspaces.

But that's where the idyllic, picture-perfect artist's studio ends. Fiona's studio is filled with *stuff*. Some of it's art supplies—tubes of paint, coffee cans stuffed with paintbrushes, discarded sponges and rags—but the rest of her things would look out of place if I didn't already know she made works of art out of everyday items. At least three separate stacks of newspapers sit next to the door, and an old globe, a salad bowl full of orange peels, and two dusty dictionaries are piled on top of a rusty metal table near the fan. Underneath is a giant, half-rolled rug, the edges frayed and matted. The only things that look even remotely organized are her power tools, which are lined up neatly on a table next to a rack of pristine canvases.

Fiona waves from the other side of the room. "Over here."

I start toward her, but there's an exercise bike in the way. I try going the other way, and almost trip on the rug.

"Dessa?"

I step around a potted plant. "Just a second!"

Fiona suddenly stands in front of me. "Follow me."

We pick our way toward the windows along the back wall and I take a seat on one of two soft brown leather couches. Fiona sits next to me, but before I can think of anything to say, she hops up again.

"Tea. We need tea. What do you like?"

"Oh, uh . . . anything really."

"How about *matcha*? I love *matcha* in the morning."

"Sure," I say, even though I have no clue what *matcha* is.

She hurries over to a kitchenette in the corner that I hadn't noticed. She moves gracefully but fast, like she's speeding through the final movements of a ballet. I wrap my arms around one of the many available throw pillows. When she comes back, I'll tell her the truth. It'll be like ripping off a Band-Aid. Painful, but quick.

"Here you go," she says when she comes back, handing me an oversize clay mug with a wonky handle, keeping a squat blue mug for herself. I lean my face over the edge of the cup, and breathe in the smell of grass and lemon. I say a silent prayer to the gods of tea that I don't hate whatever *matcha* is, then blow on the top and take a taste.

"Oh, it's green tea."

"It is!" she says, like she's surprised to find herself drinking it as well.

She takes a sip, places her mug on a glass table between the couches, and picks up a thick binder. I should tell her now, before she opens that binder and shows me whatever is inside. Before she starts talking about all the work we're going to do together. Before I lose my nerve. Now. Right now.

I take another sip of tea.

"As you know, I have a show coming up, and there's a *lot* to do beforehand," Fiona says. "But that doesn't mean this internship is just about my show. It's also about you and your work. That's why over the next two weeks I'll be teaching you about found art, since that's my specialty, as well as a bit about painting since that's your primary medium."

I can't help but smile. *Primary medium* sounds so official.

Fiona picks up her mug and turns it around and around in her hands. "You've made a good decision in choosing UCLA," she says.

Her words are an icy breeze, chilling me from the inside out. This is it. My chance to either tell the truth or commit to my lie. It's tempting to keep up the act, but then I remember my dad, sitting on that blanket in the park, convinced he's lying to my mom to protect her, when the truth is, he's lying for the same reason I lied to Fiona. Because he's ashamed.

I don't want to live like that.

"Fiona, I have to tell you something." I lower my mug to the table, my hands shaking a little. "I didn't get into UCLA."

She frowns. "Where are you going then?"

I take a deep breath, ignoring the metallic taste in my mouth. My face is probably tomato red, but there's nothing I can do about it. "I'm not going anywhere. Technically I was still 'college bound' when my friend applied for me, but . . . I'm not anymore."

"Wait—your *friend* applied for you?"

My cheeks burn. "Yeah . . ."

"I see." She sits back, her arms crossed over her chest. "Then you got the internship and . . . what? You decided that lying was the best option?"

"No, I just . . . I panicked. I'm sorry." I stare down at my hands, waiting for her to pass judgment. Will she fire me? Tell my parents? I can't bear the thought of everyone knowing that in addition to being a failure, I'm a liar, too. Hot tears blur my vision.

"Why do you think you got the internship?" Fiona asks suddenly.

I open my mouth, but nothing comes out. If Cy had submitted any of my other paintings, I would have said it was because I have good technique. But Cy chose the one painting that doesn't showcase any formal technique. The sunburst.

I should look at her. I owe her that much. But I can't. "I . . . well . . ."

"You really don't have any idea? You must not think very highly of my taste after all."

"No! That's not what I meant—"

Fiona puts down her tea. I flinch at the sound of the cup clinking against the glass table. "What do you think I should do with this information? Now that I know you lied on your application, should I fire you?" She leans forward. "Would *you* fire you?"

The question catches me off guard. Would I give myself a second chance, or would I punish myself?

"I ask," Fiona continues, "because you seem to have very strong feelings about what it means to be rejected from art school, and whether you've earned this internship. So I'm wondering why I should keep someone who doesn't believe they deserve to be here."

"I understand," I say, wiping at my eyes. "I'll go."

I start to gather my things, but Fiona holds up her hand. "Dessa, I'm not asking you to leave."

"You're not?"

"If you really, truly don't think you belong here, then you can head home and I'll call another applicant. But if you want to prove to me that you deserve this, then stay. We'll call it probation." She waits for me to respond. All I can do is nod emphatically. She opens the binder on her lap. "Here's what's going to happen: Over the next week, you are going to bust your ass on every task I give you, and you're never going to question me or complain. If I say jump, you say 'how high?' Is that understood?"

I nod again, hope and fear warring in my chest.

"Good," Fiona says, and hands me the binder. "For now I want you to familiarize yourself with my upcoming show—what pieces I'm thinking of showing, where it's going to be and when, who will be attending, and what sort of press the show's been getting. That sort of thing. Can you do that?"

"Yes, absolutely," I say, hugging the binder to my chest. The next question is out of my mouth before I can stop it. "Why . . . why are you letting me stay?"

Fiona just looks at me for a second. "If you can answer that question by the time this internship is over, then I'll have done my job."

She stands and gives my shoulder the tiniest squeeze. "I've got some work to do, but let me know if you need me."

The bus is empty when I get on at six a.m. the next morning. The driver nods as I pass, a salute to stumbling out of bed before the sun, to guzzling hot coffee and forcing down dry cereal. I slump into a seat as the bus lurches forward. Seven days. That's how long I have to prove myself to Fiona before she decides my fate. It shouldn't be hard to stay busy. There's an endless list of things to do at the studio, from memorizing the pieces she's considering for the show to compiling a list of vendors to unpacking her older sculptures and making sure they aren't damaged. I just hope it's enough to prove that I deserve to be here.

Fiona's working when I arrive. I drop my bag on the floor

next to the couch before joining her at the table where she's poring over a stack of papers. The top page is covered in pencil scribbles. "Morning," I say, sliding into a seat. "Can I help?"

She doesn't look up from the papers. "Coffee?"

"I had some at home, but thanks."

She shakes her head. "Make some."

"Oh, of course, no problem."

I hurry to the kitchen. There's no coffeepot, but a shiny black-and-silver contraption squats at the edge of the counter, daring me to push one of the pulsing buttons. I glance over my shoulder at Fiona, but she's still staring down at the stack of papers in front of her. I turn back to the machine. I've seen these things on TV but I've never used one. How hard can it be? I open one of the cabinets and root around for the little pods of coffee, but I can't find any. I open another, and another. No luck.

I'm toying with the idea of asking Fiona where she keeps her damn coffee when suddenly Cy's ringtone blares through my pocket. I decline the call as quickly as I can. Why is Cy calling when he knows I'm working?

"Everything all right over there?" Fiona calls.

"Just a second!"

I shove the phone back into my pocket, and peek into a blue vase next to the sink. Three pods of coffee wait for me at the bottom. *Bingo.*

I pluck a pod from the vase, hoping it's not decaf, and hurry back to the machine. I open the top of the machine and drop the pod inside, then grab a clean mug and shove it under the spout. There are two buttons, but neither is labeled, so I just push one at random and hope I'm right.

A growling rumble erupts from the machine. Steam pours out of the top. I push the button again, but nothing happens, so I push the other button. The rumble grows louder, more insistent. I yank on the top of the machine—I'll pull the pod out if I have to—but it's stuck shut. "Shit," I mumble.

"It needs water," Fiona says from right behind me.

I jump at the sound of her voice. "Right! Sorry. I'll do that—"

But she's already pushing buttons and opening compartments and pouring water, so I stand to the side, feeling stupid and useless. A moment later, a stream of coffee pours into the mug.

When her coffee's made, we go back to the table. Fiona passes me the stack of papers. "I need you to type up all the notes in this stack, and then add them to the binder. My girlfriend's handwriting is a mess, so let me know if you can't read it. Did you bring your laptop?"

Damn it. "No, sorry."

"You can use mine for now, but you need to start bringing it every day." She reaches under the table and pulls a clunky computer out of a bag. "The printer is by the bathroom. It's wireless, so you don't have to plug the laptop in." She nods to the opposite corner of the room, where an ancient printer squats on a scratched secretary desk. "Let me know when you're done."

I spend the next two hours typing up the notes, mostly feedback on her paintings and thoughts about which ones belong in the show. I don't know anything about her girlfriend, but I can tell she knows a lot about Fiona's work. She mentions tons of paintings that aren't in the binder, and occasionally sketches something in the margins. I do my best to commit everything to memory as I type, but I'm going to have to read over the notes again just in case.

"Done?" Fiona asks a short while later, as I finish adding the pages to the binder. She hands me a new sketch pad and a pencil.

I follow Fiona over to the sofa. "What are we drawing?" I ask.

Fiona taps a pencil against her bottom lip. "Let's start with something simple." She grabs an owl-shaped coffee mug off a nearby table. It's wide and blue, one wing folding into the handle. Half-moons make up the feathers, while raised orbs the size of grapes form the piercing eyes.

"For the next hour," she says, "I want you to do one sketch per minute."

I grip the pad. "That's a lot faster than I usually sketch."

"Good, that means it'll be a challenge. Here are the rules: You can move the mug, turn it over, whatever you want. But I want to see you flipping to a new page every time the timer goes off."

I tuck my feet underneath me and stare at the mug. It's not much to look at. Not much to sketch. But maybe that's a good thing.

Fiona sets an alarm on her phone for one minute. "Ready and *go.*"

I grip the pencil tightly in my fingers. I should start with the outline of the mug, the basic shape, before I worry about the feather detail and the beak. My plan in place, I carefully draw the outline of one side of the mug. The edge of the cup bows out a little, but when I try to mimic that perfect sloping edge, my pencil catches on the paper and my line veers too wide. I flip the pencil over and press the eraser to the page.

"No erasing!" Fiona says. "Just keep going."

I sigh, but flip the pencil back over and continue my line, trying to ignore the way it dips in the middle. I glance up at the mug, taking in the way the cup curves at the bottom—

The timer blares.

"That's a minute," Fiona says, resetting the timer. "New sketch."

"But I just started! Can I pick up where I—"

"Nope. Are you ready?"

I turn the page. "Ready."

"And . . . go."

I sketch the outline of the mug quickly. The pencil doesn't catch this time, but the angle's wrong. I keep going, focusing on finishing the base and the other side of the mug as quickly as I can. As soon as these elements are in place, I start on the handle, but I can't quite get the thickness right. I study the little mug, the way the handle curves sharply at the top, but then slopes gently away from the side. I'm halfway through the second curve of the handle when the timer blares again.

"Better," Fiona observes, peering at my page. I look at hers, but I've barely caught a glimpse before she turns the page. "Eyes on your own paper."

"But you already started shading the feathers—"

"Don't worry about that. Just get as much down as you can. Don't let perfection get in the way."

That's easy for her to say. It only takes her a minute to draw a near-perfect owl.

"Ready to go again?" she asks.

The minutes pass, so fast and yet never ending. My hand cramps and my brain feels like putty, but I turn the page and start again . . . and again. By the time the hour is over, I have a sketchbook full of half-formed owl mugs. None are great, but each one is a *tiny* bit better than the last.

Maybe.

Fiona shakes out her drawing hand. "Good work today. Maybe tomorrow you'll be able to get a bit more of the detail down. I'd also like to see you play with perspective more—"

"Wait, we're doing this *again*?"

"We're doing this every day." Fiona picks up the mug and carries it over to the kitchen. "I want you to take that sketch pad home with you and do thirty minutes of sketching every night, too."

My shoulders droop. I used to sketch for hours, but now thirty minutes sounds like an eternity.

"Don't look so glum," Fiona says. "At least you don't have to sketch owls at home."

CHAPTER 11

Fiona and I settle into a rhythm over the next few days. I spend the mornings working on her show, and the afternoons organizing the studio while Fiona paints. When she's finished, we sketch for an hour, our pencils flying across the page. I struggle to embrace all the terrible artwork she's forcing me to create each day, but as I sit on her couch, my sketchbook balanced on my knees, I feel a whisper of the excitement I had when Mom bought me my first sketchbook in third grade, insisting that art was just as important as long division.

The thirty-minute sketches at night are a different story. I press my pencil to the page, but nothing happens. Maybe it's because I'm exhausted by the time I get home, but it shouldn't be this hard. I should be able to do this.

One evening around seven, Fiona peeks over the top of her laptop. "Whatcha doing over there?"

I rub my eyes, glad to stop scrolling through the endless Excel spreadsheet I've been staring at for an hour. "Budget stuff."

"Yuck." Fiona takes a seat next to me. "How's it looking?"

"It's going to be tight, but I think we can get that caterer you wanted. But we can't do a full bar—just beer and wine."

"Ah, well," she says, reaching over me to scroll down the list of expenses. "At least we'll know people aren't just there for the free tequila." She checks her watch. "It's late. Let's call it a day."

I resist the urge to slam my computer shut and bolt for the door, instead taking my time saving the expense sheet, closing all my programs, and packing up. The last thing I need is for Fiona to think I'm eager to get out of here. The truth is, I'd stay all night if she asked me to.

But I'm glad she isn't.

"I'll see you tomorrow," I say, then head downstairs. Outside, the streetlights shine overhead as I walk toward the bus stop. My brain is fried, and my neck aches from bending over my work. But despite how hungry I am, how badly I want a hot shower, I'm happy about everything I've accomplished. It's been three days and I've done absolutely everything Fiona has asked, even stuff that made me sweat from nerves, like when she had me call a local newspaper to tell them about the upcoming show, or when she made me sketch her face from memory using a permanent marker. I'm not sure what the latter had to do with deserving this internship, but she seemed pleased with it anyway.

My family greets me at the door when I arrive at YiaYia's house. Even Rodney wraps his arms around me in a hug. You'd think I'd been away for weeks instead of twelve hours. But then I think about the last few days, and I feel a rush of guilt. I've barely seen them since my internship started. Each morning I leave before everyone gets up, and when I get home dinner is usually over and I barely have the energy to put two words together, let alone tell them about my day.

"I have a surprise for you," YiaYia says. She takes my hand, and leads me into the living room. Rodney and my parents follow.

"Ta-da!" she announces, pointing across the room.

It takes me a few seconds, but then I see it: Above the fireplace, where the soft yellow yucca used to hang, is the one painting I never wanted to see again.

The sunburst.

I shove my hands into my pockets to stop myself from ripping the stupid thing off the wall. "How did you find it?" I ask as nicely as I can, given the circumstances. "I thought I put it away."

"We were looking for your brother's Game Boy, and we came across your painting, all stuffed away in that cabinet by your bed." She claps her hands together. "Doesn't it look lovely above the fireplace?"

"Sure," I say, turning away. I don't want to look at it for a second longer than I have to. "I'm going to get cleaned up for dinner, okay?"

"Dessa?" YiaYia calls after me. "Are you sure you don't mind?"

"Nope," I call over my shoulder. "It's great."

I'm almost to the bathroom, when Dad stops me. "Dessa, hold on."

I sigh and stop walking. "Dad, it's fine, okay? I don't want to talk about it."

"I actually wanted to ask you . . . something else."

"Oh. What's up?"

He looks back toward the living room, where YiaYia and my mom are talking, and gestures for me to follow him into one of the bedrooms. "You didn't tell your mom I lost my job, did you?" he asks quietly, closing the door behind us.

"You told me not to."

"Good, that's good." He runs his hand down his face and leans against the wall.

I cross my arms. "But I think you should."

"Absolutely not. It'll just worry her."

"Maybe she *should* be worried." *I am*, I add silently.

He shakes his head. "You don't understand what it's like to keep this family afloat. To make this traveling thing work. And your mom—it's so important to her that we keep doing this. Her whole life, she's wanted to travel the country. I can't let her or you kids down. I can't tell her I'm failing."

His words make my heart ache. It's not fair that he's making me keep this from Mom, but I hate seeing him this way even more than the idea of keeping secrets. "You're not letting us down, Dad."

"Yes, I am. I'm not giving you the lives you deserve."

"Are you sure you can't get your old job back?"

"I called Mark today and tried to work things out, but he said his mind is made up. There's not going to be any more contract work. Not for a while anyway. There's a seasonal position, some management job, but I'd have to be in Charleston for half the year. So that's out."

"What about regular freelance work?"

"I've been looking, but it's hard to find a steady gig, and I keep getting priced out."

I hug myself. My dad's never opened up to me about this kind of thing before. I want to help him, but his words make me feel like I'm holding on to the edge of a cliff, helpless and alone.

"I'm thinking about taking out a loan," he mutters, more to himself than me. "Just enough to cover our expenses until I can find some new work."

I blanch. "But—but you always say loans are only for emergencies. What if we can't pay it back?"

"Let me worry about that."

"How am I supposed to let you worry about it, if you're telling me?" I say, my voice rising.

His face goes stony, and he straightens up. "I shouldn't have said anything."

"No, Dad, that not what I'm saying—"

"Dessa?" Mom calls through the door. "Find your dad and tell him it's dinnertime."

He holds his finger up to his lips. When her footsteps disappear down the hall, he whispers, "Remember, mum's the word."

I sigh heavily.

"Wait a sec, Dad." I reach into my back pocket and pull out the crumpled twenty-dollar bills from my art sale. Every morning I tuck the money into my pocket, waiting for the right moment to give it to him. Now seems like the time.

"I sold a painting," I explain. "I didn't make much, but I want you to have it."

"I can't take this, sweetheart."

"Yes," I say, folding the bills into his hand. "You can."

Before he can say anything else, I open the door and hurry down the hallway toward the kitchen. Part of me wants him to come after me, but at the same time, I need space. It's not fair that he is putting me in the middle, especially since there's nothing I can do to help, no way I can make things better. It's not like forty bucks is going to last long.

Except . . . maybe I *can* help. Once my internship is over, the future will be as wide open as the road I'm so sick of travel-ing. I've never wanted to be anything but an artist, but as long as my dream of going to college is over, I might as well figure out a way to support my family. Selling my art didn't help much, but I could pick up odd jobs on the road, or learn how to do web design work like my dad.

It's not what I want, but what choice do I have?

"Come on," Cyrus says over the phone later that night. "I haven't seen you in days."

"I know, I know." I put my sketch pad aside, trying to ignore the blank page. "I've been really busy with work."

"Sounds like you need a break."

I look over the back of YiaYia's couch. I can just make out Dad and Rodney in the kitchen, my brother's math homework strewn across the table next to Dad's laptop. "I'm not saying I'm leaving, but . . . where would we go?"

I can practically hear him grinning into the phone. "I'll tell you when we get there."

I laugh. "That doesn't sound suspicious at all."

"Where's your sense of adventure?"

I squeeze my eyes shut and take a deep breath. I brought home Fiona's binder so I could focus on finalizing the list of pieces in the show. After I finish my stupid thirty minutes of sketching, that is. If I leave now, there's no way I'll get it all done tonight. But I haven't seen Cy since the disastrous art sale, and before that . . . Goose bumps race up my arms at the thought of his arms around me, his lips only inches away.

"Come on, Dess," Cy says, his voice so low it sounds like he's right next to me. "I miss you."

Screw it. I can look over the list of pieces for the show in the morning. "Give me five minutes."

"Wear your bathing suit," Cy says, then hangs up.

"Hey, Dad?" I call as I hop over the back of the sofa. "Is it okay if I go out with Cyrus for a few hours? I'll be back by ten-ish."

He looks up from his laptop. "What?"

"I'm going out? Back by ten?"

"Oh. Yeah. Okay." He looks back at the screen. Next to him, Rodney chews on the end of his pencil and stares into space.

I go to my bedroom and pull my bikini out of the set of drawers I'm sharing with Rodney. The navy fabric is stretched thin and the strings are still knotted from the last time I wore it. I put it on, making sure nothing is hanging out that shouldn't be, then throw my clothes back on and grab my purse off a chair by the front door. I consider saying goodbye, but I don't want my dad to change his mind about letting me go, so I quietly close the door behind me.

Cyrus is waiting for me at the end of YiaYia's driveway. A pair of black swim trunks hangs low on his hips, and his sleeveless navy shirt shows off his dark, muscled shoulders. For once I don't look away.

"Where are we going?" I ask.

"You'll see."

Twenty minutes later, we arrive outside a wrought-iron gate set into a thick brick wall. We're not far from YiaYia's house, but this neighborhood is totally different. Fancier. All the hedges are perfectly trimmed, and I heard at least three fountains bubbling behind tall hedges as we passed some of the bigger houses. But there hasn't been any sign of a public swimming pool, and this isn't the kind of neighborhood that would have a broken fire hydrant. Or at least, it's not the kind of neighborhood that would let the hydrant stay broken for long. "Cy, where are we?"

Cyrus holds out his arms, as if he's presenting the iron gate to me. "This is the Santa Fe Women's Club."

"Uh-huh . . ." I lean against the gate. "And we're here because . . . ?"

"Because they have a swimming pool and no one is here."

"We can't sneak into their pool!" I say, but already my heart is racing with the thrill of it.

"We're not. I got permission."

I roll my eyes. "Yeah, right."

"I did! I was walking by earlier and I ran into a lady who works here, and she told me the side gate's always open in case I wanted to come swim sometime at night."

"She just *told* you that?"

"I offered to help her carry some boxes from her car. She said I reminded her of her grandson, Rick."

I shake my head. "Is no one immune to your charms?"

He takes a step closer to me. I can feel the heat of his body. "You tell me."

Cy leans forward, and for one delicious moment, I think he's going to kiss me, but then he looks over my shoulder. "Did you see that? The light in the security guard's booth just went off. We have the place all to ourselves now."

"So *that's* why you didn't want to swim at my YiaYia's."

I laugh, and turn around to peer through the gate. It's dark on the other side, but the streetlight is bright enough that I can see the front door of a wide, two-story building set far back on the other side of a plush lawn. There's a tennis court to the right, and what looks like a brand-new BMW in the driveway. "There's a car. Someone is here."

Cy shakes his head. "That's a complimentary car to drive the members around town. I heard one of the other staff members talking about having to wash it every day even though no one ever uses it." He takes my hand. "You ready?"

He looks into my eyes, and my heartbeat picks up speed again. As much as I love working for Fiona, it feels good to be on an adventure with Cy. "Let's do it."

Cyrus leads me around the corner. The brick wall continues all the way around, but halfway down the block we come to a wooden gate.

Cyrus glances quickly up and down the empty street, then pushes open the gate. "Come on."

I follow him across a wide lawn, and soon we're at the side of the main building. So far it looks like Cy's right—the place is totally deserted. "Where's the pool?"

"This way."

We hurry around to the back and the pool comes into view. It's not as big as I was expecting. I figured a place this fancy would have an Olympic-size pool, but this one looks like the public pool we used to visit back in Chattanooga, all the way down to the cracked tile surrounding the water, and the bent metal ladder at one end. The familiarity makes me feel a little bit better about being here.

Cyrus pulls open the gate to the pool—also unlocked—and gestures for me to follow him. Once inside, he pulls off his shirt and drops it on a nearby pool chair, then kicks off his sandals and cannonballs into the pool. I laugh and walk over to another chair. My sandals *thwap thwap thwap* against the concrete, so loud in the silence that I might as well be wearing tap shoes. I take them off and remove my shirt and shorts.

By now Cy has resurfaced. "The water's really warm."

I sit on the edge of the pool and put my legs in. He's right—the water is the perfect temperature from sitting in the sun all day. I wiggle my toes. "This is so nice."

"It's even better if you get all the way in," he says, swimming up to me. He puts his wet hand on my bare knee. Goosebumps race up my leg.

I push myself off the edge. The water feels so good I let out a sigh. "I needed this. My hands are killing me from all the damn owl sketches I've been doing."

Cyrus raises an eyebrow. "Sounds exhausting."

I splash him, and before long we're having a water fight. It eventually turns into a race across the pool; we tie twice, and I win once. Neither of us has ever lived anywhere with a pool, but we've grown up in lakes and rivers across the country, plus the occasional public pool, so we're both strong swimmers. When we're exhausted from racing, our chests heaving from holding our breath, we play Marco Polo. Cy calls out *Marco!* at full volume, making me cringe. But he's right; there's no one here to catch us.

After an hour of messing around, I float on my back and close my eyes. Someday, when I have a house of my own, I'm going to have a pool that I can swim in every single day. It'll be twice the size of this one, and filled with salt water like the one Cy and I swam in when we visited his uncle in Toronto. I remember the face Cyrus made when he accidentally swallowed a mouthful, and laugh.

"Dessa?"

I open my eyes. Cyrus is standing over me. A droplet of water clings to the end of his nose. I reach to brush it away, but he gently catches my wrist and turns my hand over. He makes a circle with his finger, but instead of putting a dot in the middle like normal, he presses his lips to my palm. I close my eyes as his kisses continue up my wrist. His mouth is soft against my skin.

"Dessa . . . ," he says again, and I feel his hand slip around my waist. He helps me to my feet, and I wrap my legs around his hips, the water sloshing around us. The heat from his chest warms my stomach as I stare into his eyes.

"I've wanted this for so long," he says quietly. "You and me, just like this."

My heart pounds in my ears. "Me too."

Suddenly I can't wait a second longer to feel his mouth on mine. I cup my hands around his face, and lean forward. He meets me halfway, his lips pressing against mine, and for a moment, we're perfectly still, letting the realization that this is *actually happening* course through us. But then the kiss deepens, and everything—the water, the chill air—disappears until there is nothing but me and Cyrus. Cyrus and me.

I don't know how much time passes, but when we finally part, I'm breathing so hard it's as if I've been underwater this whole time.

He holds me, and I lay my head on his shoulder. I want to stay here forever.

"I know you were disappointed about college," he says after a moment, "but it's better this way."

"Better?"

He puts me down, so we're face-to-face. I immediately miss the feeling of his body against mine. I want to go back to a minute ago, when all that mattered was us, right here, right now.

"Well, I've been thinking about how, if we're going to be together, we'll have to be really careful. It's going to be hard enough explaining this to the families, you know? They think of us as family. So once we tell them . . . that's it."

I wrap my arms around myself. "What do you mean, *that's it*?"

"I mean, we'll be together. No more maybes or what-ifs. No more distractions. It'll just be you and me, and the families." He reaches through the water and takes my hand. "Now that you've got this internship, you don't need college, right? Once it's over, you'll know everything you need to be an artist, and you can go back to traveling for good."

His smile is so huge, so beautiful. I want to agree. I want to squeeze his hand, and say *yes, that's enough for me.*

But it's not.

"Cy . . . that's not what I want." But he keeps talking, like he hasn't heard me.

"Dess, by the time I realized how badly I wanted to be with you, you'd already decided you wanted to go to college. But now the only thing standing in our way . . . it's gone. We finally have a real chance to be together."

Anger flares inside me suddenly, and I yank my hand out of his. "Just because I didn't get into college doesn't mean I want to travel forever. I want more out of life than a cramped RV and the same conversations over and over again with the same people."

He rubs a wet hand over his head, frustration coming off him in waves. "I know you feel that way now, but you'll change your mind when you see how happy we can be." He looks at me with pleading eyes. "Try to see it my way, Dess. Please?"

The water shimmers between us, cold and blue. It's only a few inches, but it feels like miles.

"I'm sorry," I say, "I can't."

"Can't?" he says quietly, "or won't?"

The pain on his face is so clear I can feel it in my bones. They ache, almost as much as I ache to reach out for him again. But I can't.

Won't.

Cyrus swims to the edge of the pool and pulls himself out of the water. I watch him, my stomach churning. What I've done hits me with the force of a hurricane, the winds made of white panic, yet I know I can't take the words back. Because it's the truth.

"We should go," he says, pulling his shirt on. He doesn't look at me. "You don't want to be late for work tomorrow."

CHAPTER 12

Midmorning sunlight streams through the windows, turning the chaos of the studio a stunning gold. Fiona and I are curled on the sofa, our empty hot chocolate mugs crusting over on the table in front of us.

"Your technique is already very good," Fiona says as she swipes through photos of my portfolio on my cell phone. She points at a picture of a painting on the screen. "But there's no passion here. I don't see *you* in this."

"Those pictures are small," I argue. "Maybe if you see the paintings on a bigger screen . . ."

"It doesn't matter. Big or small, grainy or clear, these read like careful forgeries, failing to capture the essence of an original. Perfect replications void of soul."

I suck in a sharp breath. I thought these paintings were *good*. How can I call myself an artist if I can't even tell the difference?

"All artists go through this phase," she says, handing the phone back to me. "It's transitional. You start with raw talent, with color and shapes and speed. The kind of talent that makes your parents pin your work to the fridge."

I think of the countless times Mom's told me how wonderful I am, how talented, how special. Guess I was right not to believe her.

"Then your parents send you to art class," Fiona continues, "and you learn to focus on *technique*. Most people never move past this stage. Or they give up on technique entirely. Few can marry talent and technique into one."

"What if you get stuck? What if all the passion that got you started in the first place is gone, and all you can think about is technique?"

Fiona considers me for a second, her head tipped to the side. Her long black hair cascades off her shoulder like a waterfall. "Stay right here. I have an idea."

She strides over to a towering stereo with wall-mounted speakers, and flips through a stack of tottering CDs, reading the front of the cases before tossing them down again. She finally finds what she's looking for and slips the CD into her stereo. The machine gobbles it up, and a series of green lights flash.

Fiona's index finger hovers over the play button. "When my brain won't shut up, sometimes I have to drown it out."

She pushes play, and I'm hit with a wall of sound. Beating drums, so loud and insistent I feel them pounding inside my brain, my bones. She turns a dial, and the volume soars. The sound rattles the windows, my teeth. I place my hand over my heart, and I swear I can feel it vibrating inside me.

Fiona returns, a piece of charcoal in hand. "Draw!"

"Draw what?" I shout. "I can't even think."

"Exactly!" She rips a piece of drafting paper off a long roll attached to the end of a table, and holds it out to me. "Don't think. Just create."

Fiona tears off another piece for herself, and drops to the floor. She pulls a broken piece of charcoal across the page in long, sure strokes. The drums beat on.

I stare down at my blank page. *Don't think, just create.* I roll my shoulders and take a deep breath, then press the charcoal to the page. But my hand doesn't move. *Don't think, just create.* The charcoal grows slippery with sweat. I close my eyes, and try to let the pulsing of the drums quiet my worries, my fear. For a moment, I think it's going to work. But then I'm bombarded with images of my soulless portfolio, my half-formed owl sketches. Of my family's empty bank account. Of my future, as blank as the page in front of me.

Of Cyrus.

My breath hitches in my chest, and I drop the charcoal. I open my mouth, trying desperately to inhale, but my lungs stutter in my chest.

Fiona looks up, confusion written across her face. Black lines crawl across her paper, furling and unfurling. I'm going to be sick.

"What's wrong?" she yells over the music.

A thousand-pound weight bears down on my chest. "I can't—I can't breathe."

She jumps to her feet, and the whole world tips sideways. I bend over, my hands pressed against my face. A wave of sickness crashes over me, filling my mouth with sour juices. I choke them down. *Make it stop. Please please please make it stop.*

The drums halt, and my own ragged breathing fills my ears.

"I'm here," Fiona says. "You're having a panic attack, but it's okay. Just keep breathing. You can get through this."

I take a shuddering breath, and listen as my heart beats a rhythm of shame and failure against my rib cage.

You can't. You can't. You can't.

I inhale as deeply as I can, but it's still not enough. Never enough. "I can't . . . do this."

Fiona lays a steady hand on my back. "You can," she says, "of course you can. Just take your time."

We sit in silence, I don't know for how long, as I struggle to breathe normally. Fiona watches me carefully, but I can't read the look on her face. Pity? Confusion? Regret? My breathing starts to speed up again and I feel tears prick at the corner of my eyes.

"Dessa, everything is okay," Fiona says. "You are okay."

I squeeze my eyes shut and continue to breathe, in and out. In and out. Until finally . . . *finally* . . . I take a full, deep breath.

I open my eyes.

"Better?" Fiona asks, picking up the piece of charcoal.

"Yeah," I say, nodding. "Sorry—"

"Don't apologize. You did nothing wrong. This kind of thing happens when people are under stress."

"Has it happened to you?"

She laughs. "Oh, definitely."

Fiona turns the charcoal over in her fingers, leaving black marks against her skin. I remember the way the crisscrossing lines on her page looked like they were moving, like they had a life of their own. I shudder. "I don't want to feel like that every time I try to draw. How do I make it stop?"

"I'm not sure there's anything you can do to make sure it never happens again. But in general . . . well, I guess you have to figure out what's bothering you, what caused the attack." She looks up. "But you don't have to do that right now. Maybe it's better if you rest a bit."

I hug my knees to my chest. Only a few days into this internship, and I'm already in need of a rest? "No. I want to figure this out."

"Okay . . . ," she says hesitantly. "Walk me through what happened."

"I picked up the charcoal, and I couldn't think of a single thing to draw. All I could see were my problems." I shake my head. "What kind of artist can't even touch charcoal without panicking?"

"Just because our souls crave the creative process, doesn't mean it's possible to create. Sometimes the muse flies the coop, and we have to spend some time looking for him. But that doesn't mean we aren't artists. It just means we're going through some kind of change, and our creative minds are working through it."

"But it's not just my art. I'm failing at everything in my life. My family—even my best friend." I wrap my arms around myself, a sob lodged in my throat. "I feel like I'm drowning."

She hands me the charcoal. "Give yourself a chance to be weak, Dessa. Sometimes it's the only way to find out how strong you really are."

I swallow hard and turn the charcoal around in my hand. "Could we try again?"

"Absolutely. But let's skip the drums this time."

I drop my bag next to the front door on Friday afternoon. The house is silent and still. "Hello?"

No one answers.

"Mom? YiaYia? I'm home early."

The kitchen is empty, and so is the living room. I walk through the rest of the shadowy house, not bothering to turn any lights on. It feels like I haven't seen my family in forever. I thought we'd hang out on the couch, watch a movie. Maybe go swimming. But they're gone. All of them.

I make my way back to the kitchen. Did Mom say anything this morning about where they were going? All I can remember is grabbing a bagel before racing out the front door. I push away my disappointment and pull a carton of orange juice from the fridge. Half full. I look over my shoulder, just in case, then lift the carton to my lips. There's one good thing about being in an empty house—no one can tell you what to do.

I'm about to take another swig when my phone buzzes in my pocket. I'm expecting it to be my mom, but Cyrus' name lights up the screen instead. My finger hovers over the green button. Is he still mad? Should I apologize?

Should *he*?

The phone rings again. This is stupid. We've been friends for years. It's going to be okay. We'll work this out.

I clear my throat and answer the call. "Hey . . . how's it going?"

"I just saw you get off the bus. I thought you had work today?"

His voice is cool, but he doesn't sound mad. I breathe a sigh of relief. "I did, but Fiona had a doctor's appointment and then dinner with her girlfriend."

"Nice. Want to go for a walk?"

"Give me a few minutes and I'll come over."

"I'm actually already outside."

I look out the window by the front door. Cyrus is standing at the end of the driveway, cell phone pressed against one ear. He holds up his free hand in greeting. My heart does a little dance at the sight of him standing there, even though he's wearing an old sweatshirt and a pair of basketball shorts.

"Isn't it a little hot for that sweatshirt?" I joke.

"Couldn't find a clean shirt." He shrugs. "So, you coming out or . . . ?"

"Oh, um . . . yeah. Give me a minute." We hang up, and I

hesitate. He doesn't sound angry, but a peace offering after the other night can't hurt. I head back to my parents' bedroom and grab one of my dad's old T-shirts out of a drawer, then head outside.

Cyrus is leaning against the door to our RV. I toss him my dad's shirt. "Here."

"Thanks." He pulls off his sweatshirt. His chest glistens with a thin sheen of sweat, then disappears under the shirt. It's baggy and faded, and I silently curse all of Cy's form-fitting T-shirts for being unavailable.

We start walking, the sun beating down on us like it's high noon instead of almost five thirty. I walk close to the curb so I can stay in the shade from the trees, but Cy ambles down the middle of the road.

"So . . . how are you?" I ask, breaking the silence.

Cy shrugs and keeps walking. I'm about to try again when he glances at me out of the corner of his eye. "How's the internship going?"

I join him in the middle of the street. "Busy. I spent most of the morning cleaning the studio."

"What are you, her maid?" Cy asks, elbowing me gently.

I elbow him back, relieved that he's finally acting normal. "I want to show her how seriously I'm taking this, and I figure improving her workspace will only make us more productive. Besides . . . I kind of like washing paintbrushes."

Cy grins. "Nerd."

"What about you? Have you and your dad found a new bike to work on yet?"

"Still looking. We'll probably pick one by next week though."

We keep walking, our faces turned up to the late-afternoon sun. It feels nice to do nothing with Cy, like I'm vacationing in my old life. I've been so busy I haven't realized how much I've missed it. Missed him.

When we reach the end of the next block, Cy stops. "There's something I need to tell you."

This is going to be about the pool. I knew it. But maybe that's okay. Maybe he thought about what I said, and he gets it. Maybe there's still a way to make this work.

"Cyrus—about what I said—"

"No, let me go first, okay? I need to get this out." He takes a deep breath, his chest filling underneath my dad's old shirt, then lets it out in one big whoosh. "I called Rachel and we're going out again. But this time . . . it's going to be a date."

His words hit me like a punch in the stomach. This is not what I thought he was going to say. This is the *opposite*.

"I don't want you to be upset," he says, shoving his hands into the pockets of his shorts. "But I realized if you don't want to be with me, then I have to accept that and move on."

Everything inside of me screams that he's wrong, that I want to be with him. But I can't bring myself to say it. It's like something is shifting beneath me, like we're standing on a piece of ice that's breaking apart, but if I just reached out—

"I'm going to borrow my dad's bike," Cyrus continues, "and ride to Dallas to see her. I'm going to stay there for a few days."

My eyes go wide, but Cyrus shakes his head. "It's not like that. I'm not staying *with* her. My dad has some old friends that live in town, and I'll be couch surfing. But . . . I'm going to see her. Probably more than once. I thought you should know."

Suddenly the heat doesn't matter. It's like I'm stranded in the middle of a frozen sea, drifting away from land on that same piece of ice, and all I feel is cold and empty and alone. And angry. Really, really angry.

"That sounds great," I say, my voice hard. "Really great. I'm sure Rachel will be super happy you're coming all that way to see her."

Cy looks unsure. "Thanks . . . ?"

"But are you sure staying that long is a good idea? Don't you think it'll look . . ." I search for the right word, the word that'll hurt the most. "Desperate?"

"Excuse me?"

"I mean, a guy drives all the way to Dallas from Santa Fe, and he stays in town for a few days . . . all for a second date?" I shrug. "Seems kind of extreme for someone you barely know."

"What do you know about second dates, Dessa?" Cy says, his voice low and dangerous. "You've never been on a *first* date."

I tighten my hands into fists. "Shut up."

"I'd be surprised if you've ever even kissed a guy. And don't tell me about that dude in Portland last summer. We both know that was bullshit."

"Oh yeah? Well . . . it wasn't bullshit when I made out with a guy that night in Oklahoma."

Cy frowns. "What guy?"

"No one you know," I say, folding my arms. "He's a cowboy, and he's in his twenties. And he was *gorgeous*." And a total douchebag I hope I never see again.

"You're lying," he growls. "You're trying to make me jealous."

He stares at me, his chest heaving like he ran here. The silence feels alive and furious, pressing in from all sides. Suffocating.

When he speaks, it's hardly more than a whisper. "So a random dude in a bar is good enough for you, but I'm not. Why is that?"

I swallow, but don't answer.

"You think you're too good for me. For the families. Admit it."

I flinch. "That's not true, I just—I can't— Please, Cyrus, don't make me."

"Don't make you *what*?" Cyrus demands, his face flushing. "Come on, Dessa. Tell me once and for all. And don't give me any bullshit about wanting to go to art school or being tired of traveling. For once just tell me the fucking truth."

"Fine!" I shout. "I can't be your girlfriend because if I am, that's all I'll ever be!"

His eyes are darker and more icy than I've ever seen them.

165

He takes a step back, like he can't stand to be near me. "I'm going to Dallas tomorrow, and I don't know when I'll be back. In the meantime, do me a favor."

I wipe my nose, just barely holding back tears. "What?"

"Get over yourself."

He walks away, leaving me standing alone on the side of the road. I watch him go, my head a jumble of words and feelings so loud I can't think. Then he disappears around the corner, and I sink down to the grass and cry.

CHAPTER 13

"Pass the sugar," Rodney says on Saturday morning.

I roll my eyes. "Say *please*, dorkus."

Rodney sticks out his tongue.

"Consider yourself lucky, Dessa," YiaYia says, taking a sip of her coffee. "It's going to be his middle finger he's sticking up at you in a few years."

"My baby would never do that." Mom kisses Rodney on the side of the head and hands him the bowl of sugar. "Only take a little."

"What are you doing today, Dessa?" Mom asks, turning to me. "Got any plans for your first day off?"

"Not sure," I say, my eyes on Rodney as he spoons sugar into his cereal. "Fiona mentioned that her website needed to be updated so I thought I might look into that. . . ."

Mom crosses her arms. "I thought you'd want to spend some time with the families. You haven't been around much lately, and I hear you've already decided to skip our trip to Albuquerque."

"Mom, I have to *work*."

"Dessa's not coming to Albuquerque, but she *is* cleaning the garage today," Dad says as he opens the newspaper, the dry pages rustling. He looks at me over the top of the Politics section. "Don't think we forgot your little adventure."

I cringe. "Dad, I'm really busy. . . ."

"Too bad."

"Where's Cyrus?" YiaYia asks. "I'm sure he'd be happy to help out."

I dig my nails into the palms of my hands under the kitchen table. I know she's trying to make my punishment more bearable, but after yesterday, the last thing I want to do is hang out with Cyrus. Not that I could, anyway. By now he's probably halfway to Dallas, with nothing on his mind but wrapping his arms around Rachel, whispering what a terrible person I am into her ear.

Dad shuffles the pages of his paper. "Dessa will be cleaning the garage *by herself*. Besides, Jeff says Cyrus went to Dallas this morning."

"Never stop moving," Mom says with a sigh.

"Never stop moving," Dad answers automatically.

We eat in silence for a while, Rodney slurping up his milk, me focused on chewing as slowly as possible just in case someone else tries to ask about Cy.

Then Mom clears her throat and looks pointedly at me. "The McAlisters mentioned taking a short trip to see the Grand Canyon tomorrow, after Albuquerque. The girls have never been there, and Rodney hasn't seen it since he was little."

I swallow a painful bite of unchewed cereal. "Mom, I already told you, I can't leave. Fiona needs me."

"It's just a few days. Surely she can spare you?"

I think of the pile of work back at the studio, and shake my head. "She really can't. Let's just go when the internship is over, okay?"

"We've already put our lives on hold for this internship."

I drop my spoon into the bowl. "Are you kidding? When I came home yesterday to hang out with everyone, no one was even here."

"We can't be expected to wait around for you."

"I didn't say that—"

"*And* this internship is why we left Asheville early."

"It was raining anyway!"

YiaYia holds up her hands.

"Now let's all *calm down* a minute." She turns to my mom. "Geri, if you want to go so badly, then go. Dessa can stay here with me."

"Yeah," Rodney says, sneaking another teaspoon of sugar. "Dessa can just stay here."

I look to Dad, and I can see from his expression that he's thinking the same thing as me. He and mom have never left me behind, not even for a long weekend. It's one thing for the families to split up for a few days, but leaving just one person behind? We've never done that before.

"Is that what you want?" Mom asks me. "To stay here?"

Everyone looks at me.

It's just a week in Santa Fe, I remind myself. But the way my mom is staring at me, I know it means more to her. Like I'm drawing a line in the sand between one life and another. And maybe I am. I finally have a life of my own, a life I care enough about not to up and leave it.

"I want to stay."

Mom's nostrils flare. "I guess that's settled then." She turns to Dad. "What do you think? A few extra days away? I'm sure Jeff wouldn't mind getting out of town. He's been working around the clock at that auto shop."

Dad frowns. I can practically see him counting the dollar signs.

"Aren't tickets to the Grand Canyon kind of pricey?" I ask. When Dad doesn't answer, I give him a little kick under the table. He ignores me.

Mom takes a sip of her coffee. "They're not too expensive. Around fifteen dollars a person, according to the McAlisters, plus thirty dollars for parking the RV. So that's, what . . ." She looks around the table. "Seventy-five dollars plus food and gas? Not bad."

I nudge Dad under the table again. He kicks me back.

"You should leave today," YiaYia says. "It doesn't make sense to drive all the way to Albuquerque and back if you're just going to leave again right away."

"That's a good point," Mom says, standing up. "I'll talk to Jeff and the McAlisters. The twins will go nuts over that old train you can ride to the canyon." She wipes a little milk off my brother's face. "Rodney, finish your cereal, then come pack."

She hurries out of the kitchen. Dad and I lock eyes for a moment, then he follows her. I slump back in my seat. Why isn't he even *trying* to convince her they shouldn't go?

"Well," YiaYia says, "it looks like it's just going to be you, me, and the Lord this weekend, Dessa."

Across the table, Rodney dumps the entire bowl of sugar into his cereal.

I sink even lower in my chair. "Sounds great."

YiaYia and I stand together, me drinking a soda, her nursing a glass of white wine. She's watched me off and on all day, but there's nowhere to sit out here, and there's only so long she can stand on crutches. Meanwhile, I'm covered in dust and dirt, my sweaty hair is sticking to my forehead, and the sun is turning my skin a pale pink. It took all morning to pull the haphazardly stacked boxes out of YiaYia's garage, and all afternoon to move them back inside. But at least it kept my mind off Cyrus.

"I'm terrible at throwing things away," YiaYia says, holding up her wineglass as if to toast the packed garage.

"I can see that."

"But it looks much better now. Thank you."

I examine my work. Boxes and boxes of books and VHS

tapes are off to one side, next to a baby grand piano and three racks of clothes—mostly heavy coats she won't wear again for months. On the other side of the garage is a bulky piece of wooden furniture she informs me is an *armoire*, plus three rolled rugs and a second refrigerator filled with frozen food on one side, and beer and soda on the other. After years of living in the RV, I can't imagine having this much stuff.

I pick up the last box from the driveway and carry it inside the garage, adding it to a low pile near the front. We're about to go back into the house, my punishment complete, when YiaYia lets out a soft "oh!"

"What is it?" I ask as she taps the bottom of one crutch against a box.

"I forgot all about these," she says. "Can you open it for me?"

I kneel on the dusty floor and flip the top off the box. Inside, four stacks of colorful southwestern tile shine up at us, blue and red and green and yellow, each one a different pattern. I pick up a tile printed with a plump orange sun and another decorated with a blue geometric pattern that reminds me of waves. They look like the kinds of tiles that decorate the staircases in fancy Santa Fe hotels, or like the tiles they sell for twenty bucks a pop in the tourist shops on the plaza. "They're in perfect condition. What were you saving them for?"

"I wasn't. Those are the last of the tiles your grandpa made before he shut down his tile yard and retired. He used to bring home pieces of the ones that broke, and we'd find little ways to use them. Have you noticed those pieces of tile around the edge of the pool? Those were his."

"They're in the garden wall, too."

"That's right. Maybe you could use them in your art someday."

"They're already so beautiful on their own." I pull out a few more, each more colorful than the last, and run my fingers over the surface. The tiles are bumpy and uneven, not like the sort of thing they make in factories.

"Look at the back," YiaYia says.

I turn the red sun tile over in my hand, and I spot a squiggle carved into the back. *D. Rhodes.*

"Dmitri Rhodes," YiaYia says with a small smile. "Those immigration officers were hard of hearing so I had to write the spelling down myself." She brushes her fingertips over his signature. "He was the love of my life."

My stomach twists at her words. What if Cy is the love of my life? If he is, would I feel like this, like everything I want is wrong and selfish? I know love is sometimes about making sacrifices, but doesn't that mean *both* people should be giving something up? Why should it just be me?

I turn the tile over in my hands, and press the smooth surface to my cheek. "YiaYia, how do you know when you've found the right person?"

She gently takes the tile from me and places it carefully

back into the box, like a single piece sliding into a jigsaw puzzle. "The right person just . . . fits."

"And if they don't?"

She takes my hand in hers. "Then you keep looking."

Fiona picks me up on Sunday a few minutes after YiaYia leaves for her midmorning church service. We drive to the Railyard Art District, and Fiona parks her VW Rabbit in front of a building with glass doors. She pokes around the cup holders until she finds a few quarters, then climbs out of the car, leaving me to peer out the window. I've been to galleries all over the country, usually during free art walks or student shows sponsored by local colleges, but this will be the first time I've ever gone as more than a random stranger wandering in off the street.

"You coming?" Fiona calls through the window.

I get out of the car and straighten my dress, but it's hopelessly wrinkled from being folded up in the storage compartment under the RV since last spring. I glance out of the corner of my eye at what Fiona's wearing. She looks effortlessly cool in her navy blue blazer and chunky red heels, her jeans ripped artfully at the knee. Her hair is a little messy too—like she started to comb it and got distracted halfway through by something much more fabulous than getting ready. But I bet Fiona could show up in a potato sack and she'd still look fantastic. It's something about the way she holds herself, something about the way she wears that paint-stained T-shirt like a badge of honor, that makes her look chic and confident.

I look down at my scuffed, hand-me-down ankle boots and my faded sundress. I should have dressed up more. I should have borrowed something fancier. Something flashy to use as a diversion in case I say something stupid. I think of my panic attack the other day, and cringe. Maybe I shouldn't have come at all.

Fiona links her arm with mine, as if she can read my mind. "You're nervous, which is natural. But you belong here, Dessa. You'll see." She pulls a sleek leather planner out of her bag and hands it to me. "Until then, I sometimes find props to be helpful."

She opens the glass door to the gallery, and a blast of air conditioning hits us. A gorgeous black girl rushes forward to meet us. "Welcome!" she says in a clipped British accent, pulling Fiona into a hug. They kiss on both cheeks. "You're late."

"Of course I'm late," Fiona says, throwing her hair over her shoulder with an exaggerated flourish. "I have a reputation to maintain."

"And who is this?" the girl asks, turning to me. She looks about twenty-five, and is ridiculously fashionable. I squirm a bit under her gaze.

"Jordan, meet Dessa," Fiona answers. "Dessa, this is Jordan. She manages the gallery."

Jordan gives me a quick hug and plants an air kiss on either side of my face. "So nice to meet you. You're her assistant, yes?"

"She's my right hand," Fiona says before I can explain that I'm just an intern.

Jordan raises an eyebrow. "Really."

Her disbelief sucks the air out of the room, but Fiona doesn't seem to notice.

"Show us the space?" she asks.

We follow Jordan across the tiled lobby to a double door. She pushes it open and ushers us inside a large, square white room, almost twice the size of Fiona's studio.

"A blank slate," Jordan says, sweeping her arms out. "I took down the temporary walls as you requested, but I was thinking we could—"

Fiona holds up her hand. "Don't tell me. If I know where everything is going, I'll just obsess about whether it's in the right place. You and Dessa figure it out."

"Are you sure?" I ask, but Fiona's already pulling out her cell phone and walking away.

I reluctantly turn back to Jordan.

"So," she says, "do you have any ideas?"

"Um . . . I've got a few for where we can put the larger pieces."

Jordan rolls her eyes. "We can't simply hang the larger pieces and then throw the small ones up around them."

"I know that. What I meant was—"

"We need a concept. Something to pull the exhibit together." She taps one of her manicured fingernails against her chin.

"Right . . ." I chew on my lip, flipping through Fiona's book of thumbnails in my mind. "Well . . . she likes to do the unexpected. Not just her materials, but with the pieces themselves."

"You're saying the pieces should be displayed randomly? That's not a concept."

"No, not randomly. But I don't think we should group the pieces based on medium, or theme, or something like that, either."

"Then what would you suggest?"

"They should speak to each other through . . . uh . . ." I search for the right term. I want people to see that Fiona's pieces have something in common, but that they aren't all the same. That they're in conversation with each other, and that the conversation is sometimes an argument. "The pieces should speak to each other through their differences."

"That's called juxtaposition." Fiona strides toward us. "And it sounds like a good idea to me, especially since I'm working with so many different mediums this time around."

Jordan plasters a smile onto her face. "Conversation through conflict," she says, like it was her idea in the first place. "Wonderful. I'll draw up a few concepts."

"The two of you should do it together," Fiona says. "There's a lot Dessa can learn from working with you, Jordan, and she's already shown that she has great ideas."

Jordan nods, but her lips twitch with annoyance. Spending more time together sounds unpleasant. But Fiona said I have great ideas, and that's all that matters.

"I'll give you a call and let you know when you can come by," Jordan says, her eyes traveling from my face down to my too-short dress. She smiles, but it's not quite as warm as the one she gave us when we first walked in.

Fiona gives me a pointed look and wanders outside, leaving Jordan and me alone. *Crap.* Fiona can't regret bringing me. I clear my throat.

"Actually," I say, summoning my courage, "I'll come by on . . . um . . ." I open the planner Fiona gave me and flip through a few pages, pretending to check my schedule. "Tuesday?"

She gives me another tight-lipped smile. "Tuesday it is, Tessa. Be here at five."

"It's *Dessa* . . . ," I say, but she's already walking away, her heels *clickclickclick-ing* across the floor.

"Wait!" My voice bounces off the empty walls of the gallery. "Don't you think that's too late to meet? We may need a few hours."

She stares at me, and I can practically hear her weighing the pros and cons of arguing. My hands start to sweat, but I resist the urge to wipe them off on my dress.

"Fine," Jordan says at last. "How's ten a.m.?"

"Perfect."

We nod at each other, and Jordan walks away. I let out a sigh of relief. If Cy were here instead of running around Texas with his new girlfriend, he'd be proud of me for standing up to her.

On the way back from the gallery, Fiona stops at a taco stand and orders us both three tacos de carne asada and a tall glass bottle of Coke. We eat our food in the car, the doors thrown open since the air conditioning doesn't work. I take a sip of my Coke, and for a second I consider saving the bottle— the rounded edges that make the bottom would make interesting shards for my box of glass back in the RV—but then I put it down and take another bite of my taco.

Fiona tilts her chair back and kicks off her heels, folding her legs against the steering wheel. "What do you think so far?"

I swallow a bite of taco even though I haven't finished chewing. It goes down rough. "What do you mean?" I choke out.

"About the glamorous life of a starving artist, of course." She gestures around us—at the broken AC, the empty bottles on the floor of the back seat, the sunroof that won't close. "Is it everything you wished for?"

"Actually, it is."

Fiona laughs like she thinks I'm kidding, but I shake my head. "I'm serious. Your work is going to look incredible in there."

She leans her head back against the seat. "From your mouth to the art god's ears."

As we finish our food, I flip through the binder. Now that we've decided on juxtaposition, I want to come up with a plan that'll wow Fiona. But Jordan's right: It's not enough to just have the pieces scattered randomly. We have to make the contrast purposeful. We have to *say* something. I turn another page in the binder, and I come to the list of Fiona's pieces. I drag my finger down it, past the paintings and the tire wolf that I convinced Fiona to have flown in for this show, until I come to a seven-foot-tall sculpture made of colored bottles.

Bingo.

"I know you said you don't want to talk about where we put everything, but I've got an idea that I want to run by you."

"Hit me."

"What would you think about including a light installation in your show? I saw one online a few nights ago, and it was incredible. It's at the Richard Levy Gallery in Albuquerque, and I think it'll really complement—*contrast*—your bottle sculpture. Both are made of glass but the colors . . ."

I trail off as I see her eyes go wide.

"I totally understand if you don't want to bring in someone else's work, though," I say, scrambling. She wants me to go above and beyond, but that doesn't mean telling her what to do with her own show. "Maybe we should forget I even said that—"

"No, Dessa, that's a really good idea. I've seen that exhibit, but I never would have thought to integrate something like it into my work."

"Really? You like it?"

"Absolutely." She drums her fingers on the steering wheel and stares out the front window. "You should talk to Jordan about it. Tell her to look into the rental details."

I cringe at the idea of telling Jordan to do *anything*, but I agree.

"What do you say we go back to my studio and work for a little while?" Fiona asks suddenly. "I know this was supposed to be a half day, but I'm feeling inspired. What about you?"

I glance down at my cell phone. For once no one's texting me around the clock, wondering when I'll be home. No one's wishing I was there for dinner, or asking me to take a walk.

But that's good, I remind myself. *I wanted a life of my own, and here it is.*

"So?" Fiona asks.

"Let's do it."

Colors sweep across the canvas, sticky and raw, waiting for Fiona to turn them into something beautiful. Sharp cliffs build beneath her brush, jutting out along the California coastline of her imagination. I breathe in the sharp pine tree and licorice scent of turpentine, and exhale with longing. If I could paint like this . . .

I shove my hands into the pockets of my dress. We came back to the studio to work, but I couldn't will my fingers to curl around a brush. Even the sight of canvas made my heart speed up. I'm not ready. Not yet.

"I'm not sure you should be watching me," Fiona says, her eyes full of worry. "I was hoping you might want to try something on your own."

"I'm still learning, I swear." I point to the upper right corner of her canvas, where she's been working on a twisted cypress tree growing straight out of a shelf of jagged rock. "The way you used that burnt orange along the underside of the branch, and how it reflects in the water? I never would have used those colors."

She puts down her paintbrush and steps away from the easel. Without the presence of her shadow, the early afternoon sun burning through the windows turns her half-filled canvas a blinding white. "Talk to me, Dessa. Why aren't you working?"

"I can't."

"You can't? Why not?"

"Because." I stare down at my boots, concentrating as hard as I can on the cracked leather, the scuffed toe—anything but Fiona's face. "I'm stuck, okay? I've been trying to sketch every night like you told me to, but it's not working. I just keep thinking, what if all those colleges were right? What if I'm really not good enough?"

Fiona leads me over to a paint-stained ottoman. We sit down, and she rests her chin in her hand. "Why do you think you have to go to college to be an artist?"

"Because I need to know more. I need real teachers. Real classes. Everything I know I learned from online tutorials and community classes. I need to learn from professionals."

"Do you know who taught Vincent van Gogh to paint? He taught himself. Yes, he attended art school for a year, but that wasn't until he had *years* of learning from the work of other artists. And Picasso? He dropped out of art school after only a year because he hated formal instruction."

"But they're both famous! I'm never going to be van Gogh or Picasso."

Fiona narrows her eyes. "Well . . . what about me?"

I pause. "What *about* you?"

"You're a fan of my work, right? I mean, you wanted to be my intern, you seem to like the pieces I'm putting in the show. Would you consider me a successful artist?"

"Obviously."

Fiona crosses her legs and leans back. "I didn't go to college."

My mouth drops open. "Really?"

"Nope. I wanted to, don't get me wrong. I thought I was going to become an accountant, because that's what my dad did. But it was too expensive, and I was already working part-time for my dad's firm, so . . ." She shrugs. "I never made it."

"But how did you become an artist? How did you learn to do *that*?" I ask, pointing to her half-finished painting.

"I taught myself. I studied art books. I took classes in town. I entered contests where all contestants were guaranteed feedback, and I listened *very* carefully to what the judges had to say. Especially when I disagreed with them. Eventually I got to know people in the Santa Fe art scene, and I worked with artists in the area, like you are now."

"But how do I know if I'm any good?"

Fiona sighs. "No one ever really knows that, I'm afraid. All you can do is make your best work, and continue to improve as best you can. But I can tell you right now that you have talent. You really do, Dessa. When I saw your sunburst painting, it didn't matter that the technique wasn't perfect. It made me *feel* something. That's why I chose you."

I stare at her, caught off guard by the sudden compliment. "I . . . thank you. That means a lot to me."

"You're welcome." She tips her head to the side, studying me intently. "But Dessa, I was very tempted to fire you when I found out you lied to me. Do you know why I didn't?"

I shrug helplessly. "You felt bad for me?"

"No. I let you stay because I could tell that punishing you wasn't going to help. You were already punishing yourself."

My eyes threaten to fill with tears. "I was ashamed. I felt like a failure. I still do."

"Listen to me." Fiona leans toward me, so close her face is only a few inches away. "The only thing that can make you a failure is giving up."

"But I'm afraid—"

"Exactly! You're afraid. You're afraid of failure, of not being good enough, of letting your family down. Right? But that's the problem—you're letting your *fear* of failure define you. That's why you can't pick up a paintbrush. You're letting fear get in the way of your *voice*."

Fiona takes my hands in hers.

"But it doesn't have to be like that. You can find it again."

I stare down at our hands. Everything she's saying—I want so badly for it to be true. For everything that's happened to be part of my journey, and not the end of it.

Fiona goes to the couch and pulls the binder out from under the table, then hurries back.

"You've done a great job this week. You've pushed yourself creatively, you've been up to every task I've given you, and just now, you stared your own shortcomings in the face and didn't crumble beneath their weight. That's the kind of person I want working for me. So if you still want to be here, I'd love for you to stay."

"Really?"

"Really. But there's something else, too." She opens the binder and flips through a few pages until she comes to the handwritten list titled "Gallery Pieces." I've edited it so many times my handwriting appears just as frequently as hers.

"We're adding a new piece to the show." Fiona picks up a red pen and scribbles something. Then she turns the binder to face me.

Untitled by Dessa Rhodes

I inhale sharply. My work, hanging in Fiona's gallery show.

I picture all of her wonderful paintings, her sculptures, and next to them—what?

"You deserve this," Fiona says.

"But—what will I display? The sunburst?"

Fiona closes the binder. "I think you should create a new piece for the show."

I shake my head. "Fiona, I haven't created something new in *months*. I'd have to do this in a week. I'm not sure I can—"

"I wouldn't ask you to do it if I didn't think you could," she says firmly. "I also have something that might help." She pulls a small drawstring bag out of her shirt pocket and hands it to me. "This is for you."

Frowning, I peer inside. The delicate yellow flower from the art fair sits at the bottom.

I shake my head. "I can't take this."

"Yes, you can. But on one condition: I want you to take that flower, and break it into pieces. Don't crush it—just separate the petals."

"*What?*"

"If I've learned one thing working with discarded and used things, it's that just because something seems broken doesn't mean it can't be made into something beautiful."

I pull the delicate flower out of the bag and rest it in my palm. "I love it, but I don't understand. How is it going to help me come up with an idea for the show?"

"You applied for an internship with an artist who works primarily with found art, right?" A sly smile creeps over her face. "Maybe it's time you tried to make some found art of your own."

CHAPTER 14

The plaza is mostly empty. A few old men play chess in the sun, while a family stands outside the church waiting for a morning service to begin. I should take advantage of this extra time to get some work done, but I can't bring myself to hurry to Fiona's. She's going to want to talk about my piece for the show, and I'm not ready. I was up till two a.m. trying to come up with something, but everything sounded cliché, or too simple, or just plain stupid.

My phone rings.

"Hey, Taryn," I answer, relief flooding through me. This is exactly the kind of distraction I need right now. "What's up?"

"Dude, I have amazing news. Guess where I am right now?"

I check the time. "Hmm . . . do bars in Oklahoma serve breakfast?"

"Screw you," she says, laughing. "I'm in Santa Fe!"

Ten minutes later, Taryn drops her backpack on the grass and throws her arms around my neck.

"I can't believe you're here," I say. "Wait. Why are you here again?"

"Well that's a fine *how do you do*," she says. "I came to see you. I hitched a ride from Amarillo."

"With who?"

"Ben Mathers! The singer, remember? I drove all the way from Oklahoma City with a few friends to see him play at this huge-ass Texas steak house, and he recognized me! Can you believe it?"

"I can, actually. Didn't you tell me you've seen him play, like, ten times?"

"Yes!" She throws her arms around me again and squeals. "We stayed up all night dancing, and when he said they were driving to Albuquerque for another show, I asked if I could catch a ride and he said yes. I had to hitchhike the rest of the way to Santa Fe, but here I am."

"Wow," I say, shaking my head. "Where are you staying?"

"Well, now that's an interesting question. . . ."

My mouth drops open. "Tell me you didn't come all this way without figuring out where you're going to sleep."

"I hoped maybe *you* would have someplace I could stay." She bats her eyelashes at me. "Pretty please?"

I chew the inside of my cheek, picture my mom's face when she picked me up on the curb in the middle of the night. "I'm not sure my parents will be psyched when they find out you're the girl I met in Oklahoma."

Her face falls. "Oh, yeah. Of course. I get that. I'll just . . ." She looks around the plaza. "Do you have a sleeping bag I can borrow?"

Shit. I can't leave her stranded like this, not when she came all the way here to hang out with me. Besides, my family is out of town anyway. "No, no. You can stay, but we've got to clear it with my grandma first."

"Easy," Taryn says, flopping down on the grass. She kicks off her boots and lies back. "Grandmas love me."

In the time we've been talking, a bunch of people have wandered into the plaza. I want to stay with Taryn, pretend that I don't have responsibilities outside of lying in the sun and making whistles out of grass, but I figure she can entertain herself for a few hours. "I've got to go to work, but I'll be done by five. I'll call you?"

Taryn looks around, and catches sight of a group of guys hanging out near the church at the other end of the plaza. She grins. "Take your time."

Fiona is waiting for me at the top of the stairs when I arrive, a damp rag in her hands. "Was that you I saw at the plaza on my way in? With a girl whose head looked like it was on fire?"

I laugh. "That's my friend Taryn. She's visiting from Oklahoma for . . . I don't know how long she'll be here, actually."

"Why didn't you invite her in?" Fiona swats at me with the rag. "Tell her to meet us downstairs. We're going on a field trip today anyway."

I stand next to the front window, fidgeting with the edge of a piece of newspaper covering the thin glass. Taryn is great, but I'm not sure it's a good idea to introduce her to my boss. Fiona needs to see me as a serious artist, not some teenager with wild friends. Even if Taryn *is* awesome. I decide to bluff. "I thought we were going to talk about price points for the show?"

"I came up with a complete price list last night," Fiona says. "I'll show it to you later."

"What about the lighting?"

"Dessa, I promise that as soon as our outing is over, we'll come straight back here and talk about the lighting and the prices and whatever else you want," Fiona says, ushering me back into the hall and locking the door behind us. "But you've got a lot of work ahead of you if you're going to have a piece ready for the show, and I think reconnecting with your creative side is going to help. So that's what we're going to do." She puts her hand on my shoulder. "Trust me, okay?"

I take a deep breath. "I do."

"Great. Now call your friend."

A few minutes later, Taryn rounds the corner a block away from the studio. When she catches sight of Fiona, her eyes get a little wider and her steps slow. I glance at Fiona, wondering why Taryn is being such a weirdo, but then I see the way the sun is shining on her hair, and how her colorful wrap dress looks like an explosion of paint. No wonder Taryn looks nervous. That's exactly how I felt the first time I saw Fiona too.

"Hi," Fiona says when Taryn stops in front of us.

Taryn looks at me. "Dessa, you didn't tell me your boss was, like, a model."

Fiona throws back her head and laughs. Maybe having Taryn along today is a good idea after all.

The three of us climb into Fiona's car and immediately roll down all the windows. Taryn has to hold a big plastic bin on her lap because there's so much random stuff in the back seat, but she doesn't seem to mind.

"Where are we going?" she asks.

"You'll see," Fiona says with a grin. "Seat belts!"

Thirty minutes later we pull in front of a junkyard that's right off the highway. On the other side of a tall metal fence, smashed cars are piled one on top of the other, at least ten high. "Whoa," I say, leaning forward so I can peer up at the top of the stack.

We get out of the VW, and Fiona spreads her arms wide, as if she's presenting us with Shangri-la instead of a pile of broken-down cars. "What do you think?"

Taryn looks dubious, but I grin. "I think it looks like we're going shopping."

Fiona puts her arm around me. "Exactly."

We walk inside, and a large man comes out of a mobile home parked off to the side. "Fiona, I didn't expect you for another couple weeks."

"Hi, Ricky." She gives him a hug, her arms barely reaching all the way around him. "I woke up this morning and I thought, this feels like a day to go hunting."

"You already know the deal, but would you like me to tell

it to your friends here?" he asks, looking at Taryn and me.

"Yes, please," she says.

He pulls himself up to his full height and clears his throat. "Welcome to Ricky's junkyard, home of abandoned, repossessed, and shitty cars. Plus other people's crap that they don't want no more."

Taryn laughs, and Ricky grins at her.

"Tell them the rules," Fiona prompts.

"Right. No stealing, no pulling something out from the bottom of a pile, no climbing in or on the cars. Just . . . don't be stupid, you know? Oh, and anything you find, you bring it to me. I'll give you a fair price." He points back at his mobile office. "Shopping carts are back there, in case you find something too heavy to carry, or you're like Fiona here, and you find about ten things too heavy to carry. Got it?"

"Got it," Taryn and I say.

"Okay," Ricky says, already walking back to the trailer. "Have fun."

"Let's go to the back," Fiona says. "That's where all the good stuff is."

We grab a shopping cart, and the three of us make our way down the aisle. The cars tower so high overhead that they block out most of the sunlight. I peer between the cars, but there's nothing holding them up but the support of the next car. One good earthquake could bring the whole towering mass of metal down on our heads.

"Don't worry," Fiona says, catching sight of my face. "Most of these cars have been here for years. They're not moving."

I nod, but walk a little faster.

We reach the end of the car jungle, and a massive yard stretches before us. It's full of odds and ends organized into surprisingly neat rows. Taryn rushes forward, but Fiona stops her. "Be careful what you pick up. You never know what's going to be sharp or rusted or falling apart, and sometimes you'll find something nasty living underneath the junk." She sees our confusion, and says, "Scorpions."

Taryn and I clutch at each other, but Fiona just laughs.

"Are we looking for anything in particular?" Taryn asks.

"Anything that speaks to you," Fiona answers. "Dessa—I want you to find at least one thing to bring back, okay? Maybe for the show, maybe not. But don't overthink it, okay?"

I take a steadying breath. "Okay."

"Great. Meet back here in thirty minutes." She gives me a wink, then disappears down the aisle, leaving Taryn and me behind.

"What show is she talking about?" Taryn asks.

"It's her art show," I explain, fighting off the feeling of anxiety pooling in the pit of my stomach. "It's in a little over a week at a gallery in town."

"And she's letting you put a piece in it? That's amazing! What are you making?"

I bite my lip. "That's kind of the problem. I don't know yet."

"Oh, well you have some time, right? You'll figure it out. Maybe I can help you find something cool to jumpstart your artsy-fartsy brain." She looks around. "Where should we start?"

I bend over a bunch of broken picture frames. "Here, I guess." I pick one up, but it's barely in my hands before one edge falls off. I put it back.

"What are you going to do with this stuff?" Taryn asks, lifting an old pair of cracked leather boots by their laces.

"Not sure. Hopefully, turn it into something new. Something beautiful."

"You're definitely not going to be needing these, then," Taryn says, dropping the boots onto a pile of gardening gloves.

We continue exploring, peeking into boxes and looking over old VHS tapes and the occasional cassette player. I think about picking one up for my YiaYia—I noticed a big box of cassettes in her garage—but I don't have the money to spare, not if Fiona wants me to pick out something today.

When we reach the end of the row, Taryn turns left, toward some leather jackets, and I make my way down another aisle to the right. I can't bring back just anything. I have to find something really great, something that will impress Fiona and pull me out of my art funk.

I walk past stuff that feels too obvious: toilet seats, bottle caps, silverware, and coat hangers. She'll expect me to bring that kind of thing back. I briefly consider a set of mismatched dining room chairs, stacked ten high, their wooden legs locked in a rickety embrace, but I decide it'll be too hard to untangle them. Plus, I have no clue what I'd actually *do* with a chair once I got one down.

I keep walking, quickly skipping over a creepy chest full of porcelain baby dolls, most of them missing at least one eye, and turn left at a broken-TV graveyard. None of this is right. None of it makes me feel anything, except a growing sense of panic that I'm going to come back empty-handed. I check my phone again—it's been almost twenty minutes since we got here, and I haven't found a single thing worth taking home.

I walk faster, barely even glancing at the junk in front of me. I'm walking so fast I'm practically jogging, when I hit a cul-de-sac of trash.

I sink onto a scratched-up steamer trunk and kick at a cardboard box in front of me. This isn't working. None of this is good enough. I should have stuck with Fiona, watched what sort of things she picks up, asked about her process. I drop my head into my hands. Fiona gives me a once-in-a-lifetime chance to be in a real art show, and I'm already blowing it.

"Dessa?"

Taryn is standing at the mouth of the aisle, her red hair a blaze against a sea of gray and brown and twisted metal.

"There you are," she says. "Did you find anything?"

"Not unless you count a place to sit."

She strolls toward me and looks around. "You've got a nice

selection here," she says, toeing a rusted bicycle tire. "But I may have found something better."

We weave back through the rows, Taryn leading the way. She strides forward without slowing, taking each turn as if she's navigated this lot a thousand times before. I hurry to keep up, and when she stops, I almost run into her.

"Ta-daaaa," she says, holding out her arms.

An antique vanity mirror leans against an upended sofa. It's missing about a third of the glass, and what's left is cloudy and cracked. At first I don't see the appeal, but then the sun comes out from behind a cloud, and it catches the mirror just right, and I understand. The faded glass glows gold, the warped iron frame struggling to contain it. It looks old and magical and alive.

"There's something about it, right?" Taryn asks.

"Totally," I say. "I have no idea what I'm going to do with a broken mirror, but . . ." I pick it up. It's a bit unwieldy, but not too heavy. "How much do you think it is?"

Taryn shrugs. "No idea, but I bet you can get a good deal since it's broken."

With Taryn's help, I hold the mirror at arm's length so I can look directly into the cracked glass. Pieces of my reflection are missing, turning my face into a patchwork.

"It's perfect," I say. "Let's go find Fiona."

"Oh, you poor thing," YiaYia says, patting Taryn's hand. "That Luke sounds like a real piece of work."

Taryn and I are sitting at YiaYia's kitchen table, clutching glasses of lemonade. "He's a piece of something," Taryn agrees.

"Well, don't you worry about staying here with us. I'll smooth things over with Dessa's parents."

"Are you sure?" I ask. "I could call them—"

"No, no, you two have fun. Maybe go swimming?"

I lead Taryn back to my bedroom and give her one of my mom's hideous one-piece bathing suits. I step behind the open closet door for privacy, but Taryn strips down to her underwear in the middle of the room.

"You have a tattoo!" I exclaim, instantly jealous. "Is it a butterfly?"

"No." She yanks her shirt back over her head.

"Oh. Um, okay."

"Sorry," she says, sighing. "It's just, I don't want to talk about it."

"No problem." I sling a towel over my shoulder. "Ready to go?"

We set ourselves up in two pool chairs. Taryn tosses me a pair of sunglasses, then squirts a blob of sunscreen into her palm. "Your grandma's awesome. Do you see her a lot?"

"Nah, only a few times a year. We try to stop by her house whenever we're in the Southwest, though."

"She's got a superbig cross in the bathroom. Catholic?"

"Greek Orthodox." I hold out my hand for the sunscreen

bottle, and she passes it to me. "She's really into all that stuff. But I'm not religious."

"Me neither." Taryn smears lotion onto her legs. "But I always thought it would be cool to date a guy who was super into, like, Hinduism or something."

"But what if he didn't eat meat? Would you become a vegetarian? Or just not eat meat when you were together?"

She wrinkles her nose. "Yeah, never mind. I like ribs way too much." She lies on her side so we're facing each other. "Speaking of dating, whatever happened to that guy on your phone? The friend you were hung up on at the bar?"

I feel a little jolt at the mention of Cy. I forgot I told her about him. "We kissed." I drop the bottle of lotion into my lap. "But it didn't work out."

"What happened?"

A litany of excuses sneaks up the back of my throat, but there's no reason to lie, especially not to Taryn. "I told him I didn't want to settle down and be a traveler forever, and Cyrus decided that meant I didn't want to be with *him*. And I don't know . . . maybe he's right. Maybe I don't want to be with him. Not if it means I'll never get out of my RV and into the real world."

"Is traveling really so bad?"

"No, it's . . . it's great. Or it can be. But it's not me. I love it, and I love my family. And I love—" I take a deep breath. "I love Cyrus."

Taryn sighs. "But you want more."

"Is that terrible?"

She shakes her head solemnly. "No. Not at all. You're allowed to want something different than he does. You're allowed to choose for yourself. And honestly, if he's not willing to stop traveling for you, it's not really fair of him to ask you to give up your plans for him."

Taryn lies back and closes her eyes. I do the same, letting her words play over and over again in my head. Why *shouldn't* Cy have to give something up too? Why does what I want always have to be wrong?

"What I said before," Taryn says suddenly, "about my tattoo. It's my mom's initials. I had the guy write them in this awesome pattern called an ambigram, where both sides are mirror images of each other. From far enough away it kind of looks like wings. Or a butterfly."

"You must be really close with your mom, huh?"

"I was. Before she died."

I suck in a breath. "Oh my god. I'm so sorry, Taryn. I wouldn't have—I didn't realize—"

"You didn't know," Taryn says. "How could you? Anyway, I decided to come visit you because I needed a break from my dad. He's not much fun since my mom died. It messed him up."

"What about you?" I ask quietly.

She throws her arm over her face to shade her eyes from the sun. "I don't know, man. Sometimes I think it messed me up, and sometimes I think I was messed up to begin with, and I just didn't know it."

She closes her eyes, and I get the feeling she doesn't want to talk about this anymore, so I let it go. It must be awful for Taryn not to have a mother, and for her father to lose his wife. I try to envision what it would be like if I suddenly lost a member of my family, or of the other families, but I can't. My parents drive me nuts sometimes—a lot of the time, lately—but I can't imagine losing them entirely. Even when I used to lie awake at night dreaming about college, I never worried how it would feel to be apart. I always knew the families would still be there, waiting for me each summer.

Except, with everything that's going on with my dad, is that still true? If he can't figure out a way for us to keep traveling, will there be a caravan to come home to?

Taryn scratches her nose, and I realize with a jolt that my eyes are wet. I quickly wipe them, then pull out my cell phone. I open Instagram, and scroll through my feed and watch the parade of selfies stream by. Girls I've met on the road pose in skinny jeans and scarves, holding corgis and fancy coffee drinks. I scroll faster, past boys I haven't seen since elementary school, who traded their dinosaur T-shirts for plaid hipster button-downs. I scroll so fast I almost miss the one photo that matters: Cyrus and Rachel, their arms around each other as they laugh into the camera. She's even prettier than I remembered, with her silver lip ring and her striking blue eyes.

But it's Cyrus I can't stop staring at. It's not that he looks any different—he looks exactly like he always does. But that's the problem. Even though we're in a fight, even though we're hundreds of miles apart, he looks . . . happy.

Without me.

CHAPTER 15

Jordan is smoking outside the gallery. For a split second I wish I'd brought Taryn along, instead of leaving her to sleep away the day in Rodney's bed. I take a deep breath, then cross the street.

"You walk rather slowly," Jordan calls, her British accent as sharp as her cheekbones.

I pretend not to hear her. Today is going to be different. I'm not going to let her intimidate me. I'm going to be strong and confident and stick to my guns. Fiona trusts me. Now I just have to find a way to trust myself.

When I reach her, Jordan drops her cigarette on the ground and grinds it with the toe of her high-heeled shoe. "Where did you get that shirt?"

I look down at my old black Beatles T-shirt, the sleeves cut off two years ago in an attempt to make it look less like it came out of a water-damaged box in YiaYia's basement, and more like a sweet thrift store find. When I picked it out last night, I thought it looked good with my skinny jeans and silver flats, especially when I wound a few necklaces around my wrist and pulled my hair into a low, messy ponytail. But under Jordan's piercing gaze, I suddenly feel like a sloppy poser.

"My dad gave it to me," I say, bracing for her inevitable eye roll, or maybe a lecture on how it's not *proper attire* for an art gallery, even on a Tuesday.

"Huh. I like it. Well, I suppose we should get to it," she says, pushing the glass door open. "After you."

I step through, then follow her across the foyer.

"Fiona says you have an idea about what to do with the bottle sculptures?" Jordan says over her shoulder as we step into the main gallery room. I have to hurry to keep up.

"I think so."

"Fantastic. So do I."

"Great," I mutter.

We cross the empty gallery space and come to a doorway in the back that I didn't notice the first time I was here. She opens it, revealing a small room with nothing inside but a wobbly desk, laptop, notepad, and a chair. No windows, no art, just cinderblock and concrete. Basically a closet pretending to be an office. "Wow, this place is depressing," I say.

Jordan crosses her arms. "This is my office. The gallery owner uses the bigger one upstairs." She pulls out her chair and sits down, leaving me to stand next to her.

My cheeks grow warm. "Sorry. I thought—"

"Do you have the thumbnails?"

"Just a second." I quickly pull out the binder Fiona gave me, and place it on the desk. She flips to the first set of thumbnails, and starts to scribble on her notepad.

"I'm going to find a chair," I say. "Um . . . be right back."

She doesn't answer, so I step back into the gallery. There's a lone chair against the far wall, so I grab it and hurry back to Jordan's office. But it's too cramped in there to fit another chair, let alone a second person. I put the chair down just outside her office, and chew on my lip as I watch Jordan's hand hurrying across the page, filling it with her ideas for Fiona's show.

"Would it be okay if we worked out here so I can help? I should, you know, since I'm Fiona's . . ." I trail off, trying to remember what Fiona called me when she introduced me to Jordan. "Her . . . right hand?"

Jordan keeps writing. I grind my teeth. I may be just a teenager and an intern, but this . . . it's bullshit. If Taryn were here, she wouldn't let Jordan walk all over her. So neither will I.

"Jordan," I say, my voice echoing in the empty gallery.

Her head jerks up. "What?"

"We need to work somewhere else." Before I can lose my nerve, I reach into her office and pluck the binder off the desk. "There isn't enough room for two people in here, and Fiona wants *me* to tell *you* my ideas for the show."

We stare at each other, neither of us speaking. But then the corner of her mouth curls up. "Where would you suggest we work?"

I look around the gallery. She's got a point—there's nowhere to work in here. But just as I'm about to admit defeat, I remember Fiona dropping to the floor in her studio to sketch, and I grin.

"There's plenty of room for both of us right here." I sit down on the floor, crossing my legs in front of me, and look back at her. "See?"

Jordan's lips purse in disapproval. "I can't sit on the *floor*," she says, smoothing her dress. "This is silk."

"I hear you can dry-clean anything these days," I say with a shrug, and flip open the binder.

Jordan joins me in the gallery and reluctantly lowers herself to the floor. She stretches her legs out in front of her, careful to keep her knees pressed together, but her dress is so tight it rides up her legs. She tries crossing them like me, but quickly changes her mind. "This is undignified," she mutters.

I bite down on my lip to stop myself from smiling.

"So," she says when she's finally settled into an extremely uncomfortable-looking position, her legs bent off to the side, right arm propping her up. "The bottle sculptures. We should probably start there."

"Right." I turn the binder to face her. "So let me tell you about this light installation . . ."

"Oh my god, I'm so full." Taryn collapses onto the couch next to me and pats her stomach. "YiaYia is a crazy good cook."

I smile, but don't look up from my sketch pad. The meeting

with Jordan ended up going so well that we decided to celebrate by eating *way* too much of YiaYia's incredibly rich pastitsio for dinner. But now that the celebration is over, I'm faced with reality: I have exactly five days to come up with a piece for Fiona's show, and I have no clue what I'm going to do.

Taryn looks at the pad in my lap and points to a few quick sketches of the junkyard mirror. "Are you going to use it?"

"I really want to, but I have no idea what to do with it. What do you think?"

Taryn picks up the remote and turns on an *X-Files* rerun. "Don't look at me. I found the mirror. My job is done."

I put aside the sketch pad and watch as Scully runs down a long hallway, her chunky FBI heels clacking against the linoleum. Taryn leans her head on my shoulder. "I don't want to go home tomorrow."

"Then stay another night. But I'm going to be busy during the day tomorrow. Fiona wants to go over her expenses in case she forgot to pay any of the vendors that are helping with the event. But I'll be done by five and then we can hang out."

"I can't," she says, stretching. "I have classes on Thursday mornings, so I've got to get back the night before."

"Classes?"

"Community college. I've only got a few units left, and then I'm hoping to transfer to Texas A&M or maybe Arizona State. I've got to get out of Oklahoma."

I feel a prickle of jealousy at the mention of college, but I ignore it. "How does your dad feel about you leaving the state?"

"Not great, but it might be good for him if I'm not around. Like, maybe he thinks he has to be sad all the time because otherwise I'll think that he doesn't care my mom's gone."

There's a knock at the front door. YiaYia calls from the kitchen, "Dessa? Can you please get that? I'm covered in pie dough."

"Sure." I force myself off the couch and make my way toward the foyer. Behind me, Scully is being kidnapped by yet another alien. You'd think she'd have more skills as a kick-ass FBI doctor.

"Who's visiting your grandma at nine o'clock?" Taryn calls over Scully's screams.

"Probably someone selling magazines," I call back. But when I open the door, it's not a stranger with a clipboard.

It's Cyrus.

"Hey." He smiles nervously. "I'm back."

I stand there for a second, my eyes traveling over every inch of him. Gorgeous brown eyes, smooth skin, rumpled white T-shirt. He looks exactly like he always does, but seeing him there, standing under the porch light . . . it's like I haven't seen him in years.

I clear my throat. "Hey."

"Can I come in?"

I step back, and he edges past, like he's afraid to touch me.

At the sound of the door closing, YiaYia hurries out of the

kitchen. "Welcome back," she says, placing her slightly damp hands on his cheeks. "Are you hungry?"

"No, I'm okay," he says, glancing over at me. "I grabbed McDonalds on the way here."

YiaYia makes a *tut-tut* noise and goes back into the kitchen, leaving Cyrus and me standing alone by the door. I stare at my bare feet, unsure of what to say.

Cyrus sighs. "About what I said before I left—"

"I don't want to talk about that."

I see a flicker of doubt in his eyes. "Dess, I want to apologize. I need to."

Taryn appears in the doorway to the living room. She's got one hand on her hip. "Who's this?"

"Taryn, this is Cyrus. He travels with us." I widen my eyes at her, willing her not to say anything that'll give away that we've been talking about him. "And this is Taryn. She's the one I met in Oklahoma City."

"Ah," Cyrus says. "The girl who turned Dessa into a criminal."

"The one and only," Taryn says dryly. "So you're back, huh?"

Cyrus shifts uncomfortably. "Yeah. I wanted to see if Dessa wanted to hang out. But you guys seem busy, so . . ."

He looks at me expectantly, wondering if I'm going to invite him to stay. I consider it, I really do. It would be the easiest thing in the world. We'd all go into the living room and turn on the TV, and I'm sure everything would be forgotten by the time we finished our third episode of *The X-Files.*

But then I remember the way I felt as he walked away from me. The way he was smiling in that Instagram picture. Why should I make this easy on him? Why should I pretend everything is okay when it's so clearly not?

"Tonight's sort of a girls-only thing." I open the front door again. "But I'll talk to you tomorrow, okay?"

Cy frowns, and something passes between us, a specter of our former friendship, waving goodbye as we step into unknown territory.

"Good to see you, Dess," he says, and walks down the steps and into the night.

I close the door, my hands shaking, and find Taryn watching me closely, her arms crossed. "Girls only, huh?"

I shrug. "It's your last night."

She throws her arm around my shoulders and escorts me back to the couch. "Damn straight."

We drag ourselves out of bed at eight a.m. on Wednesday morning and catch a bus to downtown Santa Fe, where Taryn's meeting a friend of a friend for a ride back to Oklahoma City. We get to the plaza with time to spare, so we plop into a booth at a place called Tia Maria's. The yellow walls are decorated with hanging red chile ristras and landscape paintings, mostly of the surrounding desert, punctuated by small adobe homes like YiaYia's. Taryn orders eggs and bacon, and I order a breakfast burrito smothered in green chili, plus all the coffee they can pour.

As soon as the waitress walks away, I lay my head down on the table. It's sticky with syrup but I don't care. "We shouldn't have stayed up so late."

"No, what we shouldn't have done is made that peanut butter chocolate milkshake at midnight." Taryn shakes her head as she pours creamer into her coffee. "Sugar overload."

"I warned you," I mumble.

Taryn takes a sip of her coffee, grimaces, and dumps two packets of sugar into it. "So, Cyrus."

"What about him?" I try my black coffee. "Ew, this tastes like motor oil."

Taryn slides the creamer toward me. I pour a bunch into my coffee, barely changing the color. I take another sip. Better, but still not good.

"What are you going to do about him?" she asks.

"I'm not sure there's anything I *can* do. He wants one thing and I want another."

"So you're just going to give up?"

I put my cup down. "You said Cyrus is the one who isn't being fair. So how is it suddenly my responsibility to fix everything?"

"It's not. But that doesn't mean you shouldn't do something about it," Taryn says. "Stop letting him call all the shots. What do you want?"

We stare at each other across the table, a bubble of silence surrounding us in the midst of this noisy restaurant. I fiddle with my silverware for something to do. I've been in love with Cy for years, but last night, when I saw him standing outside my front door, little gnats flittering around the porch light, I realized something: My life doesn't have to revolve around him. We went a full three days without speaking, and the world didn't fall apart. *I didn't fall apart.*

The waitress sets two plates in front of us. Taryn twists her bacon around on her plate so it makes a smiley face under the egg-yolk eyes.

"I know I can be pushy," she says, "but it's because I don't want you to get hurt."

"I know, I know. You're right."

"Of course I am." She takes a bite of her bacon. "But enough about that. I Googled Fiona last night on my phone after you fell asleep—"

I raise an eyebrow at her.

"What? She's hot. Anyway, people pay serious money for her work."

"She's the real deal," I say, cutting into my burrito. Green chili sauce spills onto the plate. I take a huge bite. YiaYia wouldn't approve, but how else am I supposed to get egg, chorizo, hatch chilis, onion, *and* cheese into my mouth at once?

"You're the real deal, too, you know," Taryn says.

I shake my head and take another bite.

"You are," Taryn insists. "You work for an artist. You're

going to be in a real art show. You've got *skillz*." She twirls her fork in her hand, clearly pleased with herself. "You're going to kill it."

"Or I'm going to fail miserably and everyone will know I'm a fraud."

I mean it as a joke—kind of—but Taryn frowns. "Do you really think that?"

"Yeah, kind of." I poke my burrito with my fork. "I keep freezing up. Fiona says it's normal to be afraid, but that I can't let it stand in my way. But . . . I'm *terrified*."

Taryn takes a bite of her eggs. I watch her face, the way her jaw moves up and down as she chews, the way she doesn't take her eyes off me. It feels like hours are passing as I wait for her to give me advice, to save me from my stupid self.

She finally swallows. "Get over it."

"*What?*"

"I said, get over it. You're scared. So what? I'm scared all the time! I was scared when my mom died. I was scared when my dad started drinking. I was scared when I applied to community college with my shitty grades. But I kept going, one foot in front of the other. I can't stop living just because I'm scared, and you can't stop making art. It's who you *are*."

"Holy shit." I sit back in the booth. When she puts it like that, it sounds so obvious. "You're right."

"Duh."

"It doesn't matter if I'm scared."

"Nope."

"All that matters is that I never give up."

The corner of her mouth curls up in a devilish smile. "Say it again."

"What?"

"That you're not giving up. Say it again." Taryn leans forward. "Say it again and say it louder. Like you mean it."

"Come on."

"Say it!" Taryn says, a grin spreading across her face. She picks up her fork and knife and pounds them on the table. "You're not giving up."

"Taryn, people are looking."

"You're not giving up." She bangs her fork again. "Say it!"

"I'm not giving up," I say, barely louder than before.

"You're not giving up!"

"I'm not giving up," I say back, louder this time. It feels good. Really good.

"Again!"

"I'm not giving up!" I shout. "I am an artist, damn it, and I AM NOT GIVING UP!"

"And *I* am the manager," a tall man with a thick mustache says, marching up to our table. "And if you two don't keep it down, I'm going to kick you out."

Taryn and I slink down into our seats, but as soon as the manager walks away, we burst out laughing.

"You're going to get us in trouble every time we hang out, aren't you?" I ask.

Taryn picks up her bacon and smears it around in the egg yolk. "Probably," she says, and shoves the entire piece into her mouth.

CHAPTER 16

"Dessa, over here!"

I drop my bag on the ground and hurry across the studio. Fiona is struggling in the corner, her back braced against what looks like a massive birdcage on a pedestal.

"Give me a hand?" she grunts. I push my back into the cage, and together we heave the metal monstrosity back onto its base.

"What's this for?" I ask, staring at it in wonder.

"The show! I had the idea at the last minute, and I stayed up all night working on it." She sticks her arm inside the cage and waves at me. "What do you think?"

I circle the birdcage, taking it in from every angle. At first glance, it's just a huge, black birdcage, but as I examine the thick bars, I notice that they're actually made up of four or five smaller wires, twisted together, and that the artfully curled pieces every few inches are too perfectly shaped to have been done by hand. "Are these *hangers*?" I ask Fiona, pointing to one of the bars.

"Yes! You know how dry cleaning comes on those crappy hangers everyone throws away?"

"Yeah, I know the ones." There are about thirty of them hanging in my RV closet.

"I came across tons of them at the junkyard while you and Taryn were looking around," Fiona says. "At first I figured they were too much trouble. But then I couldn't stop thinking about them, so I went back yesterday and bought about two hundred."

"Where did you get the idea for this?" I ask, nodding to the cage.

Fiona walks around it, running her fingers along the bars. "I was watching TV, and one of those reality shows about models came on. Those girls are so talented, but the beauty standards in our country . . . they're just not healthy. Or realistic." She wraps her fingers around one of the bars. "Buying clothes one season, replacing them the next. Making sure you have the perfect makeup, the perfect tan, the perfect body." She gives the cage a little shake. "The more I thought about it, the more unfair it felt."

"Like being trapped in a cage," I say. "But it's not just about the cage—it's about the person inside it. I think . . . I think something's missing."

Fiona tips her head to the side and considers the cage. "What do you think it needs?"

"It's about the people, right? Not the cage itself."

"Right."

"Well . . . I think you need a person inside, then. Someone who will embody that impossible beauty, but also show how unobtainable it is."

Fiona looks unsure. "So you want to hire a model for the show?"

I picture a girl sitting inside, looking purposefully bored. It could work, but it doesn't feel quite right. Plus, we'd have to pay someone to do it. "What if we used a mannequin? Like, one of those fancy ones they have in department store windows. We could dress her up in really nice clothes, but leave her face completely blank."

Fiona narrows her eyes and walks slowly around the cage. I hold my breath, praying that she doesn't hate my idea.

She stops walking. "I love it. And I know just the place to get the mannequin. I saw a bunch at the junkyard. I'll go back tonight."

"That's great," I say, more than a little relieved.

She runs across the room and pulls a slim purple notebook out of a drawer. "Come here," she says, beckoning me over.

I watch as she flips through the notebook, pieces of loose paper slipping onto the floor. I stoop to pick them up, and see that they're covered with her plans for the birdcage. There's a perfectly scaled drawing of a hanger, complete with measurements, and then a rough sketch of the cage itself. I climb back to my feet, notes in hand, and see that she's scanning a page of handwritten notes. "Here," she says, picking up a pencil and pointing to a blank space next to yet another sketch of the birdcage, this one so big it takes up a whole sheet of notebook paper. "Add your idea."

I take the pencil from her, and in my neatest handwriting, make a few notes about the mannequin. It feels like I'm adding my mark to the Magna Carta or the Declaration of Independence. I grin as I hand the pencil back to her.

"I know Taryn just left," Fiona says as she closes the binder, "but have you had a chance to think about what you're going to make for the show? You've only got a few days left."

I follow her over to the couch, where I sink into my spot by the window. "I'm still having trouble coming up with an idea. I keep staring at your little yellow flower, but so far . . . nothing."

Fiona kicks off her shoes and curls up on the opposite side of the couch. "Whenever I'm having trouble I always go back to the beginning and ask myself, 'What am I trying to say with this piece?' I wonder if that might help you."

"But I don't have a piece yet. That's the whole problem."

"Hmm, true. Then maybe you should go back even further. Don't ask what you're trying to say, but why you're doing it in the first place."

"What do you mean?"

She holds out her hands, palms up. "You have two paths in life right now. One, the life of an artist." She holds up one hand. "The other, the life of . . . well, something else. *Anything* else. So why are you choosing the first path? Why do you want to be an artist?"

I pick up a pillow and squeeze it against my chest. I answered the "why do you want to be an artist?" question a million times in my college essays, but I never really settled on a single answer. Is it because I love the challenge of perfectly capturing my subject? Because I want to express myself? Because I love the satisfaction of finishing a piece?

"It's okay if you don't want to answer," Fiona says. "I know it's a more personal question than it sounds."

"No, it's okay." I clear my throat. "So . . . my families share everything and we do everything together, right? It's part of traveling in a caravan. Or, it is for us, anyway. We decide things as a group, and we always try to do what's best for everyone. But sometimes . . ." I take a deep breath, struggling to find the words.

"Take your time," Fiona says.

"I guess . . . I've always wanted something that I don't have to share. Something that's all mine. From the moment I start a piece to the moment I finish it, there's nothing but me and my art."

As soon as I stop talking, I feel a rush of embarrassment. Here I am, whining about how I want something all to myself, while my dad is probably beside himself with worry at this very minute, trying to figure out how to salvage the life he and my mom have built for us. "I sound really selfish, don't I?"

"Not at all," Fiona says. "Going after what you want in life doesn't make you selfish. It makes you brave."

I think of Cyrus, and the way I turned him away last night. Of my mom, and how hurt she was that I didn't want to go to the Grand Canyon, and how she'd feel if she knew I *still* wanted to leave the families, even without college on the table. "What if the only way to get what I want is to turn my back on the people I love?"

"I don't believe that's your only choice," Fiona says. "But if it is . . . then I guess you have to choose."

The families come home that night, full of stories and laughter, the bridges of their noses burnt to a crisp. We talk about the Grand Canyon over stir-fry in YiaYia's backyard, which is the only place we can all fit.

"It's huge," Rodney says, throwing his arms wide. "And everything is hot and dusty. But we took a train that looks like one from the Wild West, and they gave me soda in a glass bottle."

"That sounds a bit anachronistic," YiaYia says. "But fun!"

Across the pool, Cy dangles his feet in the water as he laughs at Mr. McAlister's story about the twins trying to make a mountain goat wear a pair of pink sunglasses. He catches me staring and gives me a shy smile. My traitorous heart speeds in my chest. Cy pulls his feet out of the pool, like he's going to stand up and come sit by me. *Shit.* Do I ask about his trip? About Rachel?

I'm not ready.

"I'll be right back," I say to no one in particular, and hurry into the house, my wet feet leaving prints along the wood floors.

I find Mrs. M and Mom inside the kitchen, scraping mostly empty plates into the trash. "Can I help?" I ask, looking over my shoulder to make sure Cy hasn't followed me inside.

"Sure," Mom says.

"I'll go collect the rest," Mrs. M says, patting my shoulder as she leaves. "It's good to see you, sweetie."

I face Mom, and suddenly I'm nervous. The last time I saw her, we were arguing about me staying here instead of traveling with the families.

"I'm glad you're home," I say. "I missed you."

She puts down a plate and hugs me. I breathe in the smell of the road and dirt from the canyon, mixed with the soapy eucalyptus of her shampoo. I'm suddenly back in the RV, hot wind streaming through the window as we drive down the highway, Mom's raspy voice singing along to the radio, even though she doesn't know all the words.

Mom kisses me on the forehead. "Dessa, I need to ask you something."

"Yeah?"

"Your dad . . . has he said anything to you recently?"

I tense in her arms. "About what?"

"I'm not sure. He just seems distracted lately. Don't you think so?"

I open my mouth to tell her the truth—that she's right, that there's something wrong—but she starts talking again before I can answer.

"I'm probably imagining it." She rests her chin on top of my head. "Ever since we got married, he's only wanted what's best for our family. That's why we started traveling in the first place. Your dad and I thought you kids deserved a life full of different people and places. We didn't want you to grow up thinking your little town was the whole world." She sighs. "I love our life, but sometimes I worry your dad's working himself into the ground to make it work. You're sure he hasn't mentioned anything?"

I bite my lip, hard, hating myself for my cowardice. I should tell her the truth about Dad's job, whatever the consequences. It's not too late. But that would hurt Dad, and he's having a hard enough time as it is. So I'll buy him more time, and maybe, *maybe* he'll figure this out. Maybe Mom will never have to know.

"Sorry," I finally say. "he hasn't said anything to me."

CHAPTER 17

Thursday morning lasts forever. First I have to argue with the caterer for almost an hour because he refuses to tell me exactly which fruit and cheeses he'll be bringing since he only purchases what's *fresh that day*. Then I spend another forty-five minutes on the phone with the Albuquerque gallery, making sure the light installation will be delivered in time for the show. When I finally get to Jordan's gallery, Fiona is already there, unwrapping the pieces we messengered over last night. I help her with each painting, taking painstaking care to remove the bubble wrap and masking tape *X*'s we've put across each piece of glass in case it shattered during the move. Then we work on the statuary. Fiona's found art pieces come in a million different shapes and sizes, and it takes a long time to remove all the protective materials and move them to their places in the gallery. By the time we're finished with the birdcage, we're all hot and ready for a break.

While Jordan runs out to grab a few bottles of water, I start to gather all the packing material into a big pile.

"How's your piece coming along?" Fiona asks from

where she's sitting on the floor, her back against the wall.

My fingers freeze over a broken-down cardboard box. "Um . . . I'm working on it."

Fiona twists her mouth to the side and considers me. "You've been working all morning. Why don't you take the rest of the day off? Go home and focus on your art. Jordan and I can throw this away," she says, gesturing to the discarded packing material. "All that's left now is to make a few phone calls to the caterer."

"I did that already."

She throws up her hands. "See? You've taken care of every-thing."

"Not *everything*. I still need to call the valet company and make sure they're sending someone. And we should also walk around the plaza to double-check the posters we put up last week."

Fiona stands. "Dessa . . ."

"I also meant to call the *Santa Fe Reporter* yesterday. They spelled your name wrong in the event announcement, did you notice? I think we can get them to print the ad again, which would be great. Double exposure."

She puts her hands on my shoulders, turns me toward the door, and gives me a little push. "Go home. Take two days off."

"Two *days*? Are you sure?"

"Yes," she says. "Make art. I'll see you Monday."

I catch the bus back to YiaYia's house, and spend the whole

ride sweating bullets. With two whole days to work, I have no excuse. I *have* to figure this out. When I arrive, I tug the thin chain around my neck out from under my tank top and use the key dangling from the end to open the RV door. The inside is boiling hot from sitting in the sun all day. I reach into the groove between dad's seat and the center console, where he keeps a spare key to the ignition, and start up the RV. Cold air pours out of the vents.

While I wait for the RV to cool down, I change into a pair of old jean shorts I have stashed in my cupboard. They're covered in paint that won't wash off, and they're so worn in some places that they're practically see-through, but I refuse to throw them away. Nothing puts me in the zone like putting them on. And today of all days, I need to be able to disappear into my work.

I pull my art bag out of the closet and kneel on the floor. I need my sketch pad, of course, but I'm not sure what to draw with. Usually I'd start with pencil, but I want something heavier today. I rummage through the bag, picking up my case of colored pencils, a box of charcoal. I settle on a set of soft pastels Cyrus bought me for my birthday last year. It's been a while since I've used them and I miss the way I can blend them with my fingertips.

When I've got everything I need, I sit on the floor with my back against the kitchen counter. There's just enough space so I can stretch my legs out under the table. I'm surprised to find it feels good to be seated here again after so long. I close my eyes and lean my head back, searching for something to draw, some-thing to get me started. But I can't see anything. My shoulders tense, and I feel that same panicky feeling from Fiona's studio coming on.

I shake my arms out and roll my head around on my neck. I can do this. I'm an artist and I can do this. I try to clear my mind. I shouldn't worry about what to draw. I should just let my hand move across the paper, like guiding the wooden marker across a Ouija board.

I open my eyes and press a robin egg blue pastel to the page. I draw a sloping line from the bottom right corner toward the top left—and the pastel breaks in two.

"Shit."

I toss the smaller of the two pieces to the side, and pick up what's left. I begin a new line, this one moving parallel to the first. But then an image of my dad's face, creased with worry as he tells the families we can no longer travel, floats across my mind, and my line goes off course, careening across the first.

"Damn it!" I toss the pad of drawing paper on the floor.

Someone bangs on the door of the RV. "You okay in there?"

I climb to my feet and peer out the window. Cy is standing outside, his hands shoved deep into the pockets of his shorts. "Just a second," I call through the glass.

I grab the pieces of broken pastel and toss them into my supply box, then shove my drawing pad under my mattress.

"Hey," he says when I open the door. "I came by to return your dad's shirt, and I heard you yelling." He peers past me into the RV. "Everything okay?"

"Yeah," I say, stepping into the doorway to block his view. "Just drawing."

"Not going well?"

I sag against the door frame. "You could say that. I've gotta figure out what I'm going to make for Fiona's show and I have no idea what to do."

"Wow, she's letting you put a piece in?"

"I didn't tell you?"

"No," he says. "You didn't."

I run through the last week in my brain, and I realize he's right. I've been so pissed at him for leaving that it never occurred to me that maybe I was being a shitty friend too. "Cy . . . I'm sorry."

"Right." He looks away, rubs the back of his neck. "Well, I'm happy for you."

"Thanks."

Suddenly it feels like a million years ago that he stood in YiaYia's house, asking me to hang out. And even longer since he told me to stop lying to myself about my feelings for him. How did everything get so screwed up? How did we go from being best friends without a secret between us to . . . this?

"Anyway, here's the shirt," Cy says, pushing Dad's shirt into my hand. "See you later." He starts back down the driveway.

"Wait!" I jump down to the pavement just as Cy turns around. He looks unsure.

"Yeah?"

I lick my lips, searching for the rights words even though I have no clue what I'm trying to say. "I want to be us again."

"Huh?"

I swallow. "I don't want to fight. But I also don't want to pretend nothing is wrong. That's not us. We always tell each other what's going on, what we're thinking."

He folds his arms over his chest. "Okay. You go first."

Damn it. I wasn't prepared for that. I take a deep breath, searching for the truth in my own heart. But all I can feel is the pain of standing so far apart from my best friend.

"I don't think I'm too good for you, Cy. I really don't. I just . . . I'm afraid, okay? I'm afraid that if we're together, it'll be so . . . so *right.*" As soon as I hear myself say it, I realize how true it is. I haven't been hiding from what's wrong with us being together. I've been hiding from what's right about it.

"Why is that a bad thing?" he asks.

"Because if we're together, I'll never be anything but a traveler because I'll never want to be anywhere that you aren't." I stare into his eyes, willing him to understand. Begging him to see that the reason I can't be with him is that I want it too badly, but also that I don't want it badly enough.

"But . . . you love traveling," Cy says. "Why would you want to leave?"

"I don't love traveling. It's never been right for me. And I think . . . I think you know that."

He takes a deep breath. "Okay."

"Okay?"

"Yeah. I get it. I mean . . . shit, I hate it, but I get it."

I expect to feel relief, but instead I just feel strange, like I've been running from something for days, only to discover I was never being chased. "Your turn."

He kicks at a rock on the driveway. "I shouldn't have said what I did about you and that cowboy. I was just jealous. And angry. And I shouldn't have . . . what I said about . . ." He rubs the back of his neck. "I never should have said you thought you were too good for us. For me. That was a dick move."

I bite the inside of my cheek to stop from smiling. Looks like I'm not the only one who's been playing our fight over and over again in their mind.

"It's just that traveling is really important to me," he continues. "I love it. And my mom . . ." He looks down at his feet. "She loved traveling too. So when you said it wasn't enough for you, I kind of freaked out."

"I get that," I say quietly. "I'm sorry, Cy."

"Nah, it's not your fault." He looks up at me, his brow creased with new worry. "Dess, there's one more thing. I shouldn't have run off with Rachel like that. I just wanted—"

I hold up my hand. "Don't, please. Not yet."

He frowns. "You sure?"

"Yeah."

We look at each other again, but this time it doesn't feel charged and horrible. It feels weird, sure, but like the kind of weird you can fix.

"So . . . is there anything I can do to help?" Cy asks. "With your art thing, I mean. For the show?"

"Oh, that." I sigh, and lean against the side of the RV. "I wouldn't say no to a brilliant idea for a gallery-quality piece of artwork."

"Hmm . . . maybe your problem is that you're all cooped up in there. Maybe you need more space, or a change of scenery."

"Like what?"

"Ocean views? Wide-open plains?" He shrugs. "Just somewhere that isn't here."

I shake my head. "Not everything can be fixed by traveling."

"No," he says. "But some things can."

CHAPTER 18

Cyrus comes to the house around seven, just as I'm biting into a piece of toast.

"Ready to go?" he asks.

"I really shouldn't. I only have a few days left before the show, and I made zero progress last night after you left."

"That's exactly why you've got to come with me today. Trust me, Dess. It's going to help."

I finish my toast, then we walk out to the curb. I start toward the bus stop at the end of the street, but Cy stops me. "We're not taking the bus."

He points to the other side of the street, where a gleaming motorcycle is parked under a tree.

"What is *that*?" I ask.

"I bought a Suzuki," he says, his face lit with pride. "I've been saving for a year, and since you've been so busy the last few weeks, I picked up some part-time work at an auto body shop. I realized I had enough money saved up last week, so I went to a garage that rehabs old bikes, and I found this beauty. What do you think?"

I walk across the street and stand in front of the bike. The smooth green metal shines in the mottled sunlight under the tree, and the curves make it look sensual, almost . . . sexy. And deadly.

"It's beautiful, but there's no way I'm riding it."

"Oh, come on," Cy says. "I bought you a helmet and everything." He picks up a light blue helmet off the back of the bike and hands it to me.

I take it and turn it over slowly. "This doesn't look like much."

"It's top of the line. I made sure."

I hand it back to him. "That's really sweet, Cy. But just the idea of all that pavement rushing at my tender skull—it's not happening."

"Please, Dess," Cy says. "I will drive extra carefully. I'll go no faster than thirty. And if you feel even a *little* bit scared, you can just squeeze me and I'll pull over. I promise."

He smiles at me hopefully, and my resolve crumbles.

"Damn you, Cyrus," I sigh, and hold out my hand.

"Yes!" He tosses me the helmet. "Make sure you buckle it under your chin. It should fit snug, but not too tight. You know what, let me do it for you."

He steps close and puts the helmet on my head, then pulls the straps down around my chin and clips them in place. I watch his face as he works, mesmerized by the way he bites his lip as he checks to make sure the helmet is in place, and how he grins when it's done.

"You look adorable," he says.

I roll my eyes. "Thanks a lot."

He throws one leg over the bike, and I notice for the first time that there's a backpack strapped to the bike. "What's that for?"

He glances over his shoulder. "Oh, nothing. Climb on."

I gingerly lift my leg and lower it to the other side. The seat is sculpted almost perfectly to fit my butt, and as soon as I sit down, I slide forward so that I'm holding Cyrus around the waist. If we weren't about to go hurtling through space with nothing between the concrete and me except my dinky helmet, I'd be super into this.

"Ready to go?" Cyrus says.

"Not really."

He's quiet, waiting for me. I take a deep breath, and press my face into the back of his T-shirt. "Ready."

He starts the bike, and it roars to life beneath me. I hold him tighter.

"Don't worry," I hear him say over the engine. "I've got you."

The bike rolls forward, slow at first. The seat vibrates a little, like I'm sitting on a really violent massage chair. We pick up speed, the engine purring now, and I chance a look over his shoulder. Houses and trees fly by us, a blur of color that I'm used to seeing through the protection of a windshield.

Cy steers us around a corner and the bike leans to the side. A shriek escapes my lips before I can swallow it down. Cy takes one hand off the handlebars and squeezes my forearm, which is pressed into his stomach—it's the only thing saving me from tumbling off the bike.

We turn again, and the freeway entrance appears.

I bury my head in his shirt as we head up the ramp, gathering speed. "Please don't let me die like this," I whisper. "I've got way too many things to do."

Cy steers the Suzuki onto a dirt road, drives for about a minute, then parks in a seemingly random spot. I turn around in my seat. The road has a slight bend to it, rendering the bike invisible from the main highway. When he kills the engine, I climb off slowly, my knees weak with relief to be back on solid ground. Cy's already got his helmet off, and he's bent over the handlebars, his eyes fixated on whatever he's fiddling with on the front of the bike. As much as I hate riding the Suzuki, I have to admit that he looks sexy as hell on it.

Cy gets off the bike and stretches his arms overhead, and the bottom of his T-shirt rises an inch, exposing a strip of smooth skin and the corner of his hipbone. He pulls the backpack off his bike and hitches it over his shoulder, then takes my hand, sending a surge of electricity through my palm, past my wrist, up my arm, and directly into my heart. "Ready?"

I nod, and he leads me down the trail into a forest of pine trees. We walk the path slowly, taking our time. There's so much beauty out in these mountains, so much to see and touch and smell, but my attention is torn between how anxious I am about wasting time that I should be spending at my easel, and what it means that Cy's fingers are curled around my own, his skin warm against mine. We've held hands dozens of times over the years, but things have never been as complicated as they are now. And he's never had a girlfriend before. Part of me still wonders if I'm doing the wrong thing by following him into the woods like this. If this were a scary movie, there would be a werewolf right around the corner, waiting to take a bite out of me—the "other woman."

We come to an old pine tree that stretches hundreds of feet into the air. I stop at the base and stare up into the green, needled canopy. "YiaYia told me these forests are in danger," I say, reluctantly letting go of Cy's hand to rest my palm against the rough, reddish bark. "Hundreds of years old, and they could be gone in the blink of an eye from a wildfire."

"It's hard to imagine what life would be like without them."

"That's a tad dramatic—"

He looks at me, and I realize he's not really talking about the tree. "Cy, I'm not going anywhere."

He looks up at the branches overhead. "So what happens now?"

I walk around to the other side and lean against the tree. It's quiet out here, so quiet I can hear a stream bubbling somewhere close by, and a bird singing above me. If I lived in Santa Fe, I could come out here all the time. Just like if I had gotten into UCLA, I could have gone to the beach every weekend. But only a traveler can do both in just a matter of days.

Cy steps around the tree and stands in front of me. He's close—too close—and yet not close enough. "There's something I need to tell you," he says. "It's about Rachel. And us."

I pick at the bark on the tree. "I know. We're just friends. You don't have to explain."

"Actually," he says, taking my hand again, "that's not what I was going to say."

I stand up straighter. "Okay," I say, struggling to keep my voice calm. "What's up?"

"The trip to Dallas was a mistake," Cy says. "A big mistake. Rachel and I . . . we're not . . ." He scrunches up his face, considering his words. "She's not you, is what I'm saying."

My heart goes into overdrive. "You're not together?"

"No. Definitely not. We didn't even kiss. I got there and realized I don't feel that way about her, and she felt the same."

I want to throw my arms around him, or shout with joy. But then he laughs. "It was sort of funny, actually."

"What do you mean?"

"I walked up to her house and I was super nervous that I was going to have to kiss her right away or something. But instead I just kept thinking about you and the fight we had before I left. And then she answered the door and we hugged, and there was this moment where it was like . . . okay, are we going to kiss? Then we both started laughing. We spent the rest of the night playing video games and hanging out with her older brother, and I came home the next day."

"You were only there for one night?"

"Yep." He's smiling now, like he's had the weight of the world lifted off his shoulders. "One night, and then I came right back. It was a *lot* of driving."

I run my hands through my hair. "Let me get this straight. You came back and you didn't come see me? You were in Santa Fe that whole weekend, and you didn't . . . what the hell were you *doing* that whole time?"

His face falls. "I was working. Saving up to buy the Suzuki."

"To hell with the Suzuki! Why didn't you tell me you weren't with her?"

He takes a step back, pushed away by my anger. "What difference would two days have made? When I came over to your grandma's, you turned me away!"

"I was pissed. I spent that whole weekend doubting myself, wondering if I was selfish and stupid. I couldn't stop picturing what you were doing together. What you were saying to each other. I thought . . . I thought you were moving on."

A muscle in Cy's jaw twitches. "Yeah, well, I tried to. But it wasn't that easy. I'm in love with you. I have been since we were fifteen."

A sob hitches in my throat. "Then why didn't you come back?"

"Because I can't just wait around, hoping you'll change your mind and say we can be together. So yeah, I came back and I spent that time doing something for *me*. Because one of these days you're going to leave, and then what?"

Tears fill my eyes, but before they can roll down my cheek, Cyrus has his arms around me. "Don't cry," he whispers. "Please."

I bury my face in his shoulder. "This sucks."

"I know," he whispers into my hair. "I know."

I press my face into his neck. He smells like he always does—like laundry and the open road. Like home.

When I finally pull away, Cy laces his fingers in mine and pulls me back onto the trail. "Come on. There's something I want to show you. It's a short hike to get there, but I promise it's going to be worth it."

We walk side by side, and when I glance over at Cy, he's looking at me, too. It fills me with a bubble of nervous excitement that I don't know what to do with, so I put my head down and walk faster. He's not with Rachel. He still wants to be with me. Nothing has changed—we're still travelers, it's still a risk—but we're different now. Both of us.

"This way," he says when the path splits. We follow a narrow, winding trail, and come to a stop in front of a towering pine tree. "Are you ready?" he asks.

"For what?"

He grins mischievously. "You'll see."

I follow him around the tree, and find myself at the edge

of a clearing. It's only about as large as YiaYia's living room, but there's a ring of stones in the middle that someone used to create a fire pit, and off to the side is a wide, flat rock, covered with a red-and-white checkered picnic blanket.

"Someone is using this space," I say as Cyrus drops his backpack on the ground.

"Yeah. Us." He walks over to the rock and picks up a duffel bag that was hidden on the other side.

"How did you know that was there?"

"Because I put it here early this morning. Along with two sleeping bags and a cooler full of food and drinks." He nods at the other side of the clearing, where the corner of a red cooler is peeking out from behind a tree. "I also brought that."

He points at the tree we just passed, and I turn around. A cardboard box, full of paints and charcoal and drafting paper, waits patiently for me against the tree, in the middle of the forest. A grin spreads across my face.

"I can't believe you did this!" I say, turning back to Cy. "This is *amazing*."

He comes to stand next to me, and takes my hand. "Dessa, I would do just about anything to make you smile like you are right now."

My cheeks burn, but Cy keeps talking.

"I knew you were struggling to come up with an idea for the show, so I went back to your RV late last night and grabbed your supplies, then drove up here and unloaded everything."

He tilts his head back to look into the canopy of pine needles. "It's not an ocean view, but—"

"Never stop moving?"

He grins. "Exactly."

I kneel in front of the box and pull out my pad of drafting paper. "What are you going to do while I'm working? Are you going back to Santa Fe?"

"Nope, I'm gonna sit right over there"—he nods to a log that someone rolled over to the makeshift fire pit—"and read. But don't worry about me. You do what you gotta do."

I hug him one more time, then grab my sketch pad and sit on the rock on the other side of the clearing. I don't want to psyche myself out again, so I tuck away all my worries—about the show, about Dad, about Cyrus—and start doodling. A broad leaf comes to life beneath my graphite, the brittle veins that stretch away from the stem branching out like the limbs of a tree from which the leaf fell. Next I sketch my shoes, the dopey way the tongue of my Converse hangs crooked to the side, how the laces are dirty near the ends from dragging in the dirt. When that's done, I draw Taryn's face in profile using a picture I snapped while she was sleeping a few days ago. I take extra care with this one, in case I decide to send it to her when I'm done. I think she'll appreciate the way I've captured the drool dripping out of the side of her mouth.

When I'm finished, I set my drawing pad aside and lie back on the rock. I close my eyes and smile up into the sunlight, letting it warm my entire body and the stone beneath me. I still need to come up with an idea for the gallery piece, but it feels so good to just *be*. This place is so peaceful. So still. Like the whole world has disappeared, leaving behind only the best parts of itself. I want to be like that. I want to be my best self, all the ugly parts stripped away. Or better yet, I want to be everything, all at once. No choice necessary. I want to be a traveler. An artist. Daughter. Friend. Failure. Fighter. I want to be the sum of all of these parts, no matter how hard it is to fit the pieces together.

The light on the other side of my eyelids dims. I open my eyes to find a cloud passing overhead. A ray of sunlight breaks free, and shines through the trees above my head. I blink into the glare, but it's too bright, so I sit up and look down at the rock beneath me. A patchwork of sunlight and shade surrounds me, broken into pieces by the trees overhead. I trace the edges with my finger, all sharp lines and geographic shapes. It feels familiar somehow—and then I remember the box of tiles in YiaYia's garage. I draw in a sharp breath.

The tiles. The mirror. The sunburst.

I know what I'm going to make for Fiona's show.

CHAPTER 19

"Earth to Dessa."

Cy stands over me, eyebrows raised. "How's it coming?"

I look up from my sketch pad for the first time in hours. The sun has started to go down, and a breeze blows through the forest. "Fantastic. But I need to borrow some supplies from Fiona. And YiaYia. And the RV."

"We can go back," Cy says with a shrug, but I can hear the disappointment in his voice. We've been together all day, but we've barely spoken since we arrived in the clearing.

"Actually . . . I could use a break," I say. "How about we camp, and leave early tomorrow morning?"

"Great!" he says with so much enthusiasm that I laugh. "I mean, yeah. Sounds good."

I climb off the rock and stretch. My back hurts from hunching over my work. "You make a fire, and I'll get the sleeping bags set up."

Cy starts a fire in the pit using some dry brush and branches, plus a lighter he brought along. While he works, I text my mom to let her know we're camping for the night, then pull a thick blanket out of his duffel bag, plus an extra sweater and two camping pillows. I hold up my hand to test the wind. Once I'm sure the smoke isn't going to blow in our faces, I lay out the sleeping bags. It isn't until they're both resting side by side that I realize that Cy and I are going to be alone, at night, in the middle of the woods. No Rachel, no parents, no siblings, nothing. Just us.

Cyrus stands next to me. The flames lick at the branches and brush, shooting sparks into the increasingly dark sky. "Do you think I put our sleeping bags too far away from it?" I ask.

"No, this should be good. Besides, we'll keep each other warm."

I nudge him with my arm. "If that was your plan, why'd you bring two bags?" Cyrus' eyes widen at my question, and I feel my cheeks heat up. "We don't have to . . . I was just kidding. . . ."

Instead of answering, he squats down and unzips both bags, then connects them to each other, making one extra-large sleeping bag. There's just enough room for us to comfortably lie next to each other, using YiaYia's blanket as a pillow. He looks up at me, his eyebrows raised.

I bite my lip. Cy and I have slept next to each other a million times, but never like this.

Cy takes my hand. "There's nothing to be nervous about." He leans in slowly, stopping just as our lips are about to touch. "We won't do anything unless you want to."

Part of me wants to suggest we crawl into the sleeping bag

and cuddle right now, but we'll end up there eventually, and I'd like some more time hanging out, just the two of us, before it's *just the two of us.*

Cy sits on the sleeping bag and pulls me down so I'm sitting with my back against his chest. He holds me tight, the fire flickering in front of us.

We eat dinner, then roast marshmallows that we eat right off the stick. When we're done, Cy pokes at the flames, sending sparks into the air.

A thumping sound rolls through the trees, deep and full of bass.

"What's that sound?" he asks, looking out into the trees.

"Music. That, or war drums."

"Wanna check it out?"

"Now? It's pitch-black out there."

"I brought a flashlight." He reaches into his backpack and takes one out. "See?"

"Hmm." I'm definitely not comfortable joining some random group of people in the middle of the night. But I can hear Taryn's voice in my head, whispering *it'll be fun.* "All right. Let's go."

He hauls me to my feet and leads me into the trees. Without the warmth of the fire, the chill of the mountain air creeps through my clothes. I pull on the sweater Cy brought for me and hurry to match his steps with my own.

It doesn't take long to find the other campers. Their music

is actually pretty loud, and their campfire is twice as big as ours. As we draw closer, I realize they're listening to a song I've heard a million times. Something with a strong bass line and a simple melody, the kind of thing you hear over and over again at malls across the country. I start to relax, like this one familiar element somehow makes these strangers less threatening.

We reach the edge of the clearing. A group of ten people are gathered near a keg. A few are dancing off to the side, bouncing along to the music, while the others sit around talking and drinking. A girl my age is lying on the ground near the fire, eyes closed, her hands tracing patterns in the air above her. A boy who looks just like her is standing guard, his lips pressed together as he tries not to laugh.

The girl sits up and looks in our direction. I shrink back toward the forest, but Cy says, "Hi."

"Hey," she says.

Cyrus strides forward. A few faces turn in our direction, but most of the people don't notice our arrival. The girl on the ground reaches for the guy's hands, and he pulls her to her feet. "Where did you come from?" he asks us.

"We're camping nearby and we heard your music," Cy says. "Thought we'd check it out."

He holds out his hand to the boy, who looks at him for a moment, then takes it and smiles. "I'm Heath. This is my sister, Alyssa."

"You can call me Liss," the girl says. Her tan skin looks

smooth and flawless in the flickering firelight. "Want to dance?"

I sigh—of *course* she wants to dance with Cy—but then she grabs my hand and leads me toward the group of people. Up close I see they're almost all my age. She jumps into the middle of the dancers, taking me with her. As she twirls me in a circle, I spot Cy standing back by the fire, an amused look on his face.

The song changes to something faster, with instruments I can't name and lyrics in a language I don't speak. Three more people join us, yelling happily when they recognize the pulsing song. For a second I stand still, Liss and her friends spinning all around me. But the beat of the music, the beautiful melody, the laughing dancers—it fills me up all at once, and I realize there's nothing to worry about. Nothing at all.

Someone grabs my shoulder from behind and twirls me toward them. It's an older woman who looks just like Liss and her brother. She turns me in two quick circles, then jumps into the air. I jump too, laughing. Someone else jumps next to me, and before long everyone is jumping and calling out, all smiles and happy screams. It's different than dancing at the Red Rooster—I'm not following a predetermined set of steps. I'm doing whatever feels right, whatever makes me happy in the moment. Sweat drips down my back, and I pull off my sweater and throw it. It disappears into the trees on the edge of the clearing, but I don't care. My heart is thumping inside me and I feel like I can dance, dance, dance all night.

The song changes and Cyrus appears in front of me. He's

got a huge smile on his face, like he's never been so happy. Without speaking, we grab each other and spin around in a circle, laughing. But it's not long before Liss tugs us apart. I reach for him, but Liss keeps pulling me, and her brother has his arm around Cyrus' shoulder, and there's no use, so I give up and keep dancing.

The group is bigger now, people coming from the trees, other campsites—who knows where. Everyone forms a giant circle, leaving room in the middle. Someone does a cartwheel into the middle of the circle before running around the edge, his hand held out for high fives as he passes. Just as he reaches me, another person runs into the circle and does the Moon-walk. When he leaves, a third girl runs forward, but just before she reaches the middle of the circle, she does a backflip. The crowd cheers, and she runs back to her place.

It goes on like this, single dancers, couples, and small groups taking center stage just long enough to show off their best moves. I run across the circle and pull Cyrus into the middle with me. We twirl around, holding hands, and then he picks me up and I throw my arms into the air. I was happy before, but it isn't until now, with his arms around me, that I feel so completely alive.

The song changes, and another couple joins us. Then another, and before I know it everyone is crowded together again. But even as they push in on us, Cyrus and I stay together, our bodies moving in sync. We don't touch, but every fiber of my being feels connected to his, like our bodies are magnetic.

Then he grabs my hand and leads me out of the circle. We step into the trees. "Dessa," he says, so out of breath he can barely speak, "I love you."

I wrap my hand around the back of his neck and kiss him. He lets out a groan of pleasure as his tongue enters my mouth. I grab his waist, pulling him toward me so that every inch of our bodies is touching. His hands travel up my back, and there is nothing, nothing in the world but this moment. The way he smells—like campfire smoke and pine. The way we cling to one another, like we need each other to breathe. It doesn't matter that we grew up together, that we're travelers. It doesn't matter that there were other guys, or other girls. It doesn't matter that the future is unsure, or that our families might not approve. All that matters is that when I'm with Cy, I know who I am and I know what I want.

When I'm with Cy, I'm home.

Cy pushes me against a tree, not taking his mouth off mine. I wrap my legs around him, my feet leaving the ground entirely. His hands travel up my stomach, his fingers warm on my skin. My heart pounds in my chest, my head, and *god* I want him to keep touching me, but just as I'm about to tear the shirt off his back, he eases me down, and steps back.

"That was—wow." He stares at me, like he's never seen me before.

"Let's go back," I say, breathlessly.

"Okay."

I catch Liss' eye. She waves, then goes back to dancing.

We run back through the trees, holding hands and laughing. I'm flush with the heat of dancing and of Cyrus' kiss. When we reach our campsite, Cy pulls me over to our sleeping bag. His mouth is on mine before we even hit the ground. The fire is totally dead now, but it doesn't matter, because within seconds I've pulled my shirt over my head and pressed myself against Cy's chest. He yanks his own T-shirt off, and then he's on top of me, kissing me deeply as his hands roam my body. I wrap my legs around his waist. He whispers my name, sending shivers down my spine, and I finally tell him for the first time—

"I love you, too."

CHAPTER 20

I wake up shivering the next morning. I feel around for my sweater, only to remember that I threw it off while we were dancing, and forgot to find it again. I could go back for it, but it's a little early to go poking around someone's campsite. Instead, I snuggle closer to Cyrus, lifting his arm so it's draped over my body, and press my back against his bare chest. I start to doze off again, but he rubs his hand up and down my arm and murmurs, "Goosebumps."

"It's cold."

He nuzzles the back of my neck and holds me tighter. "You're warm."

I roll over so we're face-to-face. "Actually, I'm freezing. Do you have an extra hoodie? I lost my sweater last night."

"Mm. Backpack." He waves his hand toward the other side of the clearing. I kiss him on the nose, and stand up, quickly pulling my shirt on over my jeans.

"Do you want breakfast?" he asks as I start to dig through his bag.

"What do we have?"

"Uh, not much. Granola bar, leftover chips . . ."

I pull his hoodie over my head and smile into the fabric. It smells like him. Cy comes up behind me and wraps his arms around my waist. "You woke up early," he says, and kisses me on the cheek. "You must have slept better than I did."

The last thing I remember before falling asleep was the sun rising through the trees as I tried to calm my racing heart. We didn't have sex, but we'd come very, very close. No one sleeps well after a night like that.

"Are you going to work when you get home?"

"Definitely. I have a ton to do."

"Then I better do this now, while I have a chance." He leans forward and kisses me, soft and sweet.

I rub my nose against his and pull away. As ecstatic as I am to be with him after all these years, I still don't want to talk about what this means for the future. I need to focus on getting through the next few days—finishing my project, helping Jordan set up the show. After that . . . we'll see.

We pack up the campsite, taking special care not to leave behind any trash. We can't carry my supplies back on the bike, but Cy insists that he doesn't mind coming back later. "It's an excuse to ride the Suzuki again," he says.

When everything is packed up and stowed behind a tree, we walk back down the path to where the bike is waiting. He throws his leg over, then hands me the helmet. "Ready?"

"I guess." I pull the helmet on, then take a seat behind him.

Cy starts the bike, sending the vibrations of the engine through my legs and up my body. He eases the bike down the dirt lane that connects to the highway, taking it nice and slow, but even at ten miles an hour I feel like the ground is flying by. When he pulls the bike onto the main road, I grab hold of him more tightly still, and fight against the urge to close my eyes. I kept them closed the whole way here, but today is a new day, and I want it to be different. I don't want to be afraid.

The road slopes down as we ride back toward Santa Fe. He picks up speed. The trees whip past, a blur of green and brown. I take a shuddering breath and force myself to ease my death grip on Cy. As soon as I do, I feel his ribs expand. I must have been holding on pretty tight.

"You okay?" he yells over his shoulder. "Should I slow down?"

"No!"

He looks back at me. "Should I speed up?"

I shake my head and scream, "Watch the road!"

His shoulders jerk up and down, and I realize he's laughing. I reach around to pinch his thigh, but then I start laughing too. Suddenly I no longer feel like I'm on a bike hurtling through space. Instead I'm perched on the wind, with only the feeling of Cyrus anchoring me to the earth. Before I can second-guess myself, I lift my hands into the air, spreading my fingers to let the wind thread through them. If I could float up into the trees, I would.

• • •

The door to Fiona's studio is open when Cy drops me off. Hard rock blasts out of the wall-mounted speakers. I scream her name three times, then finally give up and walk over to where she's standing in front of an easel, and tap her on the shoulder. She jumps about a foot in the air.

"Oh my god, you scared the shit out of me," she says when the music is finally off. "Why didn't you just say something?"

"I did, but it was so loud you couldn't hear me screaming. You're going to go deaf."

She laughs. "Anyway, I have good news. While you were gone I called the newspaper, and you were right. They gave us extra coverage for free. I also did a quick walk-through at the gallery with Jordan yesterday. We're ready to go."

"That's great." I feel a twinge of jealousy that I wasn't here for the finishing touches, but it's for the best that I got away for a few days. If I hadn't, Cy and I would still be stuck in the same awful place, full of silence and anger, and I'd probably still be staring at my blank sketchbook.

Fiona wipes the back of her hand across her forehead, leaving a smear of blue paint on her skin. "So what brings you here so early?"

"I finally figured out what I'm going to make for the show. Better late than never, right?"

"Hell yes!" she says, swatting at me with the back of her hand. "I knew you could do it. What are you making? No, don't tell me. I want to be surprised."

I grin. "Okay, but I have a favor to ask. Would it be okay if I borrow some tools from you, and maybe a drop cloth? I've got a long night ahead of me, and it's going to be even longer if I have to figure out a way to break tile with the heel of a shoe."

She sits back and taps her lip with her thumb. "Tell you what. I'm going to call my friend Sarah and see if I can work out of her garage tonight. You can stay here and use the studio, plus all the supplies you need."

"Really?" A thrill runs through me at the thought of having the entire place to myself.

"Why not? If I were you, I'd bring a couple blankets and a toothbrush and I'd camp out. Stay here until the work is done."

I look around the workspace, at the stacks of newspapers and the dirty paintbrushes, at the picture window in need of cleaning, and at the table in the middle of the room, covered in the materials we brought back from the junkyard. A few weeks ago this place felt cluttered and messy, and I couldn't imagine working amid the chaos. But now, I can see a sort of magic in the mayhem, and more than anything, I want to throw myself in the middle of it and see what I can create.

"I promise I won't make a mess."

Fiona laughs. "Do you think I'd notice if you did?"

It takes me an hour to pack up all my materials—including the box of my grandfather's tiles, which YiaYia said I could have—plus an overnight bag and a plastic container of Greek cookies to snack on. I'm almost ready to go when Mom appears in the doorway. "Do you have a minute to talk before you go?" she asks, a crease between her eyes.

"Sure," I say, and follow her into the bedroom at the back of the RV.

She sits down on the edge of the bed and gazes at my packed overnight bag leaning against the kitchen table a few feet away. "You're only leaving for one night, right?" she asks.

"Yep."

"Good, good," she says, her hands in constant motion as she twists her rings around her fingers.

"Mom. It's going to be fine. I don't know why you're so worried."

"It's not that. . . ." She glances toward the front of the RV, as if someone might actually be able to *hide* in this miniscule space. "You've been busy with your internship, and your dad's been distracted. . . ."

I sit down next to her on the bed. "I don't have to go. I could work here."

"No, no. You go. I don't want you to worry about me," she says, sniffling. "I just miss being all together on the road."

I want to tell her things will be back to normal soon, but I'm not sure that's true. Instead I just say, "I love you, Mom."

She sniffs again, and then the dam breaks and tears pour down her face. "I love you, too," she says, and throws her arms around me.

Rodney drops down from the cabover bed, his Game Boy clutched in his hand. Apparently, you *can* hide in the RV after all. "What did you do to her?" he asks me.

"Nothing!"

"It doesn't look like nothing," he says, unconvinced.

I reach over and knock the Game Boy out of his hands and onto the bed. "You're a punk, you know that?"

He grins. "At least I didn't make Mom cry."

I pat Mom on the back, and she sits up and wipes her face. "I'm sorry," she says, smiling a little. "I wanted to give you something, and here I am, old waterworks. . . ."

She reaches into the drawer next to her bed and hands me a plastic baggy full to the brim with shards of glass. But instead of just the blues and greens the families helped me collect for months, she's filled the bag with brilliant yellows, warm oranges, and shining reds.

"You probably don't want to work on the Santa Monica mosaic anymore now that you're not—well, you know what I mean," Mom says. "But that doesn't mean you can't start collecting new colors, right? Maybe try something different? I bet you can still make something beautiful even if your original plan didn't work out."

I stare down at the bag, the sharp edges of the glass poking at me through the plastic. The colors are incredible, and absolutely perfect for what I have planned. And best of all, they came from her.

"Do you like it?" Mom asks nervously.

"I *love* it."

Mom ushers Rodney out of the RV to give me space to finish packing. As soon as they're gone, I get down on my hands and knees to feel around under the bench seat in the kitchen until my fingers bump into the edge of a small box.

I pull it out and stare down into the cardboard box of broken glass. It feels like forever since this glass filled me with anything but dread and disappointment. I'd been so fixated on what these pieces of glass meant to me, that I'd completely forgotten that they originally belonged to glass bottles, to broken car windows, to light bulbs and vases. The pieces all had an initial purpose, but when they shattered on the street or broke apart in my hands, I'd imbued them with the potential to be anything. Anything at all.

Sweat drips down my brow, but I brush it away and grip the utility knife. One more cut and the drywall will be ready. I slide the utility knife down the side of the ruler, taking care not to scratch the table underneath, even though a lifetime of living in Fiona's studio already has it looking pretty beat up. When I'm finished, I hold up the drywall and examine my work.

Plink. Plink.

I look around for the source of the noise, but it's stopped. I shrug and turn back to my work, but just as I'm picking up the spare bits of drywall, I hear it again.

Plink.

It sounds like something little falling to the floor. I put down the piece of drywall, and get down on my hands and knees. Nothing.

Plink.

I crawl across Fiona's studio, peering under tables and chairs. But I can't find anything that would make that weird noise. I stand up and brush off my jeans and look around the room, but there's nothing moving, nothing falling, nothing making any sound at all.

Plink.

I spin around and look at the covered windows facing the street. Maybe the noise is coming from outside. I peel back a piece of blue construction paper and peer out into the night. Down on the sidewalk, standing under a streetlight, is Cyrus, pebbles in one hand and a paper shopping bag in the other.

He waves frantically and mouths something to me, but I can't hear him. I make a "just a minute" sign, and run out the door and down the rickety steps to the street. When I throw open the heavy front door, Cy is standing there.

"Finally," he says, throwing the rocks over his shoulder. They skitter across the sidewalk and into the gutter. "I've been out here for almost five minutes."

"Why didn't you just call?"

"Ran out of minutes. Let me up?"

My mind immediately goes to all the things that could

happen between us upstairs in Fiona's studio, and how close we came to having sex last night in the woods. One kiss could turn into two, and before I know it, it'll be morning and I'll have forgotten all about the work I'm supposed to be doing.

He must see my hesitation, because he holds up the shopping bag. "I brought food. When's the last time you ate?"

"Um, I haven't?"

"Uh-huh. I'm coming up." He pushes past me into the stairwell and starts to climb the steps. I consider stopping him, but then the incredible smell of roast chicken floats down to me. "Did you bring that from YiaYia's?" I ask, hurrying after him.

"Nope, I made it. Well, she did give me one thing, but it's a surprise."

We reach the top of the stairs and I open the door to Fiona's studio. Cyrus nods in appreciation. "This place is incredible. I can't believe you have it all to yourself. . . ."

"Don't get any ideas." I lean in to kiss him on the cheek, but he turns his face at the last second and our lips meet. It sends a shock through me. It's been less than twelve hours since the last time he kissed me, but it feels like much, much longer.

"This place is wild," Cy says, looking around the studio. He walks over to the window at the back and looks down at the park. "I should have brought a picnic blanket. But I guess it's pretty dark anyway."

"Ooh, I have an idea!" I kneel down in front of the table in the center of the room, and I pull out the rug I saw stashed there on my first day. "We can make a picnic of our own. It might be a little dusty, though."

Cy puts the paper bag down and helps me unroll the rug. It's not as dusty as I feared, but it's worn so thin in some places that the color is almost nonexistent. When it's laid out, Cy unloads our dinner.

"So tell me what you're working on," he says, handing me a paper plate full of food.

"It's a surprise."

"Hmmm. Well, I can tell you one thing about it already."

"Oh yeah, what's that?"

"It's making a mess." He nods over at one of Fiona's many scuffed-up side tables. It's covered in broken pieces of tile, and the floor is white with dust.

"I used a hammer to break up a few of the floor tiles I got from YiaYia. It got a little nuts."

"It's on your face, too," he says, reaching out to rub a streak of white powder off my nose. "So what are you going to do with the broken tiles? Tell me you're going to make a dress for *that*." He points his fork at the half-mannequin Fiona got at the junkyard, which has been leaning against the sofa for the last few days. "That thing freaks me out. What happened to its legs?"

"Fiona and I cut them off. She's going to dress the top in her best clothes, then put it in there." I point at the cage, sitting on the other side of the room.

Cy shakes his head. "Artists, man. Y'all are weird."

When we're finished with dinner, Cy stacks the paper plates and containers, then walks over to the wall and turns off the lights.

"What are you doing?" I ask.

He comes back to the rug and holds out his hands. "Come with me."

Cy hauls me to my feet, grabs the paper bag, and leads me over to the windows overlooking the park. The moonlight shines into the studio, turning what was a bright and messy space into something calm and lovely.

"I know this is going to sound sappy, but I wanted to tell you how happy I am," he says. "I didn't think you were ever going to change your mind about us. But I'm glad you did."

I open my mouth to respond, but realize I have no idea what to say. Did kissing in the woods mean we're together now? And if we are, what does that really mean? Will I have to give up on—

No. I can't worry about this, not right now. I have work to do tonight, and a show tomorrow. Everything else can wait. It has to.

"I'm happy too," I say.

Cy reaches down into the bag and pulls out two plastic cups and a bottle of champagne. It's still got a sticker on it, but he quickly pulls it off.

I gasp. "Where did you get that?"

"Your YiaYia gave it to me," he says with a grin.

I laugh as he pulls off the black cage covering the top of the bottle. "Watch out," he says, and yanks on the cork. It makes a loud *pop!* sound, and some of the champagne comes bubbling over the edge. I quickly bend down and catch it in my mouth.

"Too good to waste," I say, wiping my mouth.

He pours two cups and hands one to me.

"What should we toast to?" I ask.

"Your project?"

"Nah. Something bigger."

"Let's see. . . ." He wraps his arm around my waist. I give him a kiss, so light our lips hardly touch.

"How about we toast to that?" he says.

"Definitely."

We clink our cups together, which doesn't make much noise at all, and take a sip. The champagne is bubbly and slightly sweet, and it makes me feel light-headed almost immediately. "Why don't we drink this all the time?"

"Probably because we can't afford it."

"Oh, right." He laughs. "We will someday, though, and when we do, we'll drink champagne every night before bed."

"In the moonlight."

"In the moonlight," he agrees.

CHAPTER 21

Fiona's leather couch is warm against my skin. I throw up a hand to block the light streaming through her window. After Cyrus left, I worked late into the night, finally collapsing onto the couch just before three a.m. But I did it. I finished. Not even the crick in my neck from sleeping funny can ruin how great I feel.

I arrive back at YiaYia's an hour later, my box of supplies digging into my arms as I struggle to carry it, my overnight bag weighing heavy on my back. Luckily, I left my piece at Fiona's, propped up against the wall under the giant windows. She said she'd pick it up in two hours, just enough time for it to dry before the show this afternoon.

Halfway up the driveway, I hear a *crash* from inside the house. I run the last ten feet to the door. But before I can put my box down and get my key out of my pocket, the door opens.

Mom's eyes are red-rimmed, like she's been crying. "Did you know?"

Cold dread creeps up my spine. "Know what?"

She turns on her heel, leaving me standing in the doorway.

I drop my box by the front door and follow her into the kitchen, but I stop short at the sight of Dad seated at the table, head in his hands.

Shit.

Mom stands between us. "Did you know your father lost his job?"

I try to catch Dad's eye, but he's still staring down at the table.

"Well?" she demands.

"Yes." I swallow hard. "I knew."

"So everyone knows but me." She sinks into a chair, her face contorting with sadness. "I was going to take money out of our savings account to buy you flowers for your big show tonight—"

My heart constricts. "Mom—"

"—but the account was overdrawn. So I asked about it, and . . . and . . ." She lets out a sob and turns to Dad. "You should have told me, Peter. You should have told me as soon as you found out. We're a team." She rounds on me. "And you should have told me last night. Or days ago, in the kitchen, when I asked if you'd noticed anything was wrong. You knew I was worried and you said nothing!"

"I wanted to, Mom, but I couldn't—"

"Because he told you not to, right?" She shakes her head. "The two of you . . . Have you forgotten everything this family is about? We make decisions together, or not at all. If we can't be honest with one another, if we can't tell the truth, then we have *nothing*."

My eyes fill with tears. "I'm sorry, Mom. I'm so sorry."

"It doesn't matter. It's too late."

My heart leaps into my throat. "What's too late?"

Dad lets out a long, deep sigh, and for once I understand what Mom means when she warns us about bad energy. The whole kitchen is full of it.

"We might as well get everyone in here at once," Mom says, pushing away from the counter. Her movements are sluggish and heavy, like she's sleepwalking through water. I reach out for her hand, but she ignores me and keeps walking.

Dad finally looks at me. I can tell he wants to say something, but I look down at the table. He's lied to Mom for weeks, and I let him drag me into it. I want to go back to the moment in Fiona's studio when I finished my work and collapsed onto the couch. Or to last night, staring into Cy's eyes as I took that first sip of champagne. Or to two nights ago, when Cy's lips first touched mine. No, I want to go back even further. I want to go back to the moment when I agreed to keep this secret, and take it back.

This is as much my fault as his.

Mom appears in the doorway. Her face is so still it could be made of stone. "They're on their way."

Five minutes later, the families are crowded into YiaYia's living room, covering every available surface. YiaYia herself is perched on a chair in the corner, her eyes wide as she watches everyone talking over one another. I take a seat on the edge of the couch next to Rodney. Across the living room table, Cy frowns. He can tell something is wrong. They all can.

Mom edges past us to join Dad in front of the fireplace. She stands next to him, but they don't touch. They don't even look at each other.

"What's going on?" Rodney asks.

Cy leans forward. "I heard your mom say we're taking a vote."

I dig my fingers into the sofa cushion. Whatever's about to happen, it's going to be serious.

Dad clears his throat, and we all look up at him. The tip of the sunburst painting peeks out from behind his head, like a sharp, multicolored crown. The Fallen King of the Wanderers.

"I'm not going to beat around the bush," Dad says, quieting everyone. "The truth is, things have been hard for the Rhodes family lately. I lost my biggest client a few weeks ago, and work has been slow for months. We're pretty much broke."

I've been waiting almost two weeks for Dad to tell everyone the truth, but now that I'm sitting here, watching him admit it, I just want to cover my ears.

"Oh, sweetheart," YiaYia says. "Why didn't you tell us?"

"I was ashamed."

I look around the room, expecting everyone to be shifting nervously in their seats. But instead Jeff leans forward and says, "It's not your fault."

Dad shakes his head. "Maybe not, but the way I acted after it happened sure is." He looks around the room, and his eyes settle on me. "I wasn't fair to the people who love me, who depend on me. I tried to handle it all on my own, and I just made things worse. For everyone. And for that . . . I'm really sorry."

Dad offers his hand to Mom. "I'm especially sorry that I didn't tell you, Geri. We're a team, right?"

For one terrible second, I don't think she's going to take his hand. I'm not sure I'd blame her. But then her fingers close around his, and I breathe a sigh of relief.

"If I know anything for sure," Dad says, "it's that travelers are strongest when they're working together."

"Hear, hear!" the McAlisters say from their spot on the floor.

Dad clears his throat, and I see the beginning of a red blush creep up his neck. "I also have some news. I just got off the phone with my old boss, Mark. He doesn't have any contract web design work, but he's still looking for a Director of Strategic Initiatives to help with a major event he puts on every fall."

"What does that mean?" Rodney asks.

"It means your dad has been offered a job working for Mark, but only for half the year," Mom says. Her voice shakes a little, but she continues. "If he takes it . . . we'd be settling down in Charleston."

The living room explodes with protests, so loud that I jerk back in my seat. Across the coffee table, Jeff throws his hands up in disgust. "You're selling out."

I press my hand to my chest. It's like something is bearing down on me, so hard I can hardly breathe. Settling down? What about Mom? She loves traveling, it's her whole life. And what about the families? Will they keep going without us?

What about Cyrus and me?

"Calm down!" Dad says. "I'm not selling out, okay? I'm just doing what I have to, to take care of my family."

Across the coffee table, Cy searches my face. I don't know what he's looking for—a sign that it's going to be okay? That we'll get through this? Whatever it is, I can't give it to him. I'm as lost as he is. "You're not going to travel anymore," he says, his voice so quiet that a moment ago I wouldn't have been able to hear him over the shouting.

"We'd keep traveling," Dad insists. "Just not year-round. We would still be with y'all for half the year, but from June through December we'd be in Charleston. Probably in the RV this first year, but once we've saved up some money, we'll rent a small house or an apartment. We'd live a normal life."

The words "normal life" jolt me. "There's nothing *normal* about this, Dad, not for us. Plus, you both love traveling full-time. It's who you are."

"The only thing we've ever wanted was to provide you kids with the best possible life we could," Dad says. "Right now that means settling down for half the year."

"What about you, Mom?"

She looks down at her hands, and I can see her struggling

not to spin her rings around her fingers. "I love traveling, and I'd miss everyone *so* much. But things have changed, and we need to change with them." She looks up at me, and I'm surprised to see the corner of her mouth curl into a smile. "Seeing the way you've succeeded here, Dessa . . . it's been eye-opening." She puts her hand on Dad's shoulder. "Maybe this is our next adventure."

Dad nods gratefully at her. "But nothing's decided," Dad says, looking around at everyone. "We want to know how all of you feel about this. That's why we asked you here. So we can vote."

"You're going to vote on *this*?" YiaYia says. "But it's your *life*."

"That's exactly why we're voting," Mom says. "Because it's an important decision that'll affect everyone." She turns to me. "Especially you, Dessa."

I frown. "What do you mean?"

"If I'm going to take this job, we'll have to leave right away."

"Right away . . . meaning tomorrow?"

Dad grimaces. "In an hour."

I jump to my feet. "Dad, the show is *today*. I can't leave."

"Believe me, I did everything I could to convince Mark that starting a week or two later would be fine. But he's looking for someone right away, and I'm not exactly in a position to argue with him." His voice drops. "I wouldn't ask this of you if I had any other choice."

I look back and forth between my parents, panic rising

inside me. "But—but why do I have to go? Why can't I just stay *here*?"

"We're not breaking up this family again," Mom says, her hands curling into fists. "We're all going to do this together, or not at all."

"But—"

"I said no!"

I sink back down to the couch, my cheeks hot with frustration. So that's it. Everything I've worked for, everything I've learned . . . once again, it's all going to come down to a stupid vote.

"It's time," Mom says stiffly. She pulls out the beat-up San Francisco Giants hat from where it was stuffed between two couch cushions.

"I've got paper," Mrs. M says softly, pulling a wrinkled sheet out of her purse.

"And I've got pens." Rodney reaches under the couch and pulls out a blue and a red marker. "I dropped these last night. I knew leaving them there was a good idea."

Rodney and Mrs. M pass the materials over to my mom, who quickly rips the paper into a bunch of pieces. "You all know the rules. *Y* for "yea" if we should take half the year off from traveling, or *N* for "nay" if you don't think this is the right decision. You can also leave it blank if you don't want to vote, but I hope you will."

We pass the paper around, everyone taking a slip, and then

Rodney's markers start to make the rounds. Mom is the first person to use the red pen. The felt tip hovers over her piece of paper, and I can practically see her fears scrolling above her head. *Will we really still travel? What if we hate Charleston? What if the families fall apart?* But she glances over at my dad, who's studying the ground carefully as he waits for his turn, and something comes over her face. It's not peace, exactly—I can still tell by the crease in her forehead that she's nervous—but she doesn't look scared anymore. She looks determined.

Mom marks her page, then passes the marker on. One by one the votes are cast. "Yea" for a new adventure that will tear us apart for months at a time, "nay" for staying together even though my dad is struggling to pay our bills. It might seem like an easy decision, but I can feel the atmosphere in the room change, like how the air gets thick and still just before a tornado.

"Here," Jeff grunts, and passes Cy the red pen. He looks down at the paper clutched between his fingers. I don't want to see the look on his face when he casts his vote. I don't want to know his answer.

The blue pen finally comes to me. I grip it so hard my knuckles turn white. My head is a swirl of questions, each one battling to the top. We've all been together for so long—how can we give up traveling? What the hell are we going to do in Charleston? And what about Fiona's show? I busted my ass putting it together, and I deserve to see how it turns out. Not to mention seeing my own piece hanging in a gallery. How can I just give that up?

Someone clears their throat, and I look up to find Cy watching me, even though we're supposed to give one another privacy during a vote. I try to read his expression, but he looks just as conflicted as I feel. We've known each other for years, but it feels like we've just found each other. How can I vote for a life without him?

I lower the felt tip to the paper, but almost immediately pull it up again. This is an impossible choice. I want to be a good daughter, and I want to do what's best for my family. I don't want to let them down. But I also want to be happy.

"Has everyone cast their vote?" Mom asks.

I look up at the sound of her voice, and my gaze lands on the sunburst hanging behind her. In the warm light of the living room, the sloppy yellow brushstrokes and stiff ridges of orange paint come alive. It's not perfect, but there's something undeniably *right* about it.

I couldn't see that back then, but I see it now. When I made it, I wasn't afraid. I didn't second-guess myself. I let go of everything I'd learned about the "right" way to do things, and this beautiful, messy, joyous painting was the result.

"I don't need to vote." I crumple the paper in my hand. "I'm staying here."

CHAPTER 22

The vote passes five to three. My family is leaving Santa Fe, and settling down in Charleston.

YiaYia voted for us to keep traveling—she announced it as soon as the count was over, insisting that she could support the family financially while we got back on our feet. I think Cy voted against us settling down too. As for the third . . . I have no idea. Maybe Mrs. McAlister. Maybe Jeff. But it doesn't matter. Mom, Dad, and Rodney will arrive in Charleston in two and a half days, just in time for Dad to start work the next morning. The other families will probably visit us for a few weeks, and then they'll move on.

But me? I'm staying here. At least for tonight. After the show, I'll figure out the rest.

I help Rodney load his suitcases into the storage compartment underneath the RV while my parents walk down the block with the other families. I imagine the conversations they're having, about how I'm breaking up the families even worse than Dad is, or how long before my family returns to traveling full-time. If we ever go back to it at all.

"Everyone's gone," Dad says as he and Mom come back up the driveway. "We better hit the road too." He puts his arm around me. "Be good, kid, and let us know how it goes."

I hug him. "I will."

Mom takes my hands in hers. "Don't do this," she pleads. "You can still come with us."

I'm not going to argue with her—there's no point. Instead, I rest my forehead against hers. "I'll see you soon."

She sighs, then kisses the bridge of my nose. "Good luck tonight."

Dad starts up the RV. "Drive safely!" YiaYia calls from the front door to the house. "Call me when you get there."

Dad waves to us. "We will."

The RV pulls out of the driveway, and YiaYia goes back into the house. I'm about to follow her, when Cyrus runs up the driveway. "Dessa, wait!"

I spin around. "What are you doing here?" I exclaim. "Your dad already left."

"I made him let me off. I didn't want you to be alone tonight."

My eyes fill with tears, and I throw my arms around him. "Thank you," I whisper. "Thank you so much."

"We should hurry, right? Doesn't it start soon?"

I check the time on my phone. "Shit! We're already late."

"Good thing I kept the Suzuki."

• • •

The motorcycle screeches to a stop in front of the gallery. I'm off the bike before Cy even has a chance to take his helmet off.

"You go in!" Cy yells through his visor as I toss him my helmet. "I'll find you."

I run into the gallery, eyes scanning the crowd for Fiona. The exhibit started twenty minutes ago, and there are people everywhere. They're dressed really nice—dresses and suits, even a few tuxedos. I'm a mess. I didn't shower, my hair is tangled and wild from blowing in the wind, and I'm wearing cutoff jean shorts, two tank tops layered over each other, and a bunch of mismatched necklaces that look like they came off a table at a roadside flea market. Which they did. But I don't care. All that matters is that I'm here, that I'm going to finally see something I made with my own hands, hanging in a gallery.

"Dessa?"

I turn to find Jordan staring at me, her mouth open. She's wearing a floor-length white gown and her head is newly shaven. She looks like she stepped off a runway in New York and landed in downtown Santa Fe. "Where have you been?" she says in her clipped British accent. "And what in god's name are you *wearing*?"

"Where's Fiona?" I ask, searching for her. I need her to know I'm here.

Jordan grabs my arm. "Come with me."

She pulls me into a bathroom. "You can't meet potential buyers like this." She yanks a paper towel out of a basket on the back of the toilet and runs it under cold water. She wipes at my face, my neck, my arms. She bats at my clothing, then tugs at the bottom of my shirt. "Now flip your head over and shake out your hair."

"Jordan, I need—"

"You're not leaving this bathroom until you're presentable."

I groan and do as she says, so that when I stand up, it lays flat. More or less.

Jordan takes a purse out of one of the folds in her skirt, and produces a black eyeliner. She grabs my chin to hold my face steady, and quickly lines my eyes. "Almost done," she mutters. Then she bends over and yanks her heels off. "Here."

"What?"

"Put them on! I'm tall enough without them and my dress is long—no one will notice."

"Are you sure?" I say, looking down at my dirty brown boots.

She rolls her eyes. "If I wasn't sure, I wouldn't have taken them off. Now hurry up. I have to get back out there before Fiona gives away everything for free."

I toss my boots under the sink and pull on Jordan's heels. They're too big, but I can still walk. And I have to admit, pairing heels with my shorts makes me somehow look purposefully casual. "Better?" I ask her.

"Much. Now get out there. Fiona is terrible with potential buyers. She's always telling them how cheap her materials are. It doesn't make people want to spend money."

I hurry back into the gallery, and immediately spot Fiona just outside the exhibit. She's wearing an incredible purple dress that skims her collarbone in the front but plummets in the back, plus chunky silver jewelry and strappy heels. She spots me and waves.

"Dessa!" she yells, startling an old lady so badly that she almost drops her glass of wine.

Fiona gives me a hug, and I feel all the muscles in my body go limp. I made it.

"Let's go in." She grabs my hand and leads me into the main exhibit area, all the way to the back. But something is wrong: The giant bicycle sculpture we'd planned on placing on the far wall is gone. Instead, there's a small, square piece of art covered with a sheet, blocking it from view. "Oh god. Was the sculpture stolen?"

Fiona shakes her head. "Nope, it's over there." She points to the front of the room, where the sculpture is sitting in a corner.

"Then what . . ." I look back at the sheet-covered square. "You're kidding. That's *mine* under there?"

"Yep. I was going to put it in the corner, but then I showed it to Jordan and she insisted it would be more dramatic if we put your piece on the far wall."

"*Jordan* said to put it there?"

"We both love the scale—your work isn't big, but that will make it stand out even more on that white wall."

A waiter wanders by with a tray of champagne. Fiona takes

two glasses and hands me one. I take a sip. It's delicious, even better than the stuff Cy and I had. "I could get used to this."

She laughs, and we clink our glasses together. "Are you ready?" she asks, nodding toward my sheet-covered art.

People have gathered around us, curious about what Fiona's about to unveil. My hands start to shake. "I'm ready."

Fiona motions to one of the gallery workers. He steps forward and picks up the top edge of the heavy white sheet, then pulls it away with a flourish.

Alternating spirals of color spin hypnotically before me. The blue and green glass of the Santa Monica coastline, rolling in like a sparkling wave; vibrant, hand-painted southwestern tiles from my YiaYia, and shards of glass in yellows, oranges, and reds from my mother; hundreds of jagged shards of the broken mirror from Taryn, each reflecting my own face back at me. Apart, these pieces each tell a single story, of where I've been, or how I cried, or who helped me along the way. But together, radiating out from the single piece of Fiona's yellow glass flower at the center, they tell the story of everything I've experienced and put myself through in hopes of finding my own path.

I look at the beautiful mosaic I've created, and I'm filled with something I haven't felt since I first made the sunburst painting.

Pride.

All around me, the gallery patrons *ooh* and *ahh* appreciatively, and a few even clap. I turn away to hide my blush.

"Oh, there's something missing," Fiona says. She reaches into her purse and pulls out a small rectangle of white paper, and then steps forward to affix it to the wall. Written across the middle in fancy cursive is a note:

Into the Unknown, by Dessa Rhodes
Price: $1,000

My hand flies to my mouth. A thousand dollars is more money than I've ever even considered calling my own. It's enough to help my family pay back some of their loan. It might even be enough to help my mom forgive me and my dad for keeping such a huge secret from her.

At the thought of my parents, my heart constricts. They should be here to see this. They should have come with me. But then I find Cyrus' face in the crowd, and remember that YiaYia will be here soon, and force myself to stay focused on the good.

"Thank you so much," I say to Fiona. "For everything."

An hour into the show, tons of people have stopped to look at *Into the Unknown*. An older man even asks Fiona who this "Dessa Rhodes" is and whether she's had an exhibit in Santa Fe before. Fiona just smiles and says this is "the artist's first show," but that he should keep an eye out for me, because my work is going to be big someday. As he walks away to tell his friends, she winks at me.

But no one has offered to buy it yet. Cy does his best to keep me calm, bringing me snacks and trying to talk to me about the art, but by the time I drink my second glass of champagne, I'm jittery with nerves, and my stomach hurts. "You might want to slow down on the booze," he whispers.

"Why?"

He jerks his chin to the front of the room. I follow his gaze, and practically drop my glass.

Standing in the doorway, looking super nervous, is my family—all ten of them, plus YiaYia. But unlike me, they're not dressed for traveling. Dad, Jeff, and Mr. McAlister are wearing hastily ironed suits, and Mom and Mrs. M are in skirts. Even the twins are dressed in their white confirmation dresses. Only Rodney seems to have gotten away with wearing jeans and a button-down shirt. Probably because he's growing so fast he doesn't fit into his secondhand dress pants anymore.

I push through the crowd, a bit unstable in Jordan's shoes—not to mention from the champagne—and hurry over to my parents, my heart hammering in my chest.

I'm almost to them when Jordan appears in front of me. "Have you seen the waiter?"

"No, sorry," I say, craning my neck to see past her. My parents are already halfway across the gallery, only steps away from my piece. My palms start to sweat. Seeing them here, in the middle of the show—it's like I've been living two different lives, and now they're crashing together.

"He's supposed to be serving canapés," Jordan whispers angrily, "but I just overheard someone commenting on cheesecake. It's way too early for desserts to be out. Dessa, are you even listening to me? This is a *disaster*."

I look at Jordan for the first time. "Jordan, it's never too early for dessert. Everything is fine, I promise. Now . . . I have to go."

I walk past her, to where my parents are standing directly in front of my piece. I wipe my sweaty palms on my shorts. This is it.

"Um . . . hi."

Mom turns around. "Dessa, you made this?"

"Yeah . . ." I clear my throat. "Yes. Last night."

"It's . . . I didn't . . ." She looks to my dad for help.

"It's okay if you don't like it," I say quickly. "But I'm really proud of it."

"Are you kidding?" Dad says. "It's *incredible*."

I let out a sort of half laugh, half sob. "Really?"

"Absolutely." Mom pulls me into a rib-crunching hug. "I'm so sorry we left, sweetheart. We should have been here for you."

Dad wraps his arms around both me and Mom. "We were wrong."

"It's okay," I say, smiling into my mom's shoulder. "You're here now."

CHAPTER 23

The crowd clears around eleven thirty. As soon as the last person is out the door, Fiona takes off her heels and grabs a piece of cheese off a mostly empty platter in the corner. "What a night," she says. "Did your family have a good time?"

"They did, but they were getting hungry for more than just cheese and cake, so they took off."

"How are you getting home?"

"My friend Cyrus is taking me. He's outside, talking to the valet guy about driving a stick shift."

"Is Cyrus the one who keeps checking on the motorcycle out front?"

"That's the one."

"Oh, good. If you didn't already know him, I was going to suggest you check the guest book for his name so we could track down his phone number for you." She winks at me.

Jordan marches into the gallery, her bare toes barely visible under the bottom of the white dress. "I've got the initial bids if you'd like to see them," she says, tapping the clipboard in her hand. "But I have a feeling we'll get more in the morning."

I suck in a shallow breath. This is it. This is when I find out if my work can hold its own in a gallery. If all this work was worth it.

Jordan hands the clipboard to Fiona, who quickly scans the page of item numbers. Her finger comes to rest on a listing at the bottom of the page. "Who made this offer?" she asks, looking up at Jordan.

"Samuel Breen. He's a private collector, but he's been thinking of donating his works to our gallery for some time. It would be a small but permanent collection, which means the public would still have access to the piece, not just Breen."

"Interesting." Fiona hands the clipboard back to Jordan and turns to me. "I have good news and bad news. What would you like to hear first?"

I look from Jordan to Fiona and back again, but their faces are identical masks of calm. "Uh . . . the bad news, I guess?"

"The bad news," Fiona says, "is that you're going to have to part with a piece of art that you have just created, and that is going to be very hard."

I stare at her for a second, the words sinking into my brain. "It . . . sold?"

"It sold."

"Oh my god!" I spin around in a circle, almost falling over in Jordan's heels. I come to a jerky stop. "Wait . . . is it rude to ask for how much?"

Fiona turns to Jordan. "Show her, please."

Jordan passes me the clipboard. She points one long, manicured fingernail at the bottom. I look closely . . . and scream.

"Twelve hundred freaking dollars! Oh my god, that's even more than what you asked for."

I throw my arms around Fiona, and she bursts out laughing. Next I hug Jordan, who gives me a little pat on the back. But when I pull away, I catch her smiling.

"Thank you, Jordan. For everything. I learned a lot."

She inclines her head. "You're welcome. But um . . . my shoes, if you don't mind?"

"Oh, sure." I pull off the heels and hand them to Jordan, who quickly slides her feet inside and heads back to her office.

"There's one last thing I want to ask you, as well," Fiona says once we're alone. "I'm sure you're looking forward to spending more time with your family now that your internship is over, but I'm wondering if you might consider a different plan."

I think of the endless hours of driving ahead of me, and the nonexistent pull of settling down in Charleston. "Like what?"

"You have a very bright future in the art world no matter what you do next, but I know college is important to you, and I agree that having a degree will benefit you no matter what you do. Especially if you choose to minor in something like business. But you have almost a year before you can apply again. So . . ." She clears her throat, and I realize she's actually nervous. *Fiona*, nervous about talking to *me*.

"In the meantime," she continues, "I want you to stay in

Santa Fe. Become my full-time, paid assistant. I'll teach you everything I know about art—the craft *and* the business side. Do a good job, which you will, and at the end of the year I'll write you the best damn letter of recommendation you've ever seen. I'll even personally deliver it to my friend on the admissions board at the University of New Mexico."

I stare at her, my mouth hanging open.

"I know it's not UCLA," she says, "but it's a great school with a wonderful art department. Your grandmother also mentioned during the show that you're technically a New Mexico resident, so going to an in-state school would help your family with tuition. We might even be able to get you a scholarship."

"I . . . that's . . ." My heart pounds so hard that I think it's going to rip through my shirt. The ground swims beneath me. "Do you mind if I sit down for a second?"

I walk to the nearest wall and sink into one of the chairs we set out for elderly guests. I press my hand to my forehead, as if with enough pressure I could contain the flood of emotions crashing through me. For months my fear has towered above me, an unscalable, unmovable wall. *But I did it.* I proved to myself that I was good enough. A smile spreads across my face, and I press my fingers to my lips. I want to memorize this feeling, lock it up tight and never let it go. The feeling of having everything I've ever wanted.

Except, if I take this job . . . will I lose Cyrus?

"This is an incredible offer, but is it okay if I give you my answer tomorrow?" I say at last. "I need to talk to my family."

"Of course," Fiona says. "Take as long as you need."

Cyrus is waiting outside to give me a ride home. I'm so shocked by Fiona's offer that I forget to be scared of riding his motorcycle. Still, my legs shake as I climb off. Cyrus takes my hand to steady me, and doesn't let go.

"Is everything okay?" he asks as we walk up YiaYia's driveway.

I shake my head. "Inside. I'll tell you inside."

My parents and Rodney are seated in the living room with YiaYia, snacking on leftovers from last night. Even though it's not everyone, my blood pressure still spikes at the sight of them all sitting there, waiting for me.

"Why are you holding hands?" Rodney demands.

I completely forgot Cy had taken my hand when I got off the bike. I try to let go, but he keeps a firm grip. I glance over at my parents, but instead of looking shocked or uncomfortable, I catch them giving each other a knowing smile.

"How did it turn out?" Mom asks, a little too casually. "Did Fiona sell any art?"

I grimace. In all the excitement, I forgot to ask Fiona how *her* sales went. "She sold a lot," I say, struggling to remember what was on the clipboard list. "I'm not sure what exactly, but definitely a lot."

"That's wonderful," YiaYia says. "Even if her art is wacky."

Rodney snorts. "I liked Dessa's better."

"Thanks, dude." I try to ruffle his hair, but he ducks away and sits on the floor in front of our parents.

"And what about yours?" Mom asks. "Did anyone . . . ?"

"I sold it," I say, grinning. "Twelve hundred bucks."

The room explodes with congratulations. Mom plants a kiss on my forehead just as YiaYia exclaims, "I'm so proud of you!" I hug everyone, taking my time when I get to Cyrus. In just a minute I'll have to tell them about Fiona's offer, but for now, I just want to bask in this moment where everyone is together, and no one is disappointed.

But eventually they all settle down, and I know it's time.

"There's something I have to tell you." I sit on the couch across from my parents, between YiaYia and Cy. I reach for his hand, and he takes it.

"What's up?" Dad asks.

I breathe in through my nose, and let it out slow. It's going to be okay. Whatever happens, it's going to be okay. "Fiona offered me a job."

There's a sharp intake of breath, as if the whole room is inhaling. Mom looks stricken. "What job? When?"

I chew on the inside of my cheek, trying to ignore the furious beating of my heart, and the way Cyrus is gently tugging on my hand, trying to get me to look at him. But if I do, if I see the doubt in his eyes, I might change my mind.

"She wants me to be her paid assistant for a whole year.

Then she'll write me a letter of recommendation." I turn toward Cyrus and finally meet his gaze. "I might have a shot of going to college after all. I have to do this."

He drops my hand like it's burned him. "So what, you're leaving us, just like that? Just when you and I—no." He stands up, his face contorted with pain. "I can't do this."

"Cyrus, wait."

I reach for him, but he pulls away and storms out of the house, slamming the front door behind him.

I stare at the space that held him just a moment ago, aching to run after him. But I can't. Not now. Not yet.

"This is all happening so fast," Mom says. "Your dad just got this job. He was able to push his start date back, but we're leaving day after tomorrow. Maybe we should all go to Charleston and think about it for a few weeks. There's no rush, is there?"

"I'm sure Fiona would understand," Dad agrees.

"No," I say softly. "I don't *need* to think about it. I want to do this."

Mom twists her hands in her lap. "I don't know . . ."

"I'd keep an eye on her," YiaYia says, patting Mom's hand. "She could live here."

"And I could use the money I make to chip in with groceries and stuff," I add, taking YiaYia's hand in mine. "And maybe even save up enough to help pay for my first year of college." I pause. "If I get in, I mean."

"You will," YiaYia says.

I smile gratefully at her. But I need more than YiaYia on my side. Not because it's a traveler rule, but because I won't feel good about this if the people I love don't support me.

"Mom? What do you think?"

She stares down at her hands, her fingers twisting her rings.

"Geri," Dad says gently. "It's okay."

She looks up at me, her eyes watery. "We've never been apart for more than a few days. I'm not sure you're ready to be on your own."

"Mom . . . maybe it's you who's not ready."

She wipes at her eyes. "I'm not."

Dad leans forward, his hands on his knees. "If you take this job, and then get into college, that's a full five years away from the families. And after that, well . . . you might never come back." His forehead creases with sadness. "Are you sure that's what you want?"

I look down at my hands, at my fingers, still stained with white tile grout from last night. A few months ago, "What do you want?" would have been the easiest question in the world to answer. *College.* But now I know there's more than one path for me. There are hundreds, maybe thousands, each one leading off into a million different directions. Maybe I'll still end up in college, and maybe I won't. Maybe the future holds something entirely new, something I haven't even considered. For once, that doesn't scare me.

"I don't know what I want," I admit. "But whatever it is, I'm not going to find it until I see what else is out there. Until I have an adventure of my own."

Mom looks at me, her eyes still a little red. "Never stop moving?"

I reach across the coffee table and take her hand.

"Never stop moving."

Cyrus opens the door as soon as I knock. "Is your dad awake?" I ask, peering into the dimly lit RV.

"He went with Mr. M for a beer after the show. The modern art short-circuited their brains."

I follow him inside, but before the door has even closed behind us, his lips are on mine. We slam into the wall, a tangle of hands and heartbeats. His mouth travels from my lips to the skin under my ear, then down my neck to my collarbone. I don't want this to stop. I don't want this to *ever* stop.

He picks me up and sets me on the kitchen table. The cool laminate sends a shiver through my legs. His lips press against mine again, his tongue slipping into my mouth. I slide my hands under his T-shirt and up his stomach, until the fabric is pushed up around his neck. What happened inside the house doesn't matter. What he said, what I did, none of it exists. The whole world disappears.

He tugs at the top of my shorts, his fingers warm against my stomach. I reach down to help him, but in the seconds it takes for him to pull away, to give me space to move, I realize what's happening. What we're doing.

"Cyrus—stop. We can't."

"We *can*."

I shake my head. "We should talk first."

"I don't want to talk. I just want to kiss you."

"I know."

We look at each other, our chests heaving. Then he sighs, and rests his forehead against mine. "You're right."

He steps back, and I immediately miss his hands on my waist. But as the air cools around us, a strange look comes over his face. Like he's remembering why I'm here, and why he left.

"Is it time for the vote?" he asks, his voice suddenly hard.

I knew he'd ask this—if I were him I'd ask the same thing. "Actually, there isn't going to be a vote. They said it's up to me."

He exhales, long and slow. "So . . . this is it. You're not going to travel anymore."

He rubs the back of his head and looks up at the ceiling. I want to know what he's thinking, but I'm not even sure what's going on inside *my* head. Kissing him leaves me breathless, but also makes me feel like I'm full of air at the same time. Like I'm floating away, my brain disconnected from my body.

"I've been in love with you for years," he says, "and now you're leaving. Just when we're finally starting to figure this—us—out."

"I know." I wrap my arms around his waist and rest my head on his chest. I used to dream of lying like this, listening to his heart and knowing that every beat was for me. But even in my wildest dreams, I didn't imagine having this . . . and letting it go.

"Maybe this doesn't have to be the end. Maybe . . . maybe we can still be together."

"I've been in love with you for years," he says, "and you've been right in front of me. I don't want to do it from hundreds of miles away. I want to do it for *real*."

"I know," I whisper. "But I have to do this."

He pulls away and slides down the fridge to the floor, cradling his head in his hands.

His shoulders shake, and a tear rolls down his nose and lands on the floor. I want to tell him that everything is going to work out, but we both know that's a promise I can't keep. Instead, I kneel and hold him as he cries. It's all I can do.

The sun shines through the trees as I walk down YiaYia's street to the parked RVs. The McAlisters left early this morning, but the rest of the families are waiting for me at the curb. As I near them, I realize this is it. The last day before my new life begins. I can't tell if I want to run toward the future or walk as slowly as possible.

"All packed up?" I ask.

"And ready to go," Dad says. "All that's left is the hard part."

"Saying goodbye," Mom says. "For now."

Jeff shakes his head. "We're gonna miss you, kid. Take care of yourself, okay?"

"I will."

"And if you change your mind, you know where to find us."

He heads back toward the RV, his gait exactly like Cyrus'. I turn back to my parents, and catch my Dad reaching into his back pocket for his wallet.

"Dad, I'm fine. I've got the money from the sale, and I'll have my first paycheck in two weeks."

"Hush," he says, and pulls two twenties out of his wallet. He hands them to me. "Recognize these?"

A familiar streak of purple ink zigzags across the top of Jackson's head. I look up at Dad, amazed. "You kept them?"

He taps the bills in my hand. "That's the first money you ever made selling your artwork. There was no way I was going to spend it on something like gas."

I hug him tightly. "Thanks, Dad."

He kisses the top of my head. "You're welcome."

Mom wraps her arms around us, and a second later I feel Rodney collide into us too. "Group hug!" he screams.

Mom throws out her arm and catches Cyrus by the shirt. "Get in here."

We all embrace, and I swear in that moment I want nothing to change. But then Rodney lets go, and so does Mom, and the feeling passes.

"Okay, it's time to go," Mom says. "We'll let you guys say goodbye."

Then they're gone, leaving only Cyrus and me standing on the curb.

"Come here," he says, pulling me around the side of his RV. As soon as we're out of sight, his lips are on mine. I lean into him, letting my mouth say everything I can't.

When he finally pulls away, I can barely breathe.

"I had to do that one last time."

Dad hits the horn in two short bursts.

"Gotta go," he says. But neither of us moves.

"I'll miss you," I say, my voice cracking.

He pulls me toward him, and we cling to each other.

The horn honks again.

"Come on," he says quietly.

We walk back around the corner. At the sound of the RV engines starting up, ready to leave without me, it feels like I'm going to split apart, right here on the sidewalk.

But then Cyrus gives me one last crooked smile as he climbs into his RV, and I wave goodbye—to him, to my parents, to my old life—as they drive down the street, and disappear around the corner.

I take a steadying breath, the hardest part over. I'm still here, still standing. I turn toward home. YiaYia's making lunch, and Fiona's coming over in an hour to talk about what's next. I told her I want to work on portraits, starting with one of Taryn. Her wild red hair is going to be tough to capture. I'll probably need to experiment with color, and maybe even metallics to get the shine just right.

But that's okay. I'm up to the challenge.

ACKNOWLEDGMENTS

Writing *Your Destination Is on the Left* was a journey. Like Dessa, I sometimes felt lost, like I was on the wrong path, or like I was failing to achieve the goals I had set for myself. There were times it seemed like I was never going to finish. Luckily, I had something else in common with Dessa—an amazing community of people who lifted me up, pushed me when I needed pushing, and above all, believed in me.

The first person I'd like to thank is my incredible agent, Jim McCarthy. Jim, you are one of the best people I've ever met. Your passion, intelligence, and humor have been a life raft and an inspiration, and I will be forever grateful for you. Thank you also to the unstoppable team at Dystel, Goderich & Bourret—I am deeply proud to be represented by such an incredible agency.

I also want to thank Catherine Laudone, my wonderful editor at Simon & Schuster Books for Young Readers. Catherine, you helped me find the heart of my story, and reminded me that the devil is in the details. You also gave me permission to write some truly mushy kissing scenes. My book is so much better for having been edited by you. I'm also extremely grateful to everyone at S&S BFYR that has worked tirelessly to make my dream a reality. From editorial to design to marketing, you guys are superstars.

I also want to thank the many, many critique partners and beta readers who gave me feedback during not only the two years it took to write this book, but the many years of writing that came before it. First and foremost, I want to thank Juliana L. Brandt. You were my first writing friend, and I learned (and continue to learn) so much from you. You are one of the most talented and empathetic people I've ever met, and you have a superhuman ability to know when I need to complain and when I need to suck it up. I feel very lucky to call you a friend.

I also want to thank the Fellowship—Bess Cozby, Hannah Fergesen, and Ashley Poston—all of whom are top-notch human beings and gorgeous writers to boot. You guys keep me sane. A special thank you to Hannah, who got me over the finish line with this book (your line edits are intense and magical, just like you), and Bess Cozby, who is aggressively supportive of me and my writing. No negative self-talk allowed! You three are the loves of my life.

I'm also very grateful to my early readers and beta readers—Corrie Shatto, Ifeoma Dennis, Shana Silver, Diana Urban, Charlie Holmberg, Fiona McLaren, Courtney Gilfillian, Jay Coles, Rebecca Enzor, and Roselle Kaes. You guys put up with a ton of early draft shenanigans, and never once complained. A special shout out to Allison Ziegler, as well—you are an amazing writer and critique partner, and I love being your friend. Let's go back to that fabulous bar in Philly and talk about books, magic, and mayhem.

Special thanks also go to Uwe Stender, Brent Taylor, and the rest of #TeamTriada, for becoming my found family in the last year—I am so grateful to you all for supporting me and welcoming me into your ranks. I'm also grateful to Bree Barton and the Electric Eighteens. You guys are inspiring and fabulous, and your books are going to take the world by storm. I'm so happy you're in my life.

I also want to thank the Highlights Foundation, for providing me with a comfy cabin, amazing food (Hi, Amanda!), and a beautiful setting. I am convinced that Cabin 16 is both haunted and magical, and I wouldn't have it any other way. I'm also grateful to Highlights for bringing Jessica Spotswood, Tiffany Schmidt and me together. The two of you have become incredibly important parts of my life over the last few years, and I am so honored to call such talented, smart, wonderful women my friends. Let's go walk in the woods.

I'd also like to express how grateful I am for the YA community as a whole. Between the wonderful publishing people I've met in New York to the brilliant writers and readers I talk to almost every day on Twitter, I have approximately 8,000 times more friends than I did when I started writing. We have the best community *ever* and I feel so lucky to be a part of it. A special thank you to Brenda Drake, for everything she does for writers, and to Jen Gaska, for hosting my cover reveal on her amazing website, Pop! Goes the Reader. I am so happy to have met you and become friends over the last year.

Okay, now it's time for the hard part. I put off writing my acknowledgements for a long time (sorry, Catherine!) because I didn't know how I was going to adequately express how endlessly grateful I am for my family. First and foremost, my sister. Diana, you're a force of nature. You are smart and kind and talented and so, so wise, and the fact that you believe in me makes *me* believe in me. I love you. Thank you also to Michael, for being relentlessly enthusiastic about my writing. I'm so happy I know you.

I also want to thank my grandma, Nonie, for supporting me and loving me and always believing in me. You are the heart of our family, and I love you more than words. Thank you also to my uncle Mark, who is brilliant and provides me with endless support. When you say something is a good idea, I know I can take that to the bank. Thank you also to my godmother, Gail, for being there for me through thick and thin. Seeing you is my favorite part of coming home.

Now it's time for the really, *really* hard part.

Dad, you mean the entire world to me. You raised Diana and I to be strong and independent, but also to be kind and hardworking and patient (I'm still working on that last one), and I am who I am because of you. Every time something happens in my life, good or bad, you're the first person I want to tell. Thank you for always believing in me, and for never letting me give up on myself or my dreams. I love you, Dad.

And finally, the biggest thank you of all goes to my husband, Patrick. You are my best friend in the entire universe, and I literally could not have done this without you. I wouldn't *want* to do this without you. The last ten years have been the best of my life, and I could not ask for a better partner. I love you, and I love who you help me to be. I can't wait for our next adventure. *Allons-y!*